TO THE
Beach

CUT TIES AND RUN

KELIE CICHOSKI

BALBOA.PRESS
A DIVISION OF HAY HOUSE

Balboa Press books may be ordered through booksellers or by contacting:

Balboa Press
A Division of Hay House
1663 Liberty Drive
Bloomington, IN 47403
www.balboapress.com
844-682-1282

Because of the dynamic nature of the Internet, any web addresses or links contained in
this book may have changed since publication and may no longer be valid. The views
expressed in this work are solely those of the author and do not necessarily reflect the
views of the publisher, and the publisher hereby disclaims any responsibility for them.

The author of this book does not dispense medical advice or prescribe the use of any
technique as a form of treatment for physical, emotional, or medical problems without the
advice of a physician, either directly or indirectly. The intent of the author is only to offer
information of a general nature to help you in your quest for emotional and spiritual well-
being. In the event you use any of the information in this book for yourself, which is your
constitutional right, the author and the publisher assume no responsibility for your actions.

Any people depicted in stock imagery provided by Getty Images are models,
and such images are being used for illustrative purposes only.
Certain stock imagery © Getty Images.

Print information available on the last page.

ISBN: 979-8-7652-5356-4 (sc)
ISBN: 979-8-7652-5358-8 (hc)
ISBN: 979-8-7652-5357-1 (e)

Library of Congress Control Number: 2024913524

Balboa Press rev. date: 09/05/2024

CONTENTS

HERE WE GO!

I was born in late August, 1967. The lifetime I was being born into was to be the most challenging lifetime my soul had ever lived. As you may or may not know, our souls live many lives, both on the Other Side (also known as Heaven) and here, on Earth. We aren't able to remember these lives most of the time, so each time we're born it's like a brand new existence. Our soul's purpose is to learn specific lessons while we're here, and of course to do good and kind things to help others. My soul is an old soul. It has lived many lives before. When my soul chose to live the life I was about to begin, it knew it was going to be challenging, but it was necessary because I needed to learn to be independent, patient, and learn how to love myself unconditionally. I would need the help of many of my guardian angels and spirit guides to make it through the challenges I would be presented, but that is the reason we're all here, after all.

My parents, Patty and Lou Drezinski, were sure I was going to be a boy as soon as my mom started to show. The two factors that led them to believe this were that my mom felt completely different during her pregnancy with me than she did during her pregnancy with my older sister, Tina. She also carried me very low, which was said to be an indication of a boy back then. From the time they married, my parents dreamed of a boy and a girl. My older sister Tina was almost four years old when they got pregnant with me, and since they waited seven years after they got married until they had Tina, they were nearing the end of my mom's optimal child-bearing years. They hoped this pregnancy would produce the son they wanted so badly, and it could be their last chance.

My family's house was built from a kit that was purchased from the Sears catalog in the 1950's. It was located in a small suburb halfway between Cleveland and Akron, Ohio called Twinsburg. My parents had a close-knit network of family and friends nearby and everyone was looking forward to my birth. The birth of Patty & Lou's son. Even though they had no way to accurately predict a child's sex back then, everyone believed I was a boy. My nursery was painted light blue and my sister's pink crib was painted red in preparation for my arrival.

My mom's belly was low and large in the last month we spent together as one. She was very uncomfortable and irritable, which is probably why a lot of things went awry with my arrival.

It was early on a Wednesday morning when my mom was awakened by the pains of labor. Thank goodness my dad, who had been on permanent midnight shift, was home when it happened. He loaded us into the family Impala and we began our trek to Bedford Hospital, about thirty minutes away.

Although my mom's labor pains were pretty severe, we made it to the hospital. Fortunately, she was given pain medicine upon her arrival. Unfortunately, my mom never handled pain medicine very well. Her labor lasted fourteen hours before I finally arrived, so having to get numerous doses of pain medicine really scrambled her brain.

On August 30, 1967 at 7:20 p.m., my mom's lengthy and intensive labor that was only moderately dulled by pain medicine resulted in the birth of me, her second daughter. When my mom was told by the doctor that I was a girl, she thought the doctor was kidding. She actually told her to stop playing around and let her see her son.

When my dad (who had been waiting in the hallway with the aunts, uncles and grandparents I was going to meet) learned I was a daughter, his smile faded for a moment. He put his hand on the "It's a Boy" cigars in his pocket and his jaw slowly dropped. He looked at the nurse as if she were kidding, but after two seconds of processing, he realized she wasn't. The aunts, uncles and grandparents were excited because I was a healthy baby, they didn't really care if I was a boy or girl. Shortly afterward, my dad was invited to see me for the first time. Of course, I don't remember meeting my parents for the first time, but I do know that I really put a wrench in their plans.

Once they learned I was a girl, my parents had to scramble to think of a name for me. They had been tossing around boys' names for months. This was attempted after my mom was given pain medicine and endured fourteen hours of labor, while my dad was pacing in a hallway for fourteen hours. Needless to say, there wasn't a lot of brain power left for them to figure out a name. Eventually my mom, in her painkiller-induced state, came up with Michelle (that is my older sister's middle name) Antoinette. Antoinette was my great grandmother, but when the nurse asked my mom to spell it she spelled A-N-N-E-T-E, so I became Michelle Annete Drezinski.

I would be called Shelly for short, and this name would end up giving my sister Tina a lot of ammunition to use against me.

IN THE BEGINNING

Tina had spent the first four years of her life being the apple of her daddy's eye and her mommy's little princess. When Tina learned she could be getting a brother, she was very excited. I'm pretty sure she was excited because she knew a boy wouldn't want to play with her toys or compete for her daddy's love.

When I arrived in Tina's life it sparked a perfect storm of jealousy and animosity. It evoked regret in my parents. My guardian angels were bracing for the challenges I would begin to face in the not-so-distant future, although I remained a naive little baby.

The summer of 1967 stretched on much longer than normal that year. I like to think it was Mother Nature's way of easing me into the cold Ohio winters, but it was probably the Universe's way of saving me from being left out in the cold, literally.

It had been about a month since I'd arrived home. My mom had me lying on the living room floor next to where Tina was playing. Since the weather was so nice, the front door and the living room windows were open. I was wrapped up like a burrito in my swaddling blanket, and Tina was busy with her dolls. My mom walked into the kitchen to get me a bottle. This allowed my jealous sister just enough time to make her move. Tina awkwardly picked me up and carried me out to the middle of the front lawn, where she placed me in the grass. She then returned to the living room and resumed playing with her dolls as if nothing had happened.

My mom reacted with a jolt of panic when she noticed I was missing. She asked Tina where I was, and as her eyes followed Tina's tiny finger, she saw me lying in the middle of the front yard. She rushed out to get me and asked Tina why she had done that. Tina matter of factly explained that she put me outside so the stork would come to get me. She said she asked him to take me away and bring the baby brother she had been promised.

Much to my older sister's dismay, I survived my first four years. Tina had openly demonstrated her dislike of me numerous times. Once I began to walk and talk, she would push me down and make me cry. As I began to comprehend more, she would scare me by saying that mom had left and wasn't coming back, or that I was adopted so our parents couldn't love me as much as they loved her. That was one of her favorites.

I remember one evening when I was about four years old. Tina and I were in the living room and all of the doors and windows were open because it was warm outside. My dad was asleep because he was on the midnight shift. My mom had told Tina she was running across the street to the neighbor's house to pick something up and she'd be right back. I wasn't aware that my mom had gone to the neighbors. Tina saw an opportunity to scare me and jumped on it. She told me that my mom had left because of me and she wasn't ever coming back. She had me so scared I wanted to call the police. I pulled a kitchen chair toward our wall-mounted phone, picked up the receiver to dial "0" for the Operator, but before I could dial, Tina blurted out "What's our address? You can't call if you don't know the address." I had a very photographic memory, and the house numbers were right next to the front door so I had long before committed them to memory. I knew the name of our street because the signpost was right where I rode my bike in front of our house, and my mom made sure I knew how to read it. Tina was surprised I knew our address and began to panic when she thought I was actually going to call the police. Then she thought to ask if I knew our ZIP code. She could see by the deflated look on my face that she had succeeded in stumping me. She said if I didn't know the ZIP code I couldn't call the police, so I placed the receiver back into the cradle and began to cry. I still remember how scared I felt because I truly believed my mom wasn't ever coming back. It was a dreadful feeling.

A few minutes later, my mom was walking back from the neighbors and heard me crying. When she got back inside she hurriedly tried to quiet me so I wouldn't wake up my sleeping dad. I told her what Tina had told me and all she said was that she was back now, as she picked me up and carried me outside.

OUT IN THE COLD

*I*n September 1971, the month after my fourth birthday, my mom's troubled third pregnancy came to an end. She had been ordered to stay off her feet as much as possible, and when she couldn't take it any more, she had labor induced to bring her long-awaited son into the world. Our little brother would be known as Randall Michael Drezinski, Randy for short. It was the name they had planned to use on me. The doctor had to perform a hysterectomy after Randy's birth due to complications blamed on her age. My mom was thirty-six years old at the time.

When the bedrest began, our grandma and great aunts stepped in to help watch us while my dad worked midnights. I loved spending time with grandma and the great aunts. They played cards and taught me games. It was the one time Tina behaved herself because they didn't approve of her bullying me and wouldn't put up with her shenanigans.

Randy was born a big healthy baby, who arrived after a much shorter period of labor than with me. But, due to the hysterectomy, my mom and Randy stayed in the hospital for a week after he was born. I didn't mind because it was just more time with grandma and the great aunts, which meant Tina would behave. There was a constant presence of family members in and out as mom healed from her surgery. It was like the second family reunion of the year.

After my mom's surgery healed and grandma and the great aunts stopped coming over as frequently, the divide in our immediate family expanded. Randy's natural place in our family was with my mom, who had waited eight long years for his arrival. She had endured a troubled pregnancy and had finally been rewarded with her long-awaited son. He was her treasure. My dad and my sister maintained their strong father-daughter bond, but Daddy's little girl was a master manipulator and capitalized on his adoration. She was so good at manipulating him that he would never be able to see her for what she was, and God help anyone that went against her, especially me.

Things with my family had always been challenging, but now that there were three children my challenges were magnified. I was the second daughter and now the middle child. It became evident that my parents had just been going through the motions with me. As you sift through the family history, my baby book has one page filled out and no photos. Tina's book is stuffed full of memories of her arrival on this planet. Randy's is also stuffed with memories, including things like a lock of hair from his first haircut, photos, written memories, and his baby bracelet from the hospital. Family photos mostly featured Tina with only a few of me. There are no photos of my baptism, yet there are photos of both Tina's and Randy's. The only evidence I had of my baptism is being told I had a Godfather and a Godmother.

This pattern of favoritism would repeat throughout my childhood and young adult life. Whenever I asked permission to do something, the decision was strongly weighed using factors such as whether or not we had the supplies left over from Tina, or if it would eventually serve my younger brother. Many people don't understand how a child might comprehend that, but I did. It was so evident that I was an afterthought I often voiced my opinion of the unfairness in our family, which led to me being labeled as "Big Mouth." That really added ammunition to Tina's arsenal of nicknames for me. Her favorites for me so far had been "Shelly Belly" and "Annie Annie with the Big Fat Fanny…" Now I had graduated to "Big Mouth."

AN UNHAPPY MOVE

*J*ust after Randy turned one, our parents wanted to move from our Sears catalog house in the suburbs to a house in the country. I wasn't very excited about it because we lived on a dead end street that had two cool things. First, we could ride our bikes on a section of road that kept us away from cars, and second, there was a big hill with a huge dead tree stump on it we all called "The Big Tree." All of the neighborhood kids from the surrounding houses would play there, and it was always a lot of fun to get everyone together there. "The Big Tree" was right across from our house and gave us a hill to climb (which is a big deal when you're five years old) and a place to play that was close to home. Of all the houses that surrounded our house, only one didn't have kids. I could walk to any one of our neighbors' houses if my mom wasn't home after school and I was never afraid. I also really liked my kindergarten teacher and had a lot of friends in my class. I didn't want to leave.

The new house was in the middle of nowhere. There were only a few houses on the road and a lot of open fields with some woods. I remember the day we went to see it. It was really snowy and we had to park on the road because we couldn't find the driveway. The front yard was really big, and as we started to walk across the big yard toward the house it seemed to take forever. The snow was up to my butt. My mom had to carry Randy because the snow was higher than he was tall. I hoped this would be enough to convince my mom moving here was a bad idea.

When we finally made it to the front porch and went inside I didn't like it at all. The house was smelly and really dusty. There were no carpets, just wood floors, and it was really cold. When you came in the front door, there was a room to the right that was big and empty except for a wooden chair with orange cushions, a fake fireplace, and a deer head hanging on the wall. I couldn't understand why anyone would hang a deer head on the wall. How mean. When we walked through the kitchen, which was very dusty, there was another big empty room at the end. It was another living room. I was confused until my mom told me it was called the family room. She said it gave us a nice room to have company, and also a room where we could watch TV and keep our toys. There was a door in the family room that my dad said went into the garage. He was excited about that because at our house the garage wasn't attached to the house, so if it was raining and you had to come in from the garage you would get wet.

When he opened that door he held me back. When I looked to see why, I saw a big drop off. There were no steps leading down into the garage, just a door up in the air. He told me they had to build steps before we could use that door. He said the man that was selling the house had built it himself and wasn't finished yet. He had to move because he was getting a divorce. It was probably because the house was so awful.

Our reaction to this new house wasn't as positive as they had hoped, so they tried to sell us on the idea by telling us we'd have a great place to play inside during the winter. Dad said there was a whole other level to this house that was under the ground, and that it was as big as the house upstairs. He said it was where the washer and dryer were, and that he was going to set up a workshop down there. We were very excited to have a place to play in the winter. Winter in Ohio was long and cold, and when you did play outside you couldn't stay out too long because your hands and feet got wet from the snow and you had to go in.

Our excitement quickly dwindled when we saw the condition of the basement. There was a ton of dust on the floor. I remember there being so much dust it felt like you were walking on a cloud. There were also these weird poles that my dad said were holding the house up. It was freezing down there, and I didn't like it. I hoped we wouldn't have to move to this house because it was awful. However, my dad wasn't going to be discouraged at our lack of enthusiasm. He led us back upstairs and showed us a little red shed in the backyard. It was really far back in the huge yard, and with the deep snow it would have been impossible to trek all the way back there. He said there was a pony that lived in that shed, and if we bought the house the pony came with it. I was so excited about the pony, I forgot all about the basement and deer head!

We moved into that house just before Easter the following spring. Spring-time exposed the pond that took up almost the entire front yard, and now we could see just how huge the yard really was. The pony that had been promised mysteriously disappeared along with his shed. We were told he had belonged to the neighbors and they took him home. I have a feeling my dad knew the truth, but he acted as surprised as we were. He promised we could get our own ponies after he was able to clear some of the land for them. Our back yard was filled with really thick weeds that went as far back as the forest at the property line. Our land was five acres and from a five-year old's perspective that was a lot of land.

Our parents really wanted this house. They worked really hard to get the house finished and the yard cleaned up. Mom wanted a garden because she was excited to be able to grow vegetables. She used to can tomatoes and make jelly and pickles at our old house, so having a bigger garden was her dream. She worked really hard inside the house, adding tile to the floor, painting and cleaning. She even put wallpaper in the kitchen and living room to make it look better.

It seemed like our parents worked all day and into the evening for the first year. Dad got a really old red tractor that he used to clear a large area for the garden. I remember we had to go through the garden and pick up the big rocks so he could plant vegetables. Dad told us it was very important to get everything done before winter rolled around again. It felt like we spent our whole summer picking rocks out of the garden then pulling weeds. It was not very fun.

This house had the same amount of bedrooms as the old one, so I again had to share a bedroom with Tina, and I didn't like it. The older she got the meaner she got, and she still loved to make me cry.

Because the new house was farther away from the city we had less visitors. The neighbors had three kids, but unfortunately their youngest daughter was fifteen years older than me. This gave Tina even more opportunities to torment me because I was the sole focus of her day. I know our parents got tired of the constant bickering and tears, but they would never discipline Tina, only me. When our extended family would visit they would comment on Tina's behavior, but my parents used to justify it as just sibling rivalry. My grandparents and great aunts spoke out. They told my mom that sibling rivalry was a natural competition between sisters and brothers, but what had been going on between Tina and me was different. They tried to tell her that Tina being so mean to me wasn't normal, and she should do something about it. She never did. Tina continued to torment me in any way she could. She would walk up to me and pinch me really hard, then start to call me names and repeat them over and over until I broke down and cried. If that didn't work, she would whisper in my ear or get in my face and repeat the names over and over until I would explode with anger. Then she would laugh in my face. Sadly, my mom thought it was funny. I remember feeling very lost because there was no one to defend me. I used to run into the woods to hide just to get away from them.

SPREADING MY WINGS

When I became old enough to be away from home, my aunts invited me to spend weekends at their houses. At first, I was scared and would wake up in the middle of the night crying. They were so nice to me. They would call my mom and stay with me to comfort me until she came to pick me up. I don't remember why I was so afraid to be away from home, but the fear overwhelmed me.

As I got older I was able to stay the whole night and the next day. In fact, I got to the point where I didn't want to go home. My mom had to make me leave. I loved spending time with my cousins. They had little sisters or brothers but rarely fought. It was really fun to be around them.

Our parents finally got our land cleared and bought Tina a horse, and me a pony. My pony, Hot Rod, was a retired barrel racer, and he was old. He had horse asthma so bad that if I asked him to gallop he would come back gasping for air. My dad and Uncle Art called it the heaves. They said his lungs weren't working right because he was so old and he couldn't breathe well. We discovered this when my uncle set up a barrel racing area in the back yard and ran Hot Rod through it. He was impressed at how fast Hot Rod was and said it was a shame he had the heaves. I didn't mind though. I was only six and really loved him. We kept Hot Rod and Tina's horse Smokey tied on big ropes in the side yard, that way they could eat as much grass as they wanted and move around the yard. Dad moved their ropes around the yard and said the horses were his lawn mowers.

Dad had plans to build a big pole barn for our horses, and he also wanted to board race horses in the winter. He said it was a good way to save money by not having to pay to keep his horses at another farm. It only took a few weeks for Dad and some of his friends to build our new barn. It had ten stalls for horses, a feed room, and a tack room. Hot Rod and Smokey would have a great new home and a few new horse friends to spend the winter with.

Tina continued to torment me, although having Smokey and going to school took up most of her time. When I turned eight, my mom signed us up for a local 4-H club for horses. Although 4-H members had to be nine, our leader Mrs. Braun allowed me to come to meetings as an associate member. Our club held meetings at Mrs. Braun's house, which was half way around the block from our house, about one and half miles away. We had riding meetings in the summer where we'd all meet at Mrs. Braun's house and practice riding and play games in a big open field. We held our club meetings once a month in her basement, which was way nicer than our basement. We'd work through our workbooks and plan the club's activities for the summer. I really loved going to Mrs. Braun's house in the summer because she let us swim in her pool. It was like the pool at the country club, with a sliding board. Her daughters were in high school and would dive off the top of the slide and into the pool. I'd never seen anything like that before!

Not long after we joined 4-H, my mom finally gave us permission to ride our bikes around the block. She had always hesitated in the past, but since we were now riding our horses to Mrs. Braun's, there was no real reason we couldn't ride our bikes on the same roads.

The road we lived on had a lot of big trucks using it during the week. They were coming from the sand and gravel pits on the back roads near our house. The trucks would speed down the road in both directions, and there were a lot of them. I remember it was on a Saturday when my mom finally gave in to our pleading to ride our bikes around the block, and said we could. There were about seven of us that wanted to make the trip so that helped convince her it would be okay. She said we could go if Tina promised to keep an eye on me. Tina agreed, but only so my mom would give us the okay. The entire block was just over three miles around, which felt like a really long ride, but I was so excited to be allowed to do it, I didn't care.

We had made it almost all the way around, and were approaching the neighbor's house where the ride ended. Just before their driveway everyone else got a last minute burst of energy and used the gears on their ten speeds to leave me in the dirt. My three speed banana bike couldn't help me enough to keep up, so I was the last one on the road. They were all a minute or two ahead of me. I was so excited to have made it all the way without stopping that I crossed the road to turn left into the driveway, when I heard a horn blare behind me. I heard the tires screech but just pedaled harder to try to get into the driveway. The car swerved around me and sped away. I had no idea just how close I came to getting hit. Once I got into the neighbor's driveway and saw the car driving up the road, I got really scared. I had almost gotten hit by a car. It scared me so much I rode home across the front yards from the neighbor's house. I didn't ride a bicycle on that street again until I was an adult.

Later that year, Tina wanted to ride her horse to her friend's house so they could ride together through the woods and look at the fall leaves. Since Hot Rod had such a hard time breathing, my parents found me a new pony. She was smaller but was a local legend. This pony had been owned by three other families when their kids were young, and she had a great reputation for being well behaved with kids. It was now my turn to own Missy. She was a paint pony and was smaller than Hot Rod had been, but she was really well trained and patient.

My mom wanted a few hours of peace, so she told my sister to take me with her on the ride. Tina was mad that she had to have me tagging along, but she knew there was no way out of it. The trip to Tina's friend's house took us across the street, through two wheat fields, and down another street past two five-acre farms. We started our trip and crossed the road, which I wasn't allowed to cross without Tina. We rode across one field and started into the woods on a shortcut to the other field. When we got about halfway through the woods, there was a huge tree that had fallen across the trail. The woods around the trail were thick with lots of skinny trees, so there wasn't a way to go around it. Tina's horse had no problem jumping over the tree, but Missy was just too short to get over it. She tried to climb up on the tree but it was too slippery and her hoof slipped off.

15

She knew she couldn't get over it so she just stood there waiting. Tina was getting impatient and said if I didn't get over the tree she was leaving me there. I was terrified she was going to leave me alone in the woods because I couldn't get around that tree. I knew I had to do something, because Tina wasn't going to turn back and I wasn't allowed to cross the road alone. After she started to leave me, I turned around and started to go back the way we had come. I knew my pony and I would find a solution if we tried hard enough. As we made our way back down the trail, I noticed if we ran around the edge of the woods we would be able to catch up to Tina. Our route was a little longer, but at least the path was clear.

I definitely should have stayed home from this trip, just like I should have stayed home from riding bikes around the block. Tina and her friend spent the entire ride making fun of me and running away from me. I finally got fed up and headed home on my own. Tina yelled behind me to wait or I'd get her in trouble for letting me ride alone, but I didn't care. I had had enough of her and her friend's abuse. I headed back down the path I had taken to get there and crossed the road alone to get home, and nothing happened to Tina or me.

A NEW LOOK

O ur new school year always started after the Great Geauga County Fair, which was over Labor Day weekend. Starting the third grade that fall brought on a different set of challenges. The Auburn School housed only the third grade. It was in a totally different area than my last school, and there were no other schools around it, just cemeteries and the fire station. Mrs. Lindsey was my teacher and she was very nice. She reminded me of my grandma Anna, who I liked a lot. My assigned seat was in the back of the classroom, and I couldn't read the chalkboard. The reduction in the quality of my eyesight had happened gradually, so I didn't realize it had become a problem. I adapted by squinting my eyes to see better. When squinting no longer worked, I decided to ask my cousin Leah what I should do. Leah was always nice to me no matter how mean Tina was. She wore glasses and I knew she would help me.

The next time Leah was visiting, I asked her how she knew she needed glasses. She told me she couldn't read the chalkboard in school. I told her that I couldn't read the chalkboard either, so she and Tina decided to give me an eye test. They wrote some letters and words on a piece of paper and taped it to the wall. Leah conducted the eye test on me since she was familiar with how it worked. She told me to stand at the back of the room and try to read the words. I couldn't read them, so she had me move closer. Again I couldn't read them, so I moved closer. We realized I had to stand about a foot from the wall before I could read the words. Leah then had me try on her glasses. She said they probably won't be perfect, but if they made reading the words easier I probably needed glasses. I was so surprised at how crisp everything was when I put on Leah's glasses I couldn't believe it! I remember looking out the window and being able to see each individual leaf on the tree outside. What a difference! I could read all of the words and letters on the eye test they made for me. Leah said she was pretty sure I needed glasses, and went to tell my mom. Tina, always the skeptic when it came to me, started to tease me, saying I was faking it because I just wanted to wear glasses. I was just happy to know I'd be able to see clearly soon. I also might have been just a little bit happy to have something that Tina didn't have first.

THE AWKWARD YEARS

T ina, Randy, and I were all four years apart. One of the few good things about being four years apart is we never attended the same school at the same time. As Tina exited middle school, I was entering. As Tina graduated, I started high school. Randy began middle school as I began high school. There were no crossovers, which helped each of us maintain our own identity. School was difficult enough without having to worry about my evil older sister being in the same building.

As I entered middle school, I was both emotionally and physically immature. Tina was in high school, which might lead you to believe she would focus less on me and more on her experience, but amazingly she still had enough time and energy to torment me.

Middle school was really challenging for me. My friends were maturing, and I felt like I wasn't. I felt very inadequate at school. It was also a time when Tina started a new type of bullying. She liked to go through my room and take things or hide things from me. She would break into my diary and tease me about it. My mom even broke into my diary and wrote in it. I'm not sure if she was trying to show me how to journal or embarrass me, but it caused me to stop using my diary. Tina liked to take my shoes and wear them. We had a gravel driveway which would chew up heels on shoes if you weren't careful, and Tina was never careful, letting my shoes get ruined. She would then return them to my closet without telling me.

My mom took me shopping before my first band and choir concert, where I'd earned solos in both choir and band. We went to Zayre's department store and I picked out new shoes and a new dress for the concert. I took off the tags and carefully hung my new dress in the closet, and practiced wearing my new heels around the house with socks on so I could break them in before the concert. I carefully stowed them back in my closet in anticipation of my big night.

On the night of the concert I went to my closet to get my outfit. When I pulled my shoes out of the closet the heels were all torn and damaged. I was heartbroken. This was my big night and my shoes were ruined. Tina had gone through my closet and taken my new shoes. She had obviously worn them a few times because the heels were peeling and full of gravel marks. They looked like a dog had chewed on them. I showed my mom the damage as tears ran down my face. At that point there wasn't much she could do, so she tried to distract me so I would concentrate on my performances and not my shoes. She told me no one would notice my shoes, they'd be listening to me sing and play my clarinet. I wore those ruined sandals to the concert. After the concert I placed the shoes where they belonged...in Tina's closet.

As I suffered through the sixth and seventh grades, I watched my friends mature into young women. I was not developing physically at all it seemed, so that gave Tina something else to pick on me about. Her latest attacks on me included, "Fatty, fatty, two by four, can't fit through the bathroom door." That had references to my thick and unshapely mid section, as well as my lack of development in the chest area. To enhance this stage of her bullying, she began to use the new family camera to chase me around trying to take unflattering pictures of me such as in the middle of changing clothes or getting out of the bathtub. Her creativity to torment me never ceased to amaze me.

When taking embarrassing pictures of me got old, she returned to sabotaging my things, like smearing Vaseline on my glasses while I was asleep, stealing my shoe laces, or telling my parents I was doing something I wasn't to try to get me in trouble.

There were numerous times when I felt overwhelmed by Tina's incessant bullying. I would go to my parents begging them to make her stop. The only thing I'd get from them was, "Why can't you two just get along?" I should have known better than to try to get their help. They looked at me like I was the black sheep and troublemaker of the family. Anytime I'd hear them tell me that we should just get along, it triggered an explosion of anger, hurt, and frustration. These useless tirades always ended the same way. I would scream because I was so frustrated, and it would turn into me telling them I hated them, which usually resulted in a slap across the face if I didn't run away fast enough. I'd lock myself in my room and cry and yell how much I hated them. My mom would usually come to the door and tell me to open the door, and because I was obedient, I would. She would then beat my ass and say, "I'll give you something to cry about," or tell me, "This hurts me more than it hurts you." I really doubted that. This happened so frequently throughout my early teen years that I truly began to believe what Tina had been telling me since I was very young, that I was adopted and our parents didn't love me as much as they loved her.

MORE GROWING PAINS

Tina and I shared a bedroom until the summer before she started high school. I knew she had been complaining to my dad about having to share a room with me, so he decided to build her an oversized bedroom in our basement. Tina and I were both very excited to finally have our own bedrooms. Our life in that shared room had come down to having a piece of tape down the middle of the floor dividing the room in half. The only reason it worked is that we both had negotiating power. I had the doorway on my side and she had the closet. We negotiated easement access strictly for the use of the doorway or closet. I'm pretty sure our constant bickering about one of us being on the other's side is what really fueled the downstairs bedroom project, but I didn't care. I just wanted my own room.

I had no idea just how much my life would change for the better once Tina moved into her new room. When she was at home she was either in her new room, laying in the sun, or washing her car. She worked as much as she could at McDonald's, and would be getting a part-time job at an office once her vocational training was complete. I think the reason she stayed at McDonald's as long as she did was because they'd have keg parties in the parking lot after they closed on weekends. She used to lie to our parents about what time the closing shift ended so she could stay out later. I knew but I didn't care because it kept her away from me.

DAYS AT THE RACES

Throughout my life, my dad was an absent presence. What I mean by that is he was physically present some of the time, but mentally absent. He was, as I mentioned earlier, strongly bonded to Tina, and only took interest in me when my mom forced him to.

My dad's passion was thoroughbred racing. Once he was introduced to the racetrack by his work buddies in the early 1960's, he was hooked, but it wasn't the gambling that drew him, it was the horses. My dad had grown up on a farm and loved animals. He loved the athletic ability of the thoroughbred horse and learned as much as he could about the sport as soon as he was able. His buddies introduced him to their trainer friends, one of which became my uncle a couple of years later when he married my aunt. My dad built a bond with the people of the racetrack and soaked up their knowledge like a sponge.

It wasn't long before he and his buddies decided to partner together on owning a horse. It was a great way to get into horse racing without investing a lot of money. My future uncle was the trainer and my dad and two of his buddies were the owners. As opportunities arose, they traded up to better quality horses.

Throughout the years that my dad owned horses, our family spent a lot of time traveling to racetracks in Pennsylvania and West Virginia. We had a pick up truck with a camper top on it. Our parents would load us in the back with a cooler of food and drinks, and then we'd travel the ninety minutes to whichever racetrack our horses were racing. We would travel to the track and spend the entire day and most of the night there because the races took place at night. After everything was finished, we'd load up and head home. One important thing we learned while riding in the back of a truck is that Pringles potato chip cans are not waterproof when your little brother pees in one.

TOUGH TIMES

O ur lives changed dramatically after my dad tried to stop our horse trailer from slipping off of a jack when he was changing the tire. He instinctively grabbed onto it to try to stop it from falling and twisted in such a way that he damaged three discs in his spine. What was once back pain that was manageable with chiropractic care and traction was now a full blown injury that was going to require surgery. My dad was a tall man standing 6'4" so back problems always plagued him, and working in a job that required him to stand for the entire shift didn't help.

The doctor he visited referred him to a specialist. The specialist was a very prestigious doctor who performed spinal surgery. We were told he was one of the top three surgeons in the whole country. His examination concluded that my dad needed back surgery because so many of his discs were damaged. The surgery he was proposing was a total disc replacement in three lumbar vertebrae. Everyone thought and hoped this back surgery would fix his back and he'd be able to get back to normal.

It was determined that my dad was eligible for an experimental back surgery to replace his damaged discs with cadaver discs. He was encouraged by the prognosis and decided to move forward. My mom told us the doctor was going to replace Dad's bad discs with cow's bones because she didn't want to tell us that the bones were actually from a cadaver. She was extremely creeped out by the thought of parts from a dead person being put in his body and thought we would be as well. My dad was going to be one of the first people in the United States to have this experimental surgery. One of the things I remember most is my mom telling us his doctor was such a good surgeon that he wouldn't shake hands with anyone for fear that he'd injure his hands and wouldn't be able to perform surgery. Learning that about the doctor allowed us to concentrate on him rather than my dad's surgery.

A few weeks later my dad had the surgery. Mom said it went well and he would be recovering in the hospital for a few weeks.

One night my mom got home later than normal and told us there had been a problem with my dad's surgery. He had been having really bad pain, worse than it should have been for that stage of his recovery. She told us they discovered my dad's sciatic nerve was accidentally sewn into his incision and it couldn't be fixed. She told us if they cut the nerve, it might stop hurting but there was a chance he'd be in a wheel chair for the rest of his life and he wasn't willing to risk that.

Dad's recovery continued for another week or so before he finally returned home. I know it was killing him to be trapped in that hospital for so long because that is a lot of time to be stuck in bed. It was also killing him to not go to the racetrack.

At that time my dad owned four horses in partnership with a couple of his buddies. Two of those horses were scheduled to race during his hospital stay. He was sure they were both going to run well and might even win, so he sent my mom to the track to place bets for him.

The first horse to race was named Satan's Luck. My mom told me he was winning the race all the way around the track until he got to the home stretch. She had been watching him at the front of the pack when he suddenly fell down, then got back up. The rest of the horses continued on to finish the race but Satan stood where he'd fallen. The jockey came off his back when Satan went down. He knew what had happened and immediately grabbed Satan's reins to stop him from running off, which is what racehorses do. They want to finish the race. Unfortunately for Satan, this was one race he would never get to finish. He had stepped in a hole and broken his leg. The jockey held onto the reins and tried to calm him down while he waited for the vet and transport trailer to get there. My mom ran onto the track and headed for Satan. When she got there, they told her his leg was completely broken in half and he would have to be put to sleep.

In thoroughbred racing, if a horse injured in a race is able to stand, they will load him into a horse trailer and remove him from the track. Depending on the injury sometimes a horse can be saved, so the horse trailer takes them back to their barn. If the horse's leg is broken, they will take him to an area in the back of the racetrack where he is euthanized. Satan was trailered to the back of the track where he was euthanized. It's always sad to lose an animal unexpectedly, but this was not just an animal, it was also an investment. My mom didn't want to break the bad news to my dad but she knew she had to, so she went right to the hospital after the race.

Not too long after Satan's untimely death, another one of my dad's horses was scheduled to race. It was the same story, the horse was supposed to run well so my dad sent my mom to the track to place a bet. This horse's name was Krystolite. It was like deja vu. Krys was winning the race and when he got to the home stretch, right where Satan had broken his leg just two weeks earlier, Krys apparently stepped into the same hole and broke both of his front legs. Once he went down he couldn't get back up, so the vet rushed over and they put him to sleep him right there on the racetrack. Once again, my mom had to head to the hospital to break the horrible news to my dad. None of us could believe so much bad could happen so quickly.

It felt like we were covered by a dark cloud. Not only was my dad's back in bad shape, but he'd lost a lot of money when those horses died. My dad and his buddies never wanted to pay to insure the horses, so losing them was a total loss.

Shortly after that, my dad came home. The doctor said he was a good candidate to apply for Social Security Disability benefits, and referred him to a lawyer to help. He was only home for a couple of weeks before we learned that in order to apply for disability benefits, he would have to try to return to work. They said he'd have to work two weeks at his job in order for a determination to be made. He got ahold of his union hall and arranged to return to work on a temporary basis.

When he got home from his first day back, he was not in a good mood. His back was killing him, and to make it worse the conditions at his job had changed a lot in the months he'd been absent. Some of his coworkers had retired, some changed shifts, and some new younger men were brought in. I remember him complaining how much it had changed and that the younger men had stolen some of his tools while he was away. He said the new guys had no work ethic and couldn't do the job, and no one seemed to care. This concerned my dad a lot because he was a machinist for aircraft landing gear that had to be close to perfect, which is probably why he would never fly on an airplane after that.

It was evident he was suffering both emotionally and physically. My dad suffered through work for just over a week before he couldn't take the pain anymore. He went to the doctor and got a letter that said he was no longer able to perform his job and retired. He was just under thirty years at the job, but they gave him his gold watch anyway. The lawyer was able to proceed with the claim, but he told us it could take a couple of years to get approved, so my parents should do whatever they needed to do to get us through.

My mom embarked on an adventure in saving money. She sourced huge blocks of American cheese and boxes of crackers from the county welfare office, we applied for free lunches at school, and we used to visit the potato farmer's field after he finished harvesting. He would let us follow the harvester and take whatever potatoes the machine didn't pick up. Mom also shopped at the day-old bread store and bought us Hostess cakes that were on clearance. She'd buy large bags of them and freeze them. We cut back spending on clothing and only purchased what was absolutely necessary. I was told we couldn't afford new glasses since Tina had to get braces, so I was given my cousin's old frames after she got new glasses. I was just thankful I had straight teeth and wouldn't need braces. I probably wouldn't have gotten them because I wore glasses.

ENOUGH

The differences in Tina's and my childhood were blatant. Tina was allowed to do extracurricular activities and I wasn't. She belonged to the Ski Club, where she learned to ski, and spent the next three years traveling to the two local ski resorts with her friends. When I reached the age where I could join, I was told no. My mom told me I was too clumsy to ski, and that I'd break my leg. When I argued that I hadn't broken any bones yet, it turned into the familiar answer of, "It's too expensive."

When my parents weren't telling me to get along with my sister, they were telling me something was too expensive. My life had turned into a cesspool of negativity, and I hated it. I watched Tina get everything she wanted handed to her while I was constantly denied. I either had to deal with Tina's hand-me-downs or nothing.

My dad finally finished Tina's downstairs bedroom. After she moved down there and started to work full time, we saw less of her, which was fine with me. There was one weekend morning during the winter that I remember vividly because we were both wearing flannel nightgowns. Tina came into the kitchen from her bedroom downstairs and started teasing me about being fat or flat chested or something like that, I can't remember specifically. She always whispered her insults in my ear so no one else would hear her. She enjoyed sending me into an emotional rage and causing me to cry even in my teens. What I do remember is that whatever she said or did to me ignited a rage in me that had never been lit before. I turned around and lunged at her knees, tackling her like a defensive lineman. I landed on top of her as she fell to the floor. I began to hit her in the face and head, and she started to pull my hair and try to hit me back. Nothing she did made me stop. My mom was so shocked it took her a second to process what was going on. Once she realized that we were fighting, she grabbed me by the hair and pulled me up and off of Tina. I snapped back to reality and told Tina through gritted teeth to leave me the fuck alone, and then went to my room.

I am not and have never been a violent person by nature. I hate violence. But whatever Tina had whispered in my ear had struck such a nerve that it caused me to react with physical violence. That was the day that all of the suffering at the hands of my older sister ended. Our family dynamic really changed that day. I felt like my mom had developed a sense of respect for me for defending myself instead of crying to her. She never really talked about it with me, but her attitude toward me changed that day. It felt like she liked me a little more, even though she had to pull me off of my sister. It just felt different.

It was shortly after that when Tina moved out of our house, for the first time.

DRIVING TOWARDS A JOB

My sixteenth birthday couldn't come soon enough. I had long dreamed of the freedom only a driver license could offer. I would be starting my first real job and had survived the first two years of high school. Since Tina had moved out, I was able to move into the large bedroom downstairs. It felt like I had my own apartment.

Our house rules said that everyone got a job at sixteen, no exceptions. Unfortunately, when I turned sixteen in August I was in the middle of my high school driver education course and wouldn't be finished until October. The course was free and had a long waiting list, so I wasn't able to enroll until just before I turned sixteen. It was a weekend-only course so it lasted for several months. Because of that, I would have to put off getting a job until October when I would be able to drive myself to work.

One thing I didn't anticipate was my mom dictating where I could work. As was the pattern of my life, my mom made me follow in Tina's footsteps. I really wanted to work at Geauga Lake, our local amusement park, but my parents told me I had to work at McDonald's. I knew there was no fighting it, so I planned to apply for a job at McDonald's.

When the driving course was finally over, I scheduled my driver's license examination. I studied harder for that test than any test I'd ever taken in school. This was really important. We set up an appointment for late October, and unfortunately that was a year we had gotten snow early.

The snow had been on the ground for a couple of days and it remained freezing.

I had passed the written examination and was in the middle of my driving test. The man that was proctoring my driving test wasn't very friendly. He was very stoic and kind of scary. We had driven around the town square in Chardon, which is the county seat of Geauga County, where we lived. All I had left to do was the parking portion. There were four cones set up in the shape of a rectangle and one cone to represent where the front bumper was to stop. As I was entering the makeshift parking space, I hit a patch of ice. That was all it took to make me slide into the cone with my front bumper.

I failed my driver's test. My mom, desperate for me to get my license so she could relieve herself of taxiing me around, begged the instructor for another chance. He denied it and said, "You only get one chance to hit a parked car. She can retest in thirty days."

In great frustration, she drove me home. I didn't want to take a chance of hitting another patch of ice and wrecking the car. McDonald's had called offering me the job and now she knew she would have to drive me to and from work until after Thanksgiving, when I would be eligible to retake my test.

WORKING GIRL

As my mom dropped me off at work on my first day, I flashed back to the times she'd forgotten to pick me up over the years. The worst one was when I was in first grade, and I was enrolled in Saturday morning catechism. Class ended at ten thirty, then we all went to the rectory for Kool Aid and cookies. I was supposed to be picked up by 11:00 a.m., because that was when they locked the building and everyone left. Eleven o'clock came and went, and I waited. The last sister to leave asked me if someone was coming to get me, and I told her my mom was coming. The sister left and said she'd be back to check on me soon.

When the sister returned to check on me it was around twelve thirty. I had gotten really worried because I'd been waiting for a really long time and had no idea where my mom could be. The sister tried to call our house but there was no answer. I got really worried and began to cry. The sister was really nice to me and sat with me. My mom finally showed up about a half hour later. I was so relieved that when I saw her car coming into the parking lot, I jumped for joy. Before I saw her pulling in, I was starting to believe all of the things Tina had said about me being adopted and unwanted.

There were also a couple of times in middle school when I was forgotten after volleyball practice, and a time or two in ninth grade when I had been forgotten after marching band practice and I just decided to walk the three miles home. Being forgotten that many times was especially hurtful knowing it never happened to my sister.

It was exciting to start working at McDonald's. Aside from the inconvenience of having to get a ride for the first month, I loved my job. I took my responsibilities seriously and the managers loved my strong work ethic. I was eventually trained on all stations of the restaurant and given the choice of where I wanted to work when I reported for my shift. It felt great to be appreciated and valued. I made sure my bosses knew they could trust me, and I worked hard to please them. I worked a lot of evening shifts because I was in school and marching band. Sometime after football season ended and my marching band commitment was over, I was able to be more flexible with my work schedule. This gave me the opportunity to meet new coworkers and make new friends.

I remember one weekend day parking next to a 1969 Chevelle at work and seeing the driver wearing his navy blue polyester McDonald's uniform. The car was what initially caught my eye, but the guy sitting in the car listening to the radio before his shift interested me further. I told him I liked his car, then he thanked me and introduced himself. His name was EJ. I told him my name and we walked in together.

There was a break room in the back of the store where we'd all hang out until our shift started. We'd grab a soda on the way in and hang out back there until our shift started. The work schedule was mounted in a plexiglass holder on the wall. As we walked into the break room together he ran his finger across the line where his name was printed to check his schedule for the following week. I noticed his last name was Polish, like mine. He then put on his paper hat and headed to the grill area, as I made my way to the fry station where I was assigned that day. I was really excited to be put on fries that day because it gave me an opportunity to fraternize with the guys in the grill, which I fully intended to do. EJ was friendly but pretty shy, so we spent a few weeks working up the courage to really talk to each other. I began to realize he liked me because he'd show up in the break room anytime I was there. It was very exciting to think a cute guy liked me!

We had become friends at work and took every opportunity to hang out before or after our shifts when we were scheduled together. We both began trying to create opportunities for little impromptu passings in the break room, taking out trash or getting stock from the back room. We eventually started to take our breaks together so we could get to know each other. This had gone on for a few weeks with no offers for a date. When the holidays passed and he still hadn't asked me out, I began to lose hope. I started to think he didn't like me as much as I liked him so I just concentrated on work.

When spring break came about, my parents had called my manager at work and asked him to schedule me to work every day. I ended up being scheduled to work the day shift for the whole week. EJ had remained on his evening schedule throughout the week. I didn't even see him most of the week because I left before he arrived.

After my shift ended one afternoon, I found EJ sitting in his car parked right next to mine. He started in with small talk and then eventually worked up the courage to ask me out. I was so excited I couldn't believe it! I actually said to him, "Took you long enough! I've been waiting for weeks."

We grew close very quickly. EJ had a beautiful soul. We were both friendly but shy. As we struggled to find our sixteen year old selves, we clung to each other like two drowning victims. We spent every possible moment together dreaming of what it would be like after we graduated and could finally live together.

EJ lived in Solon, where McDonald's was located. Solon's school district was much nicer than mine because Solon was an actual city. My school was in a rural area called a township. We didn't even have a downtown. Our township had a bunch of churches and bars, one gas station and a couple of cemeteries. Our school looked like it had been thrown together in the middle of a hay field. His school had things like swimming pools, an auditorium, gymnasiums, and a really nice football stadium. My school did not. It was significantly less impressive. I wished I could have gone to EJ's school, and not only because it was nicer but because it was somewhere else. I had spent my entire childhood wanting to be somewhere else and embedding myself into EJ's life gave me that chance.

EJ lived with his mom on the outskirts of town. His mom treated me like the daughter she never had and welcomed me into her home. She even hung my graduation picture on the wall next to EJ's. That was the only time my graduation photo was hung on any wall. EJ's family consisted of his mom, her fiancé who lived in Aurora, the next town over, and EJ's brother and sister-in-law with two young kids, who also lived in Aurora, but closer to me. They had family dinners on most Sundays, and I was always invited. I felt loved and safe when I was around EJ and his family.

EJ and his brother were eleven years apart. When he was young, his mom worked a corporate job while depending on her older son to babysit EJ. The eleven-year age difference afforded their mom a built-in babysitter. Raising two sons as a single mom instilled in her a strong sense of independence. As her sons grew older, she came to love having her own home and living by her own rules. She didn't have room in her life for a husband, and quite frankly, didn't want one. She and her fiancé had been engaged for eighteen years and maintained their own homes. They enjoyed regular dates, but EJ's mom said she liked her own house and not having to share her bathroom. I couldn't understand why she didn't want to get married. Her fiancé was a great guy, but that mystery was solved when I was invited to a party at his house. We arrived to meet five of his six children, three of which were still living at home. The differences in the two households were immeasurable.

My constant companionship with EJ created a dream world for me. Having him to lean on gave me a strong sense of security and definitely bolstered my formerly low self esteem. I don't want to say I wasn't anything without him, but feeling the love he offered me changed my life. About three months into our relationship, we lost our virginity to each other. It happened one night on the floor in our family room. Creating that connection with EJ really strengthened our bond. Like most other couples, it was as underwhelming as can be expected. Love doesn't make much difference when losing your virginity.

Our lives centered around work and school. We usually ended up working on Saturday nights, so that gave us the other days to be together. We spent a lot of time going to car shows and swap meets because 1960's era muscle cars were a big passion of EJ's, and eventually mine. EJ ended up selling his Chevelle and upgraded to a 1969 Plymouth Roadrunner. It was a really cool car and we both loved it. It was my favorite color, aqua. The car had some engine issues so EJ set out to rebuild it. He had the block machined and replaced all of the internal parts. EJ's brother's best friend had a really nice garage with a lift in it that was only a few minutes from his house. He was kind enough to let EJ work on the car and engine there. We spent a lot of nights and weekends rebuilding the engine. He worked really hard to get the Roadrunner back together in time for our prom, and fortunately he made the deadline. I learned a lot more than I ever knew about cars by the time we finished.

We attended EJ's school's prom in the Roadrunner. It was a magical night. We went with another couple we were close to, and all of EJ's friends were there as well. None of our boyfriends would dance, so the girls danced most of the night together, then we went to an all-night after party put on by the school. It was a casino night that lasted until 2:00 a.m. My parents didn't want to release me from my standard curfew (which was 11:00 p.m.) even though it was prom night, so after begging EJ's mom, she spoke to them assuring them she'd make sure we were home right after the after party and that we wouldn't drink. The funny thing is I didn't drink anyway, that was my sister's thing. My parents' feelings about letting me stay out all night at a school sponsored event proved that they never took the time to get to know me. It hurt me deeply that they always assumed the worst from me. At that stage of my life, I didn't drink or smoke. My bad habits were having sex with my boyfriend and shoplifting.

My parents' lack of trust was further illustrated one Sunday when a big group of our friends got together at a local water park for the day. EJ and I had arranged for the day off so we could go. We carpooled because it was a forty-five minute drive to the waterpark, so we only drove three cars. It was a great day. We had perfect weather which was thankfully very hot because the waterslides were very cold. It was Cleveland, after all.

Just after lunch, one of my friends said they heard my name over the loudspeaker. They were paging me to come to the front gate. As EJ and I made our way to the front entrance, I was wondering what could have happened that would cause me to get paged. As I approached the entrance, my questions were answered. My mom was waiting for me with my McDonald's uniform in her hand. She and my dad had driven forty-five minutes to tell me that McDonald's called needing me to cover a three-hour shift, and she told them I'd be there. My friends couldn't believe they'd drive all that way just to make me work a three hour shift, but it didn't surprise me at all. It just pissed me off.

I was made to stay busy. If I didn't have a shift scheduled at McDonald's, I was told to clean my room or some other chore created to keep me at home. My parents felt the busy schedule reduced my chances of getting into trouble. I suspected a very brief conversation with my mom was the culprit. We were in our front yard washing our cars when she asked me one question that sealed my fate.

Before I get into that conversation, I think a little background is needed. My mom was an only child, but had two younger half sisters and a half brother. My mom had always had a very strained relationship with her mom because of alcohol. My mom was removed from her family home when she was fifteen by her father's sister and brother, because her stepfather made advances toward her when he was drunk. He apparently liked to drink, but wasn't good at it. When my mom told her Aunt Katie what happened, Aunt Katie sent her brother to rescue my mom immediately. By dinner time that night, my mom had a new home with Aunt Katie and Uncle John. She remained there until she married my dad in 1955. My mom never told me the story, but she told Tina. Tina only mentioned it once in passing, but I never got the whole story. Because of that strained relationship, my mom had difficulty establishing a relationship with her own daughters. There wasn't a lot of affection or bonding with us, and she ruled by fear. She always took good care of us, but when it came to having a personal relationship with us, there was a very big disconnect. A good example of this was the abbreviated conversation she and I had about sex.

My mom and I were outside in the front yard, each washing our cars, when out of the blue she blurted out, "Are you having sex with that boy?" I was shocked because she really liked EJ yet referred to him as "that boy," which gave the impression she didn't know him. Because I am so obedient, I quickly answered, "Yes." She then finished the conversation with, "You'd better go to the family planning clinic to get birth control." Because I was so shocked at the whole situation, I simply answered with, "Okay," and that was the end of it. There was no further conversation or guidance offered. We just finished washing our cars and went about our day. I realize it felt awkward for her, but she was my mom. She was the one responsible for teaching me about my body, but she couldn't bring herself to have a difficult conversation like that with me. She pushed me off on someone I didn't even know.

After I finished washing my car, I got out of there as quickly as I could. I raced over to EJ's to tell him what had just happened. Even though I hadn't gotten my period yet, we had no idea what was or was not possible, so we weren't taking any chances.

When we arrived, I was taken in the back, asked some questions and given an examination. Once we were finished, EJ was brought in and they asked us some questions together. The nurse decided to give me birth control pills, spermicidal foam, and condoms for back up. They were aware I hadn't started my period yet, but they told me to take the pills anyway. The nurse showed me how the dispenser pack worked and gave me two pills to take right there. She said I needed to take a double dose of the pills to get started, and then take one every day.

On the thirty minute ride home I began to feel nauseous. By the time we got back to my house, I felt really really nauseous and very weak. We were confused as to how I could have gotten sick so quickly, but we just thought I'd gotten the flu or something. By the time we reached my house, I felt so horrible I crawled right into bed.

The nausea got worse and worse until I started throwing up. It kept getting worse to the point where my mom started to worry, which was not like her. She brought me ginger ale and a cold towel to put on my head. Nothing helped me feel any better. As I lay curled up in the fetal position, I remember begging God to let me die. That is how bad it got. I remember EJ trying to comfort me but he was afraid to get too close because we weren't sure what was wrong with me. He didn't want to catch whatever I had, if that was possible. Although he kept his distance, I could tell how much he loved me. He was willing to stay by my side even through these horrible circumstances.

Fortunately, I was better by morning. My mom thought it was the overdose of the birth control pills that had gotten me so sick, and was mad at the clinic for having me take a double dose. I was terrified to take those awful pills but wasn't willing to risk a teenage pregnancy, so I waited a day or two before I took one.

My relationship with EJ continued to grow. He was my first love.

I loved him with all of my heart. When my school was preparing the yearbook that covered my senior year, they asked us for a quote to put under our senior picture. Mine was, "I want to marry EJ Kowalski."

I had everything I wanted in EJ, or so I thought. He loved me but because of how he had been raised, he had strong opinions against marriage. I knew his father was not a good one, but I didn't realize until later how much it had messed with his mind. I never dreamed he didn't want the same things I did.

THE BEGINNING OF THE END

Before we knew it, EJ and I had been together for almost a year. We lost our virginity together and learned to love the security of our relationship. We remained very close, even though there were changes in both of us. I was very comfortable in our relationship. I loved and trusted EJ with every fiber of my being. I thought that trust went both ways, but it didn't. EJ was starting to act a little bit jealous when I'd be around other guys. I am not a jealous person, so it was a foreign emotion to me. I did everything I could to comfort him if he seemed unsure of anything, and thought that was enough.

I think the beginning of the end of our relationship was a day I skipped my lunch period and drove to EJ's school. I was on a work release program to go to a secretarial job in Streetsboro, a couple of towns away. I was allowed to leave before my lunch period if I wanted to, and that would give me enough time to detour to EJ's school for a visit. I'd have just enough time to say hello before I headed to work. He would be in his Auto Mechanics lab at that time and they usually had the garage door open, so it would be easy for him to see me drive up. We had talked about me visiting in the past, but this was the first opportunity I had to do it.

As I arrived, it started to rain so EJ invited me to come inside the shop so he didn't have to stand in the rain. He wanted to introduce me to some of his classmates. It was nice to put faces to names after hearing so many hilarious stories about the group, especially the teacher. He introduced me to everyone, then I hit the road. I didn't want to be late for work because of the rain.

About a week or so later, EJ and I were having a conversation that gave me a weird vibe. We were talking about work and school, when he suddenly accused me of liking Dave, one of his classmates from Auto Mechanics. I thought he was kidding at first, but then his tone changed to something I'd never experienced before. He believed it was true.

All I could think to say was, "Who's Dave?" He replied, "You know who Dave is." I came back with, "No, I really don't." That wasn't enough to satisfy EJ. He was like a dog with a bone, and kept harping on it.

I was very hurt, confused, and shocked. I didn't even like anyone else, I only loved EJ. All I could remember about Dave was he had cut the sleeves off his coveralls. I didn't remember what he looked like, just the missing sleeves, which I thought was odd for someone that was working on cars. I was really caught off guard by EJ believing I was interested in anyone else. I thought he understood how much I loved him, but to help to prove it to him, I began to take extra care to show him my loyalty and how much I loved him. But no matter how hard I tried, it was clear that something between us had changed.

NEW BEGINNINGS

Before we knew it, graduation day was upon us. My commencement started before EJ's, but the times were too close for him to make my ceremony or vice versa. We planned to meet up later that afternoon.

As my class and I waited in the hallway for commencement to begin, I found a few of my old friends and gave them a hug. I knew it would probably be a while before I saw them again. My secretarial job was turning to full time in a few days, and I still worked a few evenings and weekends at McDonald's. My parents strongly encouraged me to keep both jobs since I chose skip college. I was the only one of my friends that wouldn't be attending college in the fall. I'd invited them all to my graduation party, but everyone's parties seemed to overlap so no one could commit.

It was finally time for us to line up and walk into the gym. Kenston High School's Class of 1985 would soon be free. It was an amazing feeling to know that I wouldn't have to go back to school again unless I chose to.

After we filed into the gym waving to our friends and family, we found our seats. We were told each row was to rise together, make our way to the podium, return to our seat, and remain standing until the entire row was back. We'd all sit down at the same time, then the row behind us would stand together and follow the same order. As it worked out, I was the last person in the first row.

The time had finally come for me to get my diploma. I shook hands with the principal and walked off the stage. I had been keeping a close eye on the time throughout the ceremony and realized if I left right then I would be able to make the last half of EJ's commencement. Since his last name fell in the middle of the alphabet, I just might get to see him graduate. Because I really didn't care about my own graduation, I left the stage and quickly walked to the back of the gym toward the nearest exit. Once I was out of the gym, I stripped off my cap and gown and ran to my car.

Luckily, I was able to find a parking space and get inside just in time to hear his name called. I was standing at the back of the auditorium by the exit doors as I watched him cross the stage. I remained there to see a few other friends cross the stage, then made my way outside to wait for everyone. I found EJ's mom and her fiancé while we waited for the graduates to exit the building. His graduating class was much larger than mine, so it took awhile for them to file out.

I didn't mind missing the rest of my graduation. I felt much closer to EJ's friends than I did my own. We had drifted apart when I had to quit marching band after my junior year to work. That is still one of my biggest regrets about school. I'd been in the band since fourth grade and loved marching band more than anything else, but I decided to get out of school early on work release so I could take that secretarial job. Band was the last period of the day, so I was already halfway through my work day by the time it started. It just wasn't possible to do both. EJ's friends had accepted me as one of their own. We'd gone to their prom together and spent many weekends together. They really proved to me how much I mattered to them when they all showed up at my graduation party. It was a bit of a long drive, but they came anyway. That really made me feel special.

SUMMER OF FREEDOM

Because I was still seventeen when I graduated, my parents made me adhere to an eleven o'clock curfew. They said I would have it until I turned eighteen, which wasn't for two more months. I was royally pissed. I still didn't drink, but sometimes we'd go to parties that were near EJ's house and I had to leave early so I'd be home before curfew. I swore my parents hated me.

Because I still worked at McDonald's occasionally, I became friends with one of my manager's daughters. Gina taught me how to shoplift, and we acquired all of our outfits together. We had all of the same clothes, except she wore them in black and I wore them in purple. This was the era of Billy Idol music, parachute pants, chain belts, and high tops.

Gina's family was going on vacation to a water park for Fourth of July and she invited me to come along. My parents begrudgingly allowed me to go after Gina's mom talked to my mom. Gina's mom was strict but fair at work. I really liked her. She appreciated that I was a hard worker and let me have a long leash at work. I guess my parents felt if the woman could manage me at work, she could manage me on vacation. I didn't care why, I just wanted to go. The lodge we visited was a really cool indoor/outdoor water park resort (we did live in Ohio after all) about a two hour drive from home. Since I was still struggling with EJ's jealousy, I was excited to see if my absence would make his heart grow fonder.

On our first night there we went to dinner at Ponderosa Steak House.

Gina and I ordered the fish. On the way back to the resort I started to feel abdominal cramping, and by the time we got back to the room Gina was feeling nauseous. We chalked it up to bad fish and went to bed.

The next morning I still had cramps, but Gina was fine. They weren't as bad so I didn't think anything of it. When it was my turn in the bathroom I was shocked at what I'd found. The cramping was due to the arrival of my long-awaited womanhood. I'd finally hit puberty a month before my eighteenth birthday.

As I've mentioned earlier, my mom wasn't the best at teaching me the things she should have. All I knew was what I learned in Health class, which wasn't anything I needed in this situation. I freaked out a little bit. I had no idea how bad this could be or how to use feminine products, and here I was at a water park of all places. Of course, I had a stockpile of supplies at home, since I'd been collecting the free samples we would receive in the mail, but I'd brought nothing with me. Adding to that, the resort was in the middle of nowhere, so I didn't want to ask Gina's parents to drive me all the way to the nearest store. That would only create questions that I didn't want to answer. My only hope of avoiding embarrassment was to get the supplies I needed from the gift shop. I hoped and prayed they would have the supplies I needed tucked behind the ice cream bars and sodas. I was terribly embarrassed for some reason, and didn't want anyone to know what was happening to me. I guess it was the fact that I was so late in getting my period. I was afraid if Gina's older sister found out that she'd tease me, which I hoped to avoid since we still worked at McDonald's together.

Fortunately, the gift shop offered a decent selection of products to choose from, which was great. Unfortunately, Gina's sister happened to be shopping for candy as I was shopping for my feminine supplies, and she spotted me. I tried really hard to act like I knew what I was doing and it must have worked because she just snickered as she sang in my ear, "You got your period and we're at a water park." I just laughed and said, "Of course I did." Thank goodness she didn't figure out it was my first period.

There are a lot of products in this world that come with unnecessary instructions, but in my situation at that moment in time, I certainly hoped that was not that case for the tampons I'd just purchased.

SUMMER OF CHANGE

I missed EJ terribly while I was on vacation and was eager to get home so I could see him. I promised I'd call him once in the middle of the trip, but that was all because it was a long distance call and I'd have to keep feeding coins into the phone. When I called him, one of the first things he asked during our call was if I'd met any other guys. I told him I had gotten my period and had cramps and didn't feel much like doing anything. That seemed to put his mind at ease, at least for the moment.

Gina's family lived about a mile from EJ. Since we got back early in the afternoon, I decided I'd stop by to see him. We were happy to be back together. We grabbed some dinner then I headed home. I was still feeling crampy and wanted to rest.

I had only been home for a couple of days when his jealousy once again reared its ugly head. We were in the garage working on his car. We were just talking about my trip and a bunch of nothing when he casually mentioned Dave. I could feel his eyes watching me as he mentioned Dave's name. By this time I knew who Dave was. Dave was one year behind us in school. He had been invited to EJ's best friend Rik's graduation party and got so drunk he threw up in the parking lot so then his friends had to carry him to his car, where he passed out. I also knew Rik had to help Dave get his shit together before he went home or Dave's father would kick his ass. That is the extent of what I knew about Dave.

This jealousy issue had been going on since May, and it was now late

47

July. I'd done all I could do to prove to EJ that I was in love with him, and only him, but he just wouldn't accept it. He just kept harping on it over and over. I finally realized there was nothing I could say or do to change the way things had become so I made the difficult decision to end our relationship.

My heart was broken. I had loved EJ because he was kind and gentle. He'd made me feel like I had never felt before…important. But after the jealousy switch flipped on inside of him, the EJ I knew no longer existed. Nothing I said or did to try and reassure him had worked, and I just couldn't take it any more.

It was a time of very mixed emotions for me. Because our relationship had gotten so bad so quickly, I felt relief when I walked away, but I also felt very alone. We had been constant companions and depended on each other. Not having the stability EJ offered for so long was hard to get used to. As if that weren't enough, with the loss of EJ came the loss of our friends. Most of our friends were originally his friends, and rather than choose sides, they remained loyal to him. The remainder of our friends were in relationships, so finding time to spend with them was challenging, and we eventually drifted apart.

What happened to me next can only be attributed to my immaturity, compounded by my loneliness. EJ's constant accusations that I liked Dave had taken ahold in my psyche. Although I didn't have feelings for Dave when EJ and I were together, I had somehow developed a desire to explore what could happen if we were to get together. EJ and I had been broken up for a couple of months when I decided to learn where Dave lived and stop by for a visit.

I had taken the route home from work that allowed me to pass by Dave's house, and when I saw him out back by the barn, I decided to stop. He invited me to sit on the back steps while he took a smoke break. I had only started to smoke after I broke up with EJ and I didn't like it that much, but it made me feel cool, and knowing that Dave smoked helped me grow to like it.

Dave didn't know EJ and I had broken up. I told him EJ had trust issues and I couldn't deal with it. I was so nervous. I couldn't believe I was sitting there with Dave and having a conversation. I had mixed feelings. The more time I spent with Dave, the more I liked him. He was good looking in his own way, and had this bad boy demeanor, which I was certainly not used to. I couldn't believe I was doing this.

After about twenty minutes, Dave said he had to get back to work. He had been working on his tractor and it was getting dark. Dave was starting a one-man construction company during his time off from school, and planned to grow it more after he graduated the following year. He said I was welcome to join him, so I followed him as we continued our conversation. We talked while he worked for about an hour. I wasn't sure what to expect so I just went with it. I told him I had to get going because I didn't want to keep him from his work, and was very happy when he encouraged me to stop by again.

As I continued to visit Dave, he learned how vulnerable I was, and he took full advantage of it. I fell hard for him, and he let me. Dave never acted like he wanted to date me, he just wanted to fuck me. He always encouraged me to stop by when he was working in the barn, and I gladly obliged. If I knew he was home, I'd drop everything just to spend a little time with him. I became obsessed with seeing him. It was like a secret affair.

After Dave graduated, he got a job at the local gas station as a mechanic. I began to meet him out back for smoke breaks, which always turned into fuck breaks in my car. We'd either drive over to the apartment complex next door, or if time was limited, we'd do it right behind the gas station. I didn't want to accept that I was being used, but it was obvious. Dave justified using me by telling me he was too busy to go out and we'd have to settle with seeing each other during work breaks or in his barn. I was so enamored with him by then that I didn't care. I thrived on the fact that he wanted me around, even if it was just for sex. I chose not to see that he only wanted me for sex, I saw it as someone who wanted to be connected to me, and I couldn't walk away. My life began to revolve around seeing Dave whenever I could.

After work, I'd drive past Dave's house to see if he was in the barn. If he was, I'd stop by and see if he had time to spend with me. If his dad was out there working with him, I'd be given a cold shoulder and would leave. I really didn't have any girlfriends to talk to about our relationship, so I was destined to learn the hard way. Dave's ability to string me along grew stronger over time. Our relationship eventually turned into a full-blown obsession for me. I created a world where I spent every moment of my down time longing to be around him. As Dave got older, he learned to exploit me. He would go on dates with other women, and then come looking for me when things didn't work out. I was his safety net. He was my challenge.

I almost joined the Army, but backed out at the last minute. I couldn't stand the thought of not seeing Dave for so many years. When I told him I had decided not to go, his demeanor changed. What used to be welcome visits turned into him running away from me. If I'd stop by to visit him, he'd tell me he had to go get something and leave the room, then he'd get in his truck and leave me at his house waiting. I didn't care. I'd just leave and wait to run into him next time. I just could not walk away from him. Every time I'd try, something pulled me back to him.

What confused me the most was if I went on a date with someone else, he'd get mad. He didn't want me to date other boys, but he wouldn't commit to me either. One night I was out with my younger cousin when we ran into Dave and his friend. He said he needed to talk to her alone and they left for a while. I was excited because I thought it was a conversation about me, and she'd tell me everything. Later, after we left for the evening, my cousin built up the courage to tell me he fucked her. She claimed she was sorry, but considering who she was dating at the time, I'm pretty sure she welcomed it. I overlooked it because she was one of the few friends I had at that time. This was one more reason I had to get over and away from Dave, but I just couldn't.

Another night, Dave and his best friend went to a party in Mentor, about twenty-five miles away. It just so happened, I was at the same party with a girlfriend from work. She had picked me up in Solon and we rode there together. She'd gone down to the back patio to get a drink and I was upstairs. I could see the back patio from where I was standing, when I saw Dave and Denny arrive. Dave immediately saw my girlfriend, so he started talking to her. As I watched the conversation unfold, I could tell by the body language that he was hitting on her. She got pissed, came to find me and said she was leaving. She couldn't believe he'd hit on her knowing I was at the party. Since I had met the hosts and was having fun with them, I told her I was staying and would find a ride home later. I was really hoping to get a ride home with Dave, even though he'd hit on my friend.

Dave made his way upstairs to where I was and took me by the hand.

We ended up fucking in his car. I told him it was his fault my friend had left and he should take me back to Solon, but he said he didn't have time to get me to my car and get home before his curfew, so he left.

I made my way back inside where the Denny, Dave's best friend, was hanging out with the hosts. They were handing out a new type of shot they called Harbour Lights. Denny said I had to try them because they were awesome, so I did, and more than once. One of the hosts liked them so much, he began to drink the spillage out of the serving tray, which caused us to laugh hysterically. They were a lot of fun and it was a really great party, which was a good thing because I was thinking I might end up helping them clean up in the morning if I couldn't get a ride to my car.

Denny asked me what my plans were because it was nearing midnight. I told him I had no idea. My ride had left me hours earlier, and my car was in Solon. He said, "Come on, I'll get you back to your car," and off we went. We continued laughing for most of the ride back to Solon. Denny had signaled for me to slide over next to him when we left, so I did. I thought Denny was cool and really liked him. He wasn't the pompous ass that Dave had turned out to be. I was having a lot of fun with him as he'd kiss me at each red light. He then asked me if I'd like to stop in the park for a while and I was all for it. Denny was the third guy I'd ever had sex with, and the second guy that night. I couldn't believe I had actually slept with two different guys in one night, but the Harbour Lights had cast a glow on me and I was up for anything. Denny took me back to my car and I headed home. I'd hoped our tryst would remain between the two of us, but it didn't. Denny couldn't wait to tell Dave.

When I stopped by the gas station to see Dave at work the following week, he told me Denny had told him what happened and how disappointed he was in me. He actually tried to make me feel guilty by telling me that he was just starting to fall in love with me. I broke the news to him that I'd watched him hit on my friend from the window above, which shut him up. We finished our fuck break, had a smoke, and for the first time ever, I felt a sense of power.

BOUNCING AROUND

T hings with Dave began to unravel after that, and it was okay with me. I knew I needed help getting over him, and the opportunity presented itself when I began to work at Kicks Night Club in Streetsboro as a waitress. One of the bartenders told me he was looking for a roommate. He acted like he was interested in me, and I saw an out from Dave, so I moved in with him. He lived in a trailer way out in the boonies in Ravenna. It was close to Kicks but far from everything else. He turned out to be a great roommate. I enjoyed taking charge of the cooking, and he taught me about architecture, which was his major in college. We smoked a lot of pot, which led to many deep conversations. The more he got to know me, the more he saw my scars from Dave. This alerted him that I was not a good candidate to date, so we lived together as friends. We did hook up once after a night of drinking heavily, but that was the only time.

Everything seemed to be going great until he told me he was getting back with his old girlfriend. It was sudden and out of the blue, so I was shocked. He'd never even talked about her before. I was also upset because I was afraid I'd have to move back home, and I really didn't want to. But because I didn't want to stand in his way, I immediately started looking for a place to rent. I remembered EJ's mom had an in-law suite attached to her house and that her long-time tenant had recently moved out, so I contacted her. She said she'd love to have me as a tenant and I could move in whenever I wanted to. It was the perfect place for me. It was a large room with a separate kitchen and bathroom, and all I needed. I moved in a few days later. EJ had already moved out by then, which really didn't matter because we eventually made peace with our break up and remained friends. But on the flip side, my new apartment was only about a mile away from Dave's house, and it didn't take long for him to start to show up at my door if he didn't have a better end to his night out. It didn't take long for me to fall back into the old habit of Dave, but having that year away from him helped me grow a lot. I began to use him just as much as he was using me. It was now a more level playing field.

As I settled into my first home on my own, I began to uncover a sentimental side of myself. I think it was because I had cable TV for the first time in my life and got hooked on romantic comedies. I'd watch movies in my down time and longed for that feeling of being loved. This made me cling to my on-again, off-again relationship with Dave, because I'd rather be with Dave than be alone. He was a good fall back when other things didn't work out. Dave had been the second man I'd ever slept with, then there was his best friend Denny, then my former roommate. I picked up a few one-night stands while living with my roommate and before I knew it, the number of men I'd been with was in the double digits.

One night I was watching a movie where the female character kept a list of every man she had ever slept with in her diary. I didn't keep a diary because anytime I'd tried in the past, it was exploited by my mom or Tina who would write comments in it…but I liked the idea of this list. I seemed to be racking up male conquests at a rapid rate, and I knew there would definitely be more in future, so I found a cute little heart-shaped notebook that would serve the purpose nicely. I recorded each man's name and the date of our first encounter, or as close as I could remember. To keep things simple, I made a rule that each man was only recorded once. Subsequent hook ups with the already numbered men would not be documented. No need to waste too many heart shaped pages.

NEW FRONTIERS

Now that I was living in Solon, I wanted to explore local watering holes. I had become a regular at Kicks Night Club because the DJ was awesome and I loved to dance, but it was a bit farther from my new home than I wanted to travel frequently. If I were going to be out drinking, I wanted to be closer to home. In an effort to keep my mind off Dave, I tried to start going out with friends from work. One of them introduced me to a corner bar called The Taverne. Though I'd driven past it many times while growing up, I'd never visited. When we walked in, we were greeted by the manager Jeff, whose parents owned the bar, and a group that appeared to be regulars. They were just a little bit older than us, so I felt comfortable. I also liked the fact that I didn't get the sense we were visiting our fathers' favorite watering hole. The jukebox was playing great music and the people seemed nice. We spent the rest of the evening there and had a blast. Jeff bought us a round of drinks to welcome us and we were invited to join in conversations around the bar. It was great to meet some new people and discover a new place to go in my new hometown.

My parents taught me to work hard and be honest. I was blessed with the ability to learn quickly because I learned by doing. This really helped me excel in the secretarial field due to the different types of phone systems and computer software. I also had to learn teletype because faxes weren't invented yet. Since I wasn't planning to go to college, I knew I'd have to make my own way. I had a good basis of knowledge in the secretarial field which helped me advance my career. I was driven to earn more money and gain more experience, so I'd spend an average of six to nine months at each job, then move on. My first job in my senior year of high school paid three dollars and fifty cents per hour, so getting an opportunity to make an additional fifty cents per hour was hard to pass up.

I eventually turned to working for temporary agencies because they gave me the ability to work in different types of companies and learn more. I enjoyed the short-term assignments, and quickly became an agency favorite because I caught on quickly and got along with everyone. I also have a gift of seeing through people. The most stubborn or seemingly awful people always have a reason. I enjoyed the task of diffusing their anger and getting to know them. The most curmudgeonly people liked me, and people couldn't figure out why. It was fun to conquer their moodiness.

Some of my assignments turned into permanent jobs as well. Because I am a wanderer by nature, the temporary agency stint lasted for many years. It fed my need for change and new things. I never settled for a job that didn't allow me to grow and use my talents. When I felt tethered or limited in my job I moved on. Because I was very motivated and got bored easily, I often worked part time jobs in addition to my office jobs. For a short time one summer I held seven jobs at one time. I worked in a lot of different fields and learned a lot of things. My ambition outweighed my common sense at that point in my life.

It was around my twenty-first birthday when I got hired at a company called Creative Graphics, located in Solon. I had been a temporary employee for the company, and they now decided to hire me on a permanent basis. I was excited to get a job that was close to home. It was a family-owned printing company that handled production of high-end graphic design products. After working in mail order, road paint, and plastics manufacturing, this was exciting. I was supporting twelve sales reps and a sales manager. I was hired for the position because of my multiple types of secretarial experience. This job was much more prestigious than anywhere I'd worked before, and I was honored to have been given the opportunity.

One day I found myself with some spare time before lunch, so I decided to explore my computer, which used one of the first Windows operating systems. I had experience using MS-DOS but not Windows, so the fancy screens offered by Windows tempted me to explore my computer much more than I ever had. I have a tendency to be a bit obsessive about keeping things orderly and neat, which in this case initiated the event that led to the demise of my office career.

I was amazed at how easy it was to move files around with Windows. You could just click and drag files to their new locations. After I had organized my letters and spreadsheets to my satisfaction, I began to explore the other folders which contained the operating system files. These files had strange names that I did not recognize. Computers had only been introduced into the workplace in the previous few years, so I had no idea how a computer worked. I foolishly thought all files accessible to me would be working files such as spreadsheets, letters, or pictures. I was wrong. I began to delete files I didn't recognize because I thought they were from the previous secretary and unnecessary. I had never needed to access them in the past, so I deleted them, then went to lunch.

When I returned from lunch, I attempted to open a letter I had previously written so I could update it for one of the salesman. I couldn't get my computer to work. I didn't understand what was going on, so I contacted the IT department. They sent a tech over, who was very confused as to how the computer reached that state of inoperability. I told him I had deleted some files prior to lunch, and he asked me if I could describe their names. When I told him what I could recall, he started to laugh. He told me he would have to reinstall my operating system and it would take a few hours. I couldn't believe it would take so long. I had letters to get out that day.

A short time later, I was called into my boss' office. He had a very somber demeanor as he gently explained to me that my services would no longer be needed. He told me my skill level wasn't what it needed to be to remain in my position. Not quite sure how it had come to this, I thanked him for the opportunity, then gathered my belongings and left. My pride was hurt, but I was secretly relieved. I was trying to fake it till I could make it, and it didn't work out. I also suspected there was more to my termination than my computer shortcomings.

Before the computer software deletion project, I had been working as a cocktail waitress on Friday and Saturday nights at Kicks Night Club in Streetsboro. Streetsboro was a suburban area closer to Akron than

Cleveland, so it was rare to see people from Solon there, as they tended to travel to Cleveland for fun.

It was a busy Friday night, and I was shocked to see one of the salesmen from Creative Graphics and his girlfriend show up at Kicks while I was working. He was pretty shocked to see me there as well. He was a rich kid from Solon and the best friend of the owner's son, who was also a salesman. The owner's son was a really nice guy, but his best friend was not. He was very arrogant and condescending, and he was my least favorite sales rep.

It was a busy night at the club, and I happened to find a ladies watch on the floor. I turned it into the DJ in case anyone was looking for it. At the end of the night (which was four in the morning) no one had claimed it so the DJ said I could keep it. It was a Gucci watch which was something I'd never be able to afford, so I was thrilled no one had claimed it.

When I arrived at the office on Monday wearing my new watch, the salesman that was at the club asked me where I got it. I don't know why, but I told him it was my sister's. He then proceeded to tell me his girlfriend had lost a watch just like it at Kicks. I knew I should have just returned it, but since I had already lied about where I got it I had to stick to my story. I told him I'd check with management to see if they found anything. The next day, I told him I had checked with management and no one had turned it in. I could tell by the look on his face that he didn't believe me. He got in my face and told me what an expensive watch it was, and how much his girlfriend regretted losing it. I was a terrible liar, so I'm sure he'd seen through my story immediately, but I really loved that watch and insisted to him it belonged to my sister. He immediately adopted a bad attitude toward me, and I'm sure he expressed his feelings to his best friend and my boss, which helped them make the decision to terminate me.

I was fired around three in the afternoon. I used to go to The Taverne after work for happy hour, and since it was wing night I thought a cheap dinner was just the thing for a girl who'd just been terminated. When Jeff saw me arrive so early, he asked what was going on. I told him I had been fired because I broke my computer. After we laughed about it, I asked him if he needed any help. He immediately hired me and put me on the schedule for the next night. Since I knew almost everyone there, it was an easy transition. I loved working at the bar because I wasn't sitting there spending money, instead I was making it. It gave me a much-needed break from the corporate world. Office politics were just not for me.

Since losing my daytime office job, my hours shifted to working evenings and nights. This allowed me to work as a groom at Thistledown, the local thoroughbred racetrack. I had grown up at Thistledown. My dad owned racehorses my entire life, so it was a big part of my life. As it worked out, my dad's horse trainer needed a groom and I was available so I started to work mornings for him. A groom at the racetrack takes care of the horses and works for the trainer. Grooms feed the horses, clean them and their stalls, bandage their legs, get them ready for workouts and races, and cool them out by walking them afterward. My dad taught me how to treat leg injuries when I was a child, so I knew how to do the job better than most. In addition, my cousin worked in concessions in the grandstand and pulled a few strings to get me hired there as well. The job didn't start until after my groom's duties were finished, so it worked out. Jobs in the grandstand were highly coveted because they were union jobs that paid well. They were also seasonal, so you were able to collect unemployment for the winter when the track closed.

I met a few new friends while working in the grandstand. They worked as parimutuel clerks (selling tickets for bets) in the afternoons and grooms in the morning. We hit it off because we all worked multiple jobs and were close in age. As winter approached, my friends told me they were planning to travel to Tampa for the winter. Many of the trainers took their operations to Tampa to keep earning money while Thistledown was closed for the winter. My friend Cindy's stable was one of those that travelled. My friend Willa and I were laid off for the winter, so we decided we would go to Tampa, but we'd have to find jobs when we got there. We wanted to go because we hated Ohio winters and knew we'd find jobs easily.

We did some research, which at that time meant talking to people and using the phone book, and learned about an apartment complex with a three bedroom apartment available for the winter and close to the track. Being close was important, because you had to go back and forth a couple of times a day. I remember the rent was $525.00 dollars per month, plus electric and phone. We jumped on it. We planned to leave on December 12, which would make us miss Christmas at home, but we didn't care. We just wanted to escape the cold weather.

GREENER PASTURES

I had taken a leave of absence from The Taverne and began to receive my unemployment benefits from the concession stand job. I had the car packed and was ready to go. Our caravan of three vehicles would leave Ohio around lunchtime, travel to Kentucky and spend the night with our friend Katie, then continue on to Florida so we could move into our new apartment the day before the track opened. Tampa Bay Downs officially opened on December 15 for the 1991 racing season.

Cindy, Willa and I, along with Cindy's son and my cat, Thomas, arrived at the Village at Old Tampa Bay on December 14 and moved into our new temporary home. We unloaded the trucks and cars and set everything up so Willa and I could look for work the following morning.

On the morning of December 15, Willa and I stopped by Cindy's barn to see if anyone around there needed help. Cindy's stable was the only outfit in her barn at the time, so we left and headed to the track kitchen, which is always a great place to gather information. We then went to the trainers we were told to see and both had jobs by lunch time. We got our credentials, and everything fell together seamlessly.

Cindy, Willa and I were really enjoying our new adventure. Although we worked seven days a week, our days were broken up into segments. We worked for a few hours in the morning, then left for a few hours and only had to return in the afternoon if a horse of ours was running or it was our

59

day to feed the horses dinner. Our feeding schedule rotated through the six grooms, so it wasn't too bad.

Cindy was having an affair with her stable's assistant trainer right before we left for Florida, so she spent a lot of time with him at the apartment. Meanwhile, Willa and I frequented the local bar scene along with some friends from Ohio. This was only my second time visiting Florida, and I experienced a lot of firsts that winter. My friends introduced me to raw oysters at a great local bar called the Sea Horse, Willa and I discovered Karaoke…and unfortunately, Cindy introduced me to cocaine.

The first time I'd ever tried cocaine was one night when everyone was hanging out at our house. Cindy brought her eight year old son to Florida, so we hosted a lot of house parties. He would hang out with us for awhile and then head to bed, so he didn't witness the debauchery.

After Cindy's son had gone to bed, she told Willa and me to go into the guest bathroom, where we saw white powdered lines, a rolled up dollar bill, and a razor blade on the toilet tank lid. I had never been exposed to cocaine, so I had no idea what it was. Willa laughed and showed me how to do a line, so I did. I didn't immediately feel anything, and Willa explained what I should expect. I then noticed a strong desire to chain smoke. We spent the rest of the night talking and smoking…a lot.

Once Willa found a hook up for getting more cocaine, she began to ask me to split it with her, so I did. We enjoyed using cocaine a few times a week after work when we'd go to the beach or to the bar, and it all seemed like harmless fun.

In the meantime, Karaoke had become popular in the area. We were not familiar with it, so it was a great novelty for us. There was a bar right outside the entrance to our apartment complex that hosted it twice a week, so Willa and I decided to check it out. On the first night, we met one of the bar's regulars, a very tall and handsome man named Ken. We learned he lived around the corner and worked as a machinist. Ken and I had chemistry so Willa encouraged us to pursue a relationship. Until that point, my only sexual fun in Florida had been a very adventurous one-night stand with a young man from Texas I'd met at the racetrack. I snuck him in through my bedroom window to avoid waking my roommates. Being a seasonal worker with roommates (including an eight year old), you had to get creative if you wanted any privacy. I was just glad we lived on the ground floor.

Ken and I started to date not too long after we met. He was aware of my living situation, and soon he invited me to stay at his house until I had to move back to Ohio. Since we got along really well, I jumped at the opportunity to live in a house with just one roommate, and of course my cat. I only accepted the invitation after Ken said I could bring Thomas. Ken introduced me to grilling shark steaks, which I loved. We also travelled on weekends to visit his family in New Port Richie. He taught me about the area on our time off work together. It was interesting to see different areas. I would never have done that without Ken's encouragement. Racetrack life was pretty much work, and sometimes going to the beach, so getting out and exploring other towns was great.

One afternoon as I sat home alone, I pulled out my heart-shaped notepad to add Ken to the list. I carefully penned his name and the date of our first encounter. It just so happened he was number 100.

Since it was such a symbolic milestone, I reflected back on the first ninety-nine men and remembered each one as well as I could. Many were one-night stands from being out dancing or partying in downtown Cleveland, some were coworkers, and some were guys I had dated that I'd met at either The Taverne or Kicks. A few I really loved. I was careful to never sleep with any of my bosses, even though the opportunity had arisen a few times. I seemed to gravitate to men that tried to blend in with the background. I dreamed they were the hidden gems that were beautiful souls hidden within a gruff exterior. Unfortunately, most of them were just lazy, alcoholics, or jerks. So much for that theory.

My relationship with Ken was new and exciting. After dealing with Dave's roller coaster ride of a "relationship," I enjoyed feeling appreciated. I also enjoyed that I didn't feel the need to plan anything months in advance. We both knew I'd be leaving in a little over a month so we just took things day by day. One of two things was going to happen…I would either leave, go home, and resume my flirtation with a guy named Carl from The Taverne, or I would create a relationship with Ken that might lead somewhere. I could live with either option, so I was content to just enjoy the journey.

The winter passed quickly because we always seemed to be busy. We stuffed a lot of adventures into our short time together and really grew close. About a week before I was due to travel back to Ohio for the opening of Thistledown, Ken made a knee-jerk decision to leave Florida and travel back with me. I was very excited, and said he could stay in my little apartment with me until we could figure things out. I had the feeling that he was running from something, but I wasn't sure what. It really didn't matter to me because I was going back home. If it didn't work out, at least I would be at home. I didn't object to helping another person escape an undesirable situation, so I headed home with plans that Ken would follow in about a month.

COMING HOME

Coming back from Tampa was exciting. I was excited that my new boyfriend would be joining me soon and looked forward to a great summer. I had returned to working at The Taverne, and also started working as a groom at the racetrack. In addition, it was my third year organizing the beach volleyball league at a large sports bar called Inn the Woods. They had professional referees that worked the nets, but needed someone to organize teams and keep the paperwork straight, which is where I came in. After a year, the professional referees left for greener pastures so I was promoted to head referee and continued my role as league organizer. I was a volleyball player, so refereeing wasn't a huge stretch. I'd learned a lot from the former refs, which made my transition easier. I hired a couple of my former teammates to referee with me, and we made it work. I only worked from April through October due to the courts being outdoors. The owner knew and trusted me by then, so it turned into a pretty sweet gig. We had developed a good following, therefore every league I started filled to capacity very quickly. Because our weather in Ohio was never predictable, there were early spring games that had to be played in socks or water shoes because the sand was still really cold. There were even times I'd referee in sweats and a winter jacket. That's when I learned of the warming effects of brandy.

My relationship with Ken had developed out of desperation on my part. I once again began to realize I'd picked the wrong man. I should have fled the night he told me that if I ever gained weight he'd leave me, but because I was so desperate for companionship, I just assured him I wouldn't. When he finally arrived after wrapping up his business in Florida, his disappointment in my living arrangements was evident. I could tell it wasn't what he'd expected. Again, I chose to ignore the red flag.

By the time Ken made it to Ohio, I was back to working three jobs: The Taverne, the racetrack, and the volleyball league. I had some free time, but not as much as I'd had in Tampa. When I was in Tampa, I got my license to pony, which meant I was able to ride my horse and lead the thoroughbreds to the starting gate before races. I had always wanted to be a pony girl, and was finally able to get someone to loan me a pony so I could get my license in Tampa. When I got home, my dad helped me buy a pony horse, which was a Quarter horse, so I could get started. That added some extra duties to my day, so Ken…again…wasn't happy. He'd begun looking for a job, but wasn't having any luck. I still suspected it was because there was something he was running from. His behavior had really changed between our time in Tampa to his arrival in Ohio. When we used to go out socially in Tampa, he'd have a few beers but never got drunk. He was always in control and able to drive. Now, because I usually drove us, he'd get hammered. He'd drink a lot really fast and then tell me we had to go. Of course, I resisted because on my few nights out I wanted to enjoy my friends, but he'd ruin that for me wanting to leave after only about an hour. I found his behavior selfish, and quite frankly, it pissed me off.

My close friends, the ones that truly cared about me, expressed their concern. Since these were people I really trusted, I began to take notice. After about the third time this behavior with Ken happened, Jeff, the owner of The Taverne, gave me a look. Jeff was the type of communicator that didn't need to use words to convey his message, if you were smart enough to pay attention. He had a very intuitive way of connecting with some people (and fortunately I was one of them) that spoke louder than any words. Jeff's look caused me to take notice. I'm glad it was one of the rare times I'd kept my mouth shut instead of voicing my opinion, and because I didn't immediately act, Ken ambled down a path that would lead him right out of my life.

Most bars have an in-house floozy. At The Taverne we had May, an attractive older woman that made a play for every man in the bar at one point or another. She worked at her wealthy family's business, so she had a limited view of reality as a result of their wealth. I know Jeff had bedded her a few times, but it mostly just out of convenience. You could always tell when it happened because she'd get clingy toward him. When that happened, he would jump into a relationship with someone else just to deflect her. It was pretty comical once you caught on. When I brought Ken to The Taverne for the first time, May's antennae perked up. She stood about five feet ten inches tall, so seeing fresh meat that stood about six feet four inches tall intrigued her. The fact that he was with me only slightly disappointed her. She seemed confident in her womanhood, and became one of his new friends.

On this particular night, everyone seemed to be in attendance. Ken was living up to his past behavior and was downing beers and shots as quickly as he could obtain them, which was usually at the grace of my friends buying a round since Ken still hadn't found a job. I was catching up with everyone I hadn't seen in awhile, meanwhile Ken had drifted toward May, which seemed to happen the more he drank. On my occasional glances his way, I could see Ken was fueling anger because I wasn't giving him my full attention. I didn't care, because my eyes were now open. I wasn't letting him ruin one of my few nights out. Besides, I didn't like the way things were going and I was looking for an easy solution to get him out of my life. Maybe May would take care of that for me.

On my way to the restroom, I overheard him talking and noticed slurred speech. I just shook my head and continued on. By the time I made my way through the line and headed back to the bar, he was gone. I asked May where he'd gone, and she said he told her he was leaving. I thought it was odd that he left without saying anything because we rode there in my car, but I could get a ride home from pretty much anyone so I wasn't concerned.

About an hour later, Kyle the bartender told me I had a phone call. I took the call, and it was my friend Brody. Brody's dad owned the local towing company and did all of the work for the Solon Police Department. Brody told me Ken had been arrested for DUI, and that he had my car at his lot. Wow…didn't see that coming. As I announced what had happened, everyone asked me what I planned to do. They got upset with me when I told them nothing. It was not my problem, and it wasn't going to become my problem. He was on his own. I just wanted…no needed…to get my car back. I had to work in the morning. Then, the opinionated drunks (which included May) started to berate me for leaving Ken in jail. I told them if it was that important to them, THEY should bail him out. Of course, May was anxious to run to his rescue, so she and another guy started to figure out where they could get bail money. Surprisingly the bartender donated the night's tips to the cause. I certainly didn't have or want to contribute any money. After the way he'd been acting, I was cutting ties immediately. As soon as the tip money was procured, May practically ran out the door to retrieve Ken from jail, which I thought was ballsy of her considering she'd been drinking all night as well. She was going to end up right next to him, whether it was in his cell or in her bed was anyone's guess.

Carl made his way over to me and asked me what I planned to do. I told him I needed to get to Brody so I could get my car out of hock. Carl really stepped up for me. He took me to Brody's, made sure I had enough cash to pay Brody for the tow, and insisted I spend the night at his house (in the guest room) because he didn't want Ken showing up and beating the crap out of me because he was mad. That hadn't crossed my mind, but he had a point, so I took him up on his offer. Maybe May would encourage him to stay with her, and then he would be out of my life. Fingers crossed.

Getting up early wasn't difficult because I hadn't gotten much sleep. I thanked Carl for everything he had done for me then headed home to change. Carl was concerned and asked me to check in when I could. I promised I would. When I got home, there was no sign of Ken or his belongings. I don't know what happened or where he went, I was just glad he was gone. I felt like I was just a stepping stone for him to figure out where he was going next, and that was okay, as long as where he was going was out of my life.

It was nice to come home to just Thomas the cat. I resumed my routine of going to work and going out on my designated nights. I didn't realize how much stress Ken had added to my life until after he was gone. It was like a huge weight was lifted off my shoulders. I finally understood why my intuition was flaring up when I asked him to move home with me. I proceeded with the invitation without thinking of the implications and logistics of fitting Ken into my small apartment and regimented life. Fortunately, his DUI arrest was a gift from the Universe removing him from my life.

LET GO AND LET BE

*W*ith Ken's departure came me letting go of the racetrack. Having the expense of my own pony horse and the challenges of getting people that hired me to pay me made it more of a financial hardship to me than it was worth. I'd gotten paid by about half of the people that hired me. There wasn't much you could do to try to collect, short of slashing tires and stealing, which isn't my style, so I sold my pony and left the racetrack all together. Between The Taverne and volleyball at Inn the Woods, I had enough income to sustain my lifestyle. Carl remained a constant in my life after Ken's departure as well. He began to show up more regularly at The Taverne during my shifts, and even surprised me by visiting Inn the Woods a few times. It was becoming clear to me that he was interested in a relationship, and I was flattered by his impromptu visits. I really liked him a lot and wished he'd ask me out, but he didn't.

For a few months, Carl continued to show up where I was but still didn't ask me out. It was as if he were testing the waters and deciding if we should proceed with a relationship. I hoped he would, but I enjoyed the company in the meantime. We spent many hours talking about everything. There was a time I thought he was interested in my friend Terry, but from what she told me they had the same type of relationship we had. I stopped trying to figure it out and just enjoyed our time together.

Carl lived in a caretaker's house inside a condo complex. He had a roommate that lived upstairs, and he lived downstairs. They shared the kitchen, but each had their own space. Carls' roommate was a nice guy, but liked to get stoned a bit too much, and he wasn't super ambitious. The house was the home base for occasional Taverne after-hours parties. The bartenders and waitresses and any regulars that were still around at closing used to head to Carl's house after last call. Once I left the racetrack and picked up Friday nights to work, I started going as well. This was where the coke usually surfaced.

By this time, Karaoke had finally made its way to our neck of the woods. When my former Florida roommates saw the advertisement for it at our favorite racetrack watering hole, The Winking Lizard, we made a date to get together. I explained to Carl what it was, and suggested he join us. He resisted at first, but as I continued to go and meet my friends, he eventually succumbed to the pressure and showed up. It was about our third or fourth time going when he joined us. We had about five or six tables of people every time they had Karaoke. My friend Mike (who was a jockey) and I used to sing "Stop Dragging My Heart Around" and had gotten pretty good together. Mike used to ask me out after he'd get drunk, but he dated another friend of mine on and off and I wasn't getting involved in that. I adored him, but since he was a jockey, he maxed out at 108 pounds. I weighed around 170 and couldn't imagine dating a man that weighed so much less than I did. Call me vain, but it would have bothered me. Once Carl saw that I had another "family" in my racetrack friends, I noticed a change in his feelings toward me. He seemed more comfortable around me. It was the first night he showed up when he and I started really flirting. He would tear the labels off his Heineken bottles and write notes to me on them. Then, he wrote a note on a matchbook telling me how much he wanted to ask me out. I guess he didn't have the courage to ask me, so he wrote me notes. I thought it was the cutest thing ever. I saved all of those notes, and still have them to this day.

ANOTHER NEW BEGINNING

Carl kept the promise he wrote on those notes and asked me out on a date for the following weekend. We went out for dinner and drinks, and we sat talking for about two hours. He then delivered me home and left me at the door with an unforgettable goodnight kiss. I invited him in, but he declined and he had to get home. He seemed to enjoy our evening together, but I got the sense something was holding him back. Whatever it was would eventually surface. I was just enjoying the moment.

I eventually learned that Carl was a marijuana dealer, and had been since he graduated high school just over ten years earlier. He had a specific ring of friends he supplied and was very careful about distributing it. His friends would stop by for their weed, or if he was going out he'd leave it in his gas grill and they'd leave his money in there. Carl lived in a big condo complex that wrapped around a lake, so the little bit of extra traffic went unnoticed. Once I became a customer of Carl's, I felt comfortable asking him if he had a hook up for coke. I still enjoyed using it occasionally and hadn't encountered anyone that indulged since I'd gotten home. Carl told me he did and he would occasionally partake if he could reach his dealer, but he was in downtown Cleveland so it wasn't a frequent indulgence. We lived about a half hour from downtown, and usually by the time we decided we'd want coke, we were pretty drunk. It wasn't a good idea to venture that far away from home in that condition. As we got to know each other, Carl would occasionally get some, but it was very rarely.

Meanwhile, the bar where I'd been running the volleyball league was undergoing changes. The owner had a falling out with his partner who'd moved on to open another bar a few miles away. The partner asked if I'd be willing to leave Inn the Woods and help him start a new league at his new bar. It was located in a Ramada Inn hotel and was to be called Club Iguana. It was a Mexican-themed cantina that painted your name on the wall and gave you a tee shirt if you'd successfully do a shot and eat the Mezcal worm. They wanted to build a beach volleyball court outside the bar and start their own league. The pay was the same but half the work, so I jumped at the chance. They had one court instead of two, which meant I didn't have to worry about hiring other referees or managing as many teams. They marketed the club well, and even had an old school bus that was painted green with the logo all over it. I was excited for the new opportunity.

The place took off like wildfire. I structured the levels opposite of Inn the Woods so teams could play at both places. The owners advertised on the radio and in the newspapers. The month before we were to begin, my rosters were full and the owners were thrilled. They planned events with our bus, and they offered party rides to downtown Cleveland for various events. The bus was entered into the St. Patrick's Day parade, where we thought it would be a good idea to ride on top of the bus so we could throw candy. As we made our way through an intersection, I almost got smacked in the face by a traffic light. I had to lie back so I didn't slide off the roof, which almost happened because there was nothing to hold on to. That was a one-time performance.

The owners offered a bus ride downtown to the Flats, an entertainment district on the Cuyahoga River in downtown, where a professional beach volleyball event was taking place. My bosses got VIP credentials for us, which meant we had preferred seating and were going to get to meet the players. We couldn't wait to get there as we made our way down the Interstate blasting party music and drinking. It was great fun until the bus broke down at the base of the exit ramp, which was two miles from the event. We were forced to hike through some rough areas and under a few bridges to complete our trip, but we made it, blisters and all. I don't know how, but every one of the thirty of us managed to find a ride home afterward. I'm very thankful that I ran into my friend Bernie on the way out. He stuffed four of us in his convertible made for two.

SLIPPERY SLOPE

I was eventually able to secure my own source for cocaine. Once my drinking buddies learned that I had a reliable source, I became their source. That was the easiest business I ever built. I made enough profit from selling to my friends to get mine for free, which turned into a bad thing. The more I got, the more I did.

Carl became a bit more of a constant in my life, appearing at random times during my shifts. Sometimes he would stay until I was finished, and sometimes not. I never knew what to expect. Work kept me busy, which kept me from worrying about what Carl was doing, but I was certainly excited to see him when he did show up. I slowly began to notice Carl's peculiarities. He was definitely more interested in me when he was drinking.

As time went on, we grew closer and eventually started sleeping together. I thought that would progress into more of a relationship, and it did, but not in the way that I thought it would. Carl began to show up at The Taverne during my shifts and wait for me to get off work. We'd go to his house and I'd spend the night. Sometimes I'd spend the next day at his house also, hanging out and watching movies. Our relationship seemed to be moving forward nicely, until an incident occurred that made me rethink our situation. One night, Carl showed up at The Taverne after being out with friends. He'd obviously been drinking for quite awhile and told me he shouldn't be driving, so I told him to wait for me to get off and I'd drive him home in his truck. The next morning, he and his dad were scheduled to do a handyman job, which I didn't find out about until that morning. As I got dressed, he was at his garage putting tools in the truck. His dad arrived and got in the truck. Carl came to get me in the house, and then told me I'd have to ride back to The Taverne in the back of the truck. He claimed there wasn't enough room in the cab with his dad in there. I had never met his dad, and I'm sure he had some wild thoughts running through his head as I came out of the house and climbed into the back of the truck, but I never spent enough time with him to know for sure.

That wasn't the only thing I saw that should have made me run, but being young and laser-focused on having a relationship blinded me to many things. I accepted many of Carl's quirky behaviors because I so badly wanted our relationship to work. I didn't care about me, only him. I bent over backward to make him happy and make him love me more. One thing I really loved about him was how protective he was of me without being overbearing. I always knew, no matter where I was, that he had my back. Since I hadn't had that security since EJ, I felt it was worth dealing with a few quirky behaviors.

As time went on, I learned something from Carl's roommate that helped soften the blow of some of his actions. We were deep in one of our Sunday afternoon stoner talks when he told me that Carl had been engaged just a few years before I met him. The couple had been together for a number of years, but she broke it off. She told him she couldn't marry him because she was gay. I was shocked. I also wasn't sure if he was telling me this because he was trying to encourage Carl and I to be together, or to drive us apart. I never could get an accurate read on him, but eventually chose to believe he liked the two of us as a couple and wanted to share something he thought might help me understand Carl better. We had been talking about how Carl would get very melancholy at the end of a night of drinking and play sad songs on his stereo. Now I knew why. Hearing that story broke my heart. I felt sad for both of them. They obviously loved each other but couldn't stay together if they both wanted to be happy. I couldn't imagine the heartbreak he felt after learning her news. When I learned who she was, it all made sense. I'd actually met her one afternoon when she and her cousin came to visit Carl. She seemed to be happy and relieved, but it was clear the heartbreak was still weighing on him.

Knowing that helped me let go of a lot of things. I did everything I could to make him happy and support him, but there always seemed to be a hint of sadness that just wouldn't go away.

NEW BLOOD

One evening, one of our servers came to work with an awesome new haircut and color. It was perfect for her. We all asked her who did it. She told us she had discovered a new hairdresser named Jo at a little salon in neighboring Bedford. That one hairstyle earned Jo four new customers immediately, and I was one of them. Jo transformed all of us. Once we got to know her, we encouraged her to become a part of our Taverne family. As she became known in the bar, her business grew. A lot of Taverne patrons wanted to see what magic she could create for them. She had a talent for matching the hairstyle and color to the customer's face like no one else.

Jo was recently divorced and had met Carl's roommate when he wandered into her salon. He'd invited her to join us at The Taverne then she eventually joined us on our summer outings going rafting at Ohio Pyle, Pennsylvania, and to the Lake Erie islands. He really wanted to date her, but she wasn't looking for a relationship. She had just gotten out of a bad marriage and wanted to sow her oats. Once I got to know Jo, we grew very close. There were a lot of unexplainable synchronicities between us, which made me look up to her like the big sister I always wanted. Our lives shared a lot of similarities, and we used to joke about being sisters from another mother.

One night, Jo and I were in The Taverne sitting at the bar. It was a great night and it seemed like everyone in town was there. After we had our welcome shots, we looked over the crowd and came up with a game to entertain ourselves. We called it, "How Many Men Have You Slept With in This Bar?" As we scanned the crowd and counted our conquests, I came up with six, and she came up with five. As we revealed our conquests to each other, we were shocked to find we had one man in common. We couldn't believe that we had both slept with Dr. Steve. He was a psychologist in training, who apparently got around more than we did. Because we were in my neck of the woods, I ended up winning with six over her five. That six included EJ and Dave, my first love and subsequent rebound relationship, respectively. We laughed as she said, "I'll never beat you. My number's as high as it's going to get." Jo was referring to the fact that she'd met the last man she'd ever sleep with. Bill, one of the original Taverne regulars I'd met on my first visit, had finally met his match. When I saw the sparks between the two of them, there was no doubt it was a relationship that was going to last forever.

MORE AND MORE

I was now in my mid twenties and had grown tired of the numerous jobs I had been working. Meeting Jo and seeing the success of her salon helped me decide I wanted to create a career. I wanted to pursue the dream I'd always had of going to cosmetology school. But, being a broke twenty-something forced me to ask my parents for help. Since I hadn't gone to college, they offered to help me pay for a portion of the school, but my mom tried to talk me out of it. She had a way of presenting all of the unpleasant aspects of something I wanted when she didn't want me to choose it. I'm pretty sure she was so adamant because she didn't want to cover the cost, which was around $1,500.00 dollars. She suggested I take the nail technician course instead. She said she would pay for it in full if I wanted to go, so I went to nail technician school thanks to my mom's generosity.

Luckily, they had a class starting a couple of weeks after I'd inquired, so I didn't have to wait long. The class took place in the evenings, so I worked day shift at The Taverne to cover my expenses. Carl and I had been dating for awhile when he allowed me to move in. I don't want to say he asked, because it happened more out of necessity than desire.

I had left my in-law suite at EJ's mom's house to move in with a co-worker from The Taverne. She was going through a divorce and wanted to move to Solon. She and her soon to be ex-husband had a free apartment as a part of their full-time job at their apartment complex. When they split up, the job went away. It was only offered to couples. Because we had known each other for a few years, I felt comfortable moving into a larger apartment with her. We'd been roommates for almost our entire one-year lease period when she started to act bat-shit crazy. She had been telling Carl that I was making long-distance calls to Columbia for drug deals, and that our phone bill was hundreds of dollars. I'm not sure what had brought this about because the phone bill showed only long-distance calls to Michigan, where the man she was now dating lived. Once I showed Carl the phone bill to prove I wasn't lying, he pulled me out of the apartment and "took me in." I made sure to ask him numerous times if he was comfortable with it, and he said he was. I was happy but didn't want this to cause a rift between us. Staying at someone's house is one thing, but moving in is a whole different ballgame.

Before I knew it, I was graduating from nail school and Carl and I had been together almost a year. I passed the State exam, got my license, and Jo said I could set up my nail station in her small salon. She was wonderful and supportive. Although we both desperately wanted it to work, there just wasn't enough space in the small salon. Acrylic nails, which were all the rage back then, smelled pretty horrible. We ended up opening doors more often than not to keep ourselves from getting asphyxiated from the fumes. Though I was eternally grateful for the opportunity, I had to figure something else out.

I learned about an opportunity that was actually located next door to McDonald's, where I'd spent so many years working. There was a new tanning salon that was looking for a nail tech. They already had a lady that ran her own nail business, but she was so full that she wasn't able to take on new clients. The owner saw an opportunity to expand since so many of his tanning clients were asking about nails, so he rented the other half of the room to me. It worked out really well because I was actually a customer of the other nail lady, and we got along really well. The owner of the salon helped me get started and made sure to advertise my services along with the tanning packages, so I built a good business fairly quickly.

By that time, my cocaine use had become more frequent. If I started doing it on Friday night, I lost all control and continued using it all weekend until I ran out. I would get a supply for the weekend, and instead of selling the majority of it, I would end up keeping more for myself than

I intended. I also began to develop a constant runny nose, even when I wasn't using. It became so bad that I had to keep a box of tissues on my station. I found it an inconvenience to have to deal with, but that didn't stop me from using the drug.

Carl had just purchased a home computer and we had the stacking shapes game called Tetris on it. If Carl was indulging in coke with me, we'd sit at that computer and play games all night. If he decided to go to bed, I'd stay up and play Tetris for hours. The longest streak I'd ever played was eight hours. I'd try to go to sleep because my eyes were so fatigued from the computer, but I couldn't because of the speed effect of the coke, so I would take NyQuil. Some nights it worked better than others, and some nights I'd just lay in bed looking at the ceiling until the effects would wear off. I even remember a few times when I'd taken up to six caplets of NyQuil at once. It is a miracle I didn't have a heart attack.

Then there were the nosebleeds. I'd be in the car after a night of partying and my nose would start to bleed. I tried to hide it from Carl as much as I could, but I'm sure he knew. I should have been scared when the nosebleeds would occur, but I was so wrapped up in my own haze, it didn't phase me.

HOW DID WE GET HERE?

One Thursday afternoon as I arrived home from work, I saw a bunch of brown paper shopping bags on the kitchen counter, except they weren't from a trip to the grocery store. They were not on a counter where Carl would have placed grocery bags. These bags contained my belongings, including my drug scale and the packaging supplies I used for my cocaine, some personal products and a few items of clothing. I could tell Carl was waiting for me to get home. He was standing there with a very somber look on his face. As my mind raced to try to figure out what was happening, Carl said that he had had enough of my cocaine use and I had to go. He said I needed help.

I was so shocked that I didn't react. I just stood there trying to process what he had just told me. I realized he was right, and I knew there was no purpose in arguing. I carried my bags to the car and left.

As I was loading the bags into the car, there was no feeling hurt or worried about a place to live. I only cared about the drug delivery that was due in a few hours, and I tried to figure out a solution for my situation. This is the problem with addiction…being homeless and dumped didn't occur to me, all that concerned me was not being able to get the cocaine.

We had just gotten cell phones, but they were expensive to use so we didn't use them much. We paid by the minute, with rates based on Peak and Off-Peak times. Peak time started around 7:00 in the morning and went to 8:00 on the evening. It cost around ten cents per minute. Off-Peak was from 8:00 in the evening to 6:59 a.m. and cost about three cents per minute. It was obviously beneficial to call after 8:00, but that was not possible on that day. I splurged and used the Peak rate to call a friend whose mom owned a local motel, and asked if I could get a room, which in our relationship meant a free room. He said it would be fine for that night, but they were booked solid after that. That was the best news I'd had all day.

When Carl had asked me to leave, I wasn't high. I was never high at work. But, my cocaine-addicted mind was not able to fully process what had just happened. I was so focused on completing my mission to pick up the cocaine, weigh it, package it, and then arrange to deliver it to my customers that I was actually angry at Carl because he had thrown a wrench in my plans. I just saw it as a huge inconvenience and not the life-changing event that it was.

My addiction had crept up on me. First, it started with a few lines I snorted when I lived in Florida and worked on the racetrack. Once I got home to Ohio and separated from the baggage (ex-boyfriend) I had brought home from Florida, Carl and I had enjoyed occasional purchases on drunken nights. It was when I was able to procure my own supplier that the downward spiral began. I would purchase larger amounts, sell to my friends at a profit, and keep some for myself. I got so used to having it around that I began to use it occasionally after work or on days off, which grew into craving it. It really became an issue when it started to interfere with dinner dates, as cocaine is a form of speed and I wasn't hungry when I was using it. Carl had been disappointed more than once when we'd gone to dinner and I didn't want to eat. I usually had a robust appetite, and the body to match. I was around 200 pounds at five feet, seven inches tall then. Carl and I liked to eat rich foods and eat out frequently, so I'd packed on the pounds since I'd moved in with him, but when I did coke, I had no appetite.

Then there was a time we went to the Feast of the Assumption carnival in Little Italy. I got a nosebleed on the way home that I tried unsuccessfully to hide from Carl. And now, I was being asked to leave my home. I couldn't believe how, in just a matter of months, my life was spinning out of control. I didn't understand how I went from being so much in love with Carl to constantly craving poison.

Once I accepted the fact that I was addicted, I looked for a source of strength from which to draw. Unfortunately, my sudden eviction meant I had lost that source. I was in this alone now, no matter what. I had dug this hole and it was up to me to get myself out, but I didn't want to face it quite yet. I told myself I would deal with it tomorrow.

Fortunately, I was able to sell all of the coke. It was never hard to upsell to my customers. They were always willing to buy extra. I offered quantity discounts to get rid of it so I wouldn't be tempted to use it. At least my addiction hadn't become so bad that I suffered any type of withdrawal symptoms. If I removed the temptation I was okay.

I spent the following night on my friend Anita's sofa. She said I was welcome, but her heater was on the blink, so we had to rely on space heaters. I didn't care, I was thankful to have a place to stay. Anita was a great friend. We lived in different towns so we didn't spend a lot of time together, but we went to the same school and had known each other for a long time. When we saw each other, we had a great time, but we both worked crazy jobs and never seemed to have set schedules. But when we were together, adventure ensued. I have always loved her for that.

We had a great talk about what was going on, and she really helped me. She told me it was my responsibility to accept my problem and take action. It wasn't going to fix itself. She also had a complicated past relationship with a Taverne man, so she understood the complex dynamics of my situation and how difficult life would be if Carl and I broke up. I took what she said to heart, and then went to talk to Carl. I really loved Carl and I couldn't believe I had done this to him.

My hands were shaking as I approached the door. They weren't shaking because I was high on coke, it was because I was terrified to learn what he might say. I wasn't sure if I needed to knock or if I could use my key. I decided to knock. I was so happy when he opened the door. I started to tear up as I asked him if we could talk. He agreed and moved aside so I could come in. We had a heart to heart conversation. There were tears and promises made. I told him I was done with cocaine, and that I'd thrown my supplies in the trash and that was it. He hugged me and told me to come home.

For the next few months I was fine. Carl and I put the pieces back together and our relationship was back on track. We had a few bumps in the road, as anyone would, but we had weathered the storm. We even got married, although Carl never officially proposed, I would call it more of a mutual agreement. It happened one winter night in 1992 when we were in bed after a pretty fun night at The Taverne. My liquid courage had kicked in when I asked him if he ever wanted to get married. He said, "Yes." Feeling inspired by his positive reply, I pressed on. I asked, "In 1995?" He said that was too far away. I then asked, "In 1994?" He said, "Yes." And that was how my first marriage began.

Carl was genuinely surprised when I began to plan our big day just a few days later. I wasn't willing to allow him to back out so I explained to him, in great detail, everything that had to be done for a wedding of approximately 150 people. I taught him about the food, the dress, the cake, the hall, and so on. I knew Carl had a lot of credit card debt and I had little money, but that didn't matter. We'd make it work.

Our wedding, since we had over a year to plan it, became quite the fiasco. We decided it would take place on the afternoon of June 25, 1994. As you've no doubt learned about me by now, alcohol makes me courageous. I've never been a mean drunk, just a fun drunk. So when we'd be out drinking, if I had a good time with someone I'd invite them to be in our wedding. It started with just our best friends and my brother, then I was strongly encouraged to add my sister (my mom's doing). Then I'd ask another girlfriend to be in the wedding, and then we'd have to add another groomsman so each lady would have an escort for her walk down the aisle.

Our wedding party swelled to twenty-two attendants, which included a flower girl and ring bearer. Our group photo had to be taken from the rear of the church in order to fit everyone in the picture. It was to date, the largest party I've ever thrown, which turned into the largest amount of money I've ever thrown away. We invited people we had no business inviting because we were both such jovial drunks. I think our attendance ended up around 250. It was a lot. It was so much our gifts didn't come close to covering the cost of the food. Thank goodness Jeff took it upon himself to donate a lot of the liquor from The Taverne (of course he was in the wedding party!)

It was the wedding of my dreams. We had Jack Flash, the DJ from my favorite dance club, Kicks, who played all of our favorite dance songs. All of our friends from The Taverne were there because most of them were in the wedding party, and it went off without a hitch. No drunken fights and no drama. Other than the rain right before we all got to the church, it was great. The best part was that my hairdresser, Jo, was one of my bridesmaids, and she brought all of the necessary tools to keep my hair in shape, even after we got rained on. This was another instance where Jo and I had synchronicities. She was busy helping the ten other bridesmaids do their hair and didn't have time to do her own in the style she'd hoped, and similarly I didn't have time to finish my own nails because I'd been doing the bridesmaids' nails. Because I'm left handed, I'd started doing my nails on my right hand. Before I knew it, I was out of time and never did get to do my nails on my left hand. I ended up hiding my unfinished nails under Carl's fingers for the pictures of our wedding rings.

TIME'S UP

Carl and I honeymooned in Honolulu and Maui, because we could. It had always been my dream, and Carl allowed me to experience it. He enjoyed Honolulu's big city feel, but when we got to Maui, the entertainment was much more limited. Every place near where we stayed closed by nine o'clock, so we made up for it by day drinking. We were there over fourth of July week. We learned the meaning of "summer heat" during that trip. But we also got to see some amazing fireworks. They were better than any I'd ever seen. Overall, it was a great trip, or so I thought.

When we got home, we settled into married life and talked about having a baby. I felt like it would help us leave the partying life behind and grow up. Carl owned a beautiful little stone house in the country that had been gutted. It needed a completely new interior but I hoped we could focus on finishing it. It would be a great place to raise a child. That enticed me to drink less and start to exercise. Carl didn't say he didn't want a baby, but he didn't make much effort to support the cause either. He didn't seem to want to give up any of his nights out or occasional after-hours parties.

I stopped using my birth control pills as soon as we got married, but was never able to get pregnant. This was a true example of how everything happens for a reason, and our reason was our marriage wasn't going to last through the first year.

UNHAPPY HALLOWEEN

n October, we were invited to celebrate Halloween on Put-In-Bay, an island in northwestern Lake Erie, with our friends, Scott and Liz. Carl and I always went to Put-In-Bay for Memorial Day, Fourth of July, and Labor Day weekends, but we'd never been there for Halloween. Put-In-Bay is similar to Key West, Florida, except you can't drive to the island; it is only accessible by boat or plane. There were two ferry services that carried both people and vehicles, so we took our truck on the closest ferry to the campground to avoid having to walk or deal with taxis on the island.

The Islands of Ohio thrive from Memorial Day through Labor Day with many of the businesses closing for the winter, but there is a small window of time allowed to celebrate fall and Halloween. Scott and Liz had invited us to share their family's camper for a few days, so we decided to go. Liz and I planned our costumes to coincide with each other's. Carl and I were the Flintstones, and Scott and Liz were the Rubbles. We decided to spend the evening at the Beer Barrel Saloon because they had constant entertainment and because it has the longest bar in the world, it's a huge place. We arrived, paid our admission and entered.

It was only about eight o'clock, so it wasn't yet packed. I had been walking around with Betty Rubble when Fred Flintstone decided there weren't enough people there to justify his hanging around, so he left. He apparently headed to the Roundhouse down the street because due to its much smaller size, it was packed. He didn't tell me, he just left.

Meanwhile, Betty Rubble had run into some friends from high school (because she grew up there) and I decided I'd try to find my husband. After the third trip around the bar I realized he wasn't there. Then I got pissed.

About an hour later, a few friends showed up and said they'd seen Carl, aka Fred, at the Roundhouse. I didn't have any cash on me (Fred had the wallet) so I didn't want to leave and risk not finding him and having no money. At least I had a bar tab going where I was. Fred eventually returned to find me and won me over with his usual boyish charm. I forgave him after he danced with me. He deserved being forgiven since never danced with me.

After Carl buttered me up by dancing with me twice, he told me he wanted us to drive back to the camper to retrieve the coke he'd brought. I couldn't believe he'd brought coke on this trip! Scott and Liz didn't do drugs, and of course I was fighting to stay clean. It was one thing to indulge when I wasn't around, but to bring it on this trip was a whole other level of fucked up. I told him he didn't need to drive and get busted for DUI, so I drove him because I was much better at metabolizing my alcohol than he was. True story, I learned it in my DNA test years later. I metabolize alcohol better than I do caffeine. Go figure.

As I delivered Carl to the camper to find his stash, I realized I had some hard decisions to make. This single act showed me his level of selfishness. He'd kicked me out of our home over this drug, and now he was flaunting it in my face. He didn't even have the decency to hide it from me. He actually asked me to get it for him!

I'm sorry to say, I did a little of his coke that night. I suffered a nose bleed and the embarrassment of trying to hide it from my friends. I also suffered with a terrible hangover the next morning. I was miserable, bitchy, and hated myself for slipping. I couldn't wait to leave that place and get home, but I also had to figure out what I was going to do when I got there.

When we got home that evening, Carl brought his suitcase inside then said he wanted to go out. I didn't want to go out, so I stayed home. I felt like something wasn't right but I was too miserable to care.

When I woke up the next day, I decided I needed to re-evaluate where my life was headed. I decided I needed to move home for awhile. I asked my parents if there was room for me, and they said yes. Randy had moved into an apartment near our high school, so the basement apartment-sized bedroom was empty.

Once my plan was in place, I sat down with Carl and told him I needed some time to think about what I wanted to do moving forward. I told him I loved him more than anything, but I felt betrayed by him bringing the coke to the island and telling me about it, and how angry I was that he deserted me at the bar. He didn't try to convince me of anything. He just listened and seemed relieved.

What I didn't know is that Carl had been to my parents' house at some point when I was using a lot and before he kicked me out of the house. He'd told them that if my hands weren't shaking that I was high, when in reality it was the opposite. Because my parents had no experience with cocaine, they completely trusted what Carl had told them. I had no idea this had taken place. This explained why they welcomed me home with such enthusiasm and no questions.

TO BE OR NOT TO BE...

Moving home weighed heavily on my conscience. On one hand I was glad to be out of the weird vibe that had developed between Carl and me, and on the other hand I missed him terribly. I hated that I'd failed at my marriage but I wanted time to figure things out. I thought Carl needed time too.

We didn't speak for most of November. As much as I missed him, I began to rediscover myself. I'd been so busy being Mrs. Carl that I'd lost me. This was my chance to regain my own identity.

It was early in December when Carl finally called. He asked me how I was, and we talked for a long time. I asked Carl what he wanted to do. He turned the question back on me. I told him I wanted to try to save our relationship. I was still deeply in love with him and really wanted to try to work things out. Carl said he'd like to try as well. I moved back home the next day.

I tried to show Carl how much I loved him by cooking him elaborate dinners and really spoiling him. He enjoyed it, but still had a desire to go out. Carl was a social person and really enjoyed being out in a crowd. I joined him more than I used to, but there were nights he'd want to go out and I didn't so I stayed home. I was happy to be back with him, but it felt different. At first things were quiet. Everyone knew what was going on so they didn't come by or call. They respected that we were trying, whether we'd make it or not, and gave us space.

One night Carl got a page on his beeper around midnight. I asked him who was paging him at that hour and he said it was nothing. Then he started getting more nightly pages, and some well after midnight. I also noticed he was very careful to not leave the beeper where I could see it. That was something he'd never done before.

Then he started to go out on weeknights more than he had in the past.

BITING THE HAND
THAT FEEDS YOU

Macy showed up in our lives a few months before our wedding. She acted like she knew me by telling me she had gone to school with my brother, Randy, but I had no memory of her. When I asked Randy about her, he said she was a compulsive liar and had acted less than honorably throughout their days in school. Randy said his best friend William would be able to tell me more about her if I really wanted to know. I didn't really want to know.

Macy started as a waitress at The Taverne after I'd left to start my nail business. She was that girl that got too drunk and caused drama anywhere she went. She'd broken up many good parties. Of course, she latched onto me because I was empathetic. I was the only one that would tell her to stop being an ass when she was drunk, or I'd get stuck driving her home so everyone else could resume having fun. We didn't have taxis where we lived, and the only way to get home was to drive or be driven. This is where my effective metabolism of alcohol did not serve me well. Everyone knew I was best suited to drive, so if I didn't duck into the bathroom quickly enough I'd be tasked with removing Macy and delivering her home. She even showed up at Carl's and my camper one holiday weekend asking to sleep over because she'd gotten herself ejected from her camp site.

When Carl and I were planning our wedding, I made the mistake of letting my emotions get the best of me. On one of my trips to take Macy home after drinking too much, in an effort to make her feel better about herself (she was blubbering insufferably) I asked her if she'd be in our wedding. I needed someone to fill in for one of my bridesmaids that had to drop out a month before the wedding due to health issues. The dress was paid for, we just needed a body to put in it. Macy was about the same size as the dress, so I asked her to fill in. She accepted exuberantly. I was excited to have found a replacement, but I also wanted to help Macy feel like a part of our crowd. I knew she was dating all the wrong men out of desperation. I had been there myself. Fortunately, she behaved at our wedding which amazed me because she hung out with my sister all night.

I hadn't been back home with Carl for too long when one day on my way home from work, I noticed Macy's car parked in front of our garage with the hood up. Driving past, I noticed Carl's head under the hood. I waved as I went by, but Macy didn't wave back. She stood there looking at me in shock. Then she said something to Carl, who looked up with a scowl on his face. It was obvious they hadn't planned on me coming home when I did.

Our garage was located on the back side of a separate building away from our house. Where we parked our cars was on the far side of the house, about 150 feet away. I drove up the driveway and unloaded the car. About a half hour later, Carl came in alone. I asked him where Macy was, and he said she had to get to work. Her car had been acting up and she couldn't afford to take it to the mechanic. I told him that was nice of him to help her out, and started cooking dinner.

I should have seen it sooner. Macy was a bartender and worked nights. I finally put two and two together and realized she was the source of the late night pages and Carl's new habit of going out on most weeknights. When I confronted him about it, he said they'd dated while we were separated. He'd started hanging out at her bar because he needed someone to talk to. He hadn't told her I'd moved back home. He wanted to see if it was going to work between us before he ended their relationship.

Talk about a red flag. I couldn't believe this was happening. Fortunately, I remained calm and asked him what he wanted to do. He said he wanted to try to work it out. He'd tell her to stop paging him. I believed him.

BEAT DOWN

I wanted to remove Carl from Macy's grasp long enough to see if we really had a chance, so I suggested a getaway to Punxsutawney, Pennsylvania for Ground Hog Day. I wanted to see if the town was anything like it was portrayed in the movie, so we made reservations at the historic Pantall Hotel. We drove the truck since we'd have to travel through the mountains in February. It took us about two and a half hours and the scenery was absolutely beautiful. Carl was extremely quiet on the drive, and I tried everything to engage him. Nothing worked, so I turned up the radio and started to sing *'Take this Heart'* by Richard Marx. I had decided it would be the theme song for the trip, which was a beautiful drive through the snowy mountains.

As we drove into town, I realized it was nothing like the movie. The town was very small, with less to do than in Maui. You only had a choice of bowling, the twelve seat hotel bar, or the Eagles club for BINGO. We settled on the hotel bar for dinner and drinks. We went to bed early because we were told we needed to get to the mountaintop really early the next day in order to get a parking space and place to stand to watch the Ground Hog Day ceremony. We got up at sunrise and headed up the mountain. We were shocked to see it was a huge open field full of drunk college kids that had slept there. The underwhelming ceremony consisted of a similar scene as the movie, but only lasted a few minutes and was over. We then headed back down the mountain and went to the Eagles club for the coveted pancake breakfast. We took a tour of the historic downtown area and visited Punxsutawney Phil and his wife Phyllis (the groundhogs) at their home in the front window of the public library. We shopped for a few souvenirs and then made our way home. The ride home was about as exciting as the ride there. When I heard the pager go off a few times after midnight, I knew in my heart our trip was all for naught.

After we returned home, things remained the same as before we'd taken our trip. Carl resorted to leaving his beeper on vibrate mode so I was less apt to hear it go off. I wanted to believe I could win him back, and continued to try, but my plan B was to work as much as I could so I could save up as much money as I could in case I did need to leave.

It was now March, and I'd cooked us a nice dinner of filets and lobster tails. I desperately wanted to regain the love we once had and hoped food would do the trick. After we finished dinner, we were watching '*Friends*,' one of our favorite TV shows. It was the episode where Monica's aunt was teaching the girls to play Poker so they could eventually take on the boys. Carl and I were sitting on the sofa after we'd enjoyed that amazing dinner. The show was about halfway over when I turned to Carl and said, "I really want to move to Florida." I had spent a winter there a couple of years earlier working at the racetrack and I really loved it. The winters in Ohio were dreadfully long and the cold weather just drained me emotionally and physically. Like so many others, I'd wanted to curl up in a warm blanket and hibernate until spring. I always ate like a bear going into hibernation and hated how I felt trapped inside the house. For some reason, I thought Carl would consider it. I knew if I could just get him out of Ohio and show him how beautiful Florida was, he'd love it. It would give us the opportunity for a fresh start, and we could leave the drama of our pasts behind to start a more meaningful life together. We were both multi-faceted people that could adapt anywhere we landed, so that didn't worry me. We could leave snow plowing and freezing temperatures for what seemed like half the year behind. No more hibernating, no more dry skin and chapped lips all winter. It would be awesome.

My idea caused a reaction in Carl I never dreamed possible. My sensitive husband exploded with rage and balled his hand into a fist, punching me in the face so hard it forced my head to turn away from him and hit the wall. This all happened from a seated position on the couch.

Before I could comprehend what had happened, his other hand balled into a fist and struck the opposite side of my head as he jumped up off the sofa. He then took the stance of a boxer bracing for a fight. As my head returned to center, my mind struggled to understand what had just happened. I was so confused and in shock, I just sat there. Then a second later, as I realized what happened, my vision went red. It wasn't blood, it was pure rage. I remember the moment it happened. It looked as if someone lowered little red-colored window shades down over my field of vision.

My fight or flight instinct kicked in, and I chose to fight. As I focused on him through the rage that colored my vision red, I jumped up off the sofa and grabbed whatever I could and threw it at him. Once he realized I was going to fight back, his own rage took over and he threw me down on the sofa, where I landed on my left side. He sat on top of my hip while he repeatedly punched me in the head, shoulder and arm. I fought desperately to get him off of me, but he was too heavy.

Then, as quickly as he had pinned me down and beat me, he stopped. He suddenly realized what he was doing and jumped off of me. As I slowly began to rise to a sitting position, I felt nothing as the adrenaline continued to pulse through my veins. My head began to throb, and I was stunned because everything seemed to move in slow motion. When I looked over at Carl, he looked like a trapped animal pacing around the living room furiously. The next thing I knew, he stopped and looked at me with a hateful glare, and then began yelling at me telling me it was my fault because I had hit him first.

Still fogged by the adrenaline pumping through my veins after taking such a beating, my mind switched from confusion to anger. When he told me that I had started this nightmare by hitting him first, he pushed the buttons my sister had pushed so many times before. Something clicked in my mind that took me back to the abuse I'd suffered at my sister's hand throughout my childhood. The "I'm going to tell Mom" reaction he set off in me, made me run and grab the phone. I was not going to stand by and let him accuse me of something I would never do. The feeling of the beating I just took, paired with the desperation to set the record straight, had me dialing 911 almost unconsciously. In my mind, I knew the police report would show me as the victim and him as the aggressor, I would make sure of that. He yelled at me to put the phone down, and when I started talking to the dispatcher, he ran out the door. What I didn't realize is how that phone call would set in motion a chain of events that would change my life forever.

As I explained to the dispatcher what was going on, my mind tried to minimize what had just happened. I matter of factly told her I just wanted to file a police report to document that he had hit me first. I didn't want to press charges or have him arrested, I simply wanted documentation of what happened. I'm sure the dispatcher had dealt with this type of shock before, and she handled me like a pro. She told me she had to send the police officers to create the report, and asked me if that was okay. I told her it was. She asked me if I was hurt. I told her I was bruised but I was okay. She asked me where he was, and I told her he'd run out the front door as soon as I picked up the phone. The dispatcher then told me to wait for the officers, so I did. The thought of domestic violence had never before entered my mind. I was now so wrapped up in not being blamed for something I didn't start that it never occurred to me how serious this whole situation was.

Carl and I lived in a house that had been relocated from the site where it was built to inside of a condo complex. It was tucked into a hillside, with the rear of the house looking up a heavily treed hill. The beautiful original craftsman home had rough sewn cedar siding throughout the inside of the house. It had the classic big front porch and upper balcony. The interior was original and fully in tact down to the cabinet hardware. Carl got to live in this historic home as a part of his compensation package as the complex manager.

Carl's parents lived in one of the condos in the same complex, which had its buildings placed in the shape of the letter "C." You had to drive into the complex past a few buildings and garages to reach our house, then proceed down a winding hill to the remainder of the buildings. Our house had its own address, but the 911 system didn't have a record of it being a residence. It appeared in their system like a clubhouse that was owned by the complex. When I gave them the address, they tried to cross reference it with our last name, which showed them Carl's parents' address, so that is where they sent the officers. Carl was an "oops" baby, so his sisters were considerably older than him, as were his parents. He had never been very open with his parents, probably because of the age difference. He'd tried

95

to create this illusion that he was the perfect son by keeping his personal life very separate from his family. I'd been with him for three years and only met them three times.

These lovely people were shocked when the police showed up at their door. As soon as Carl's father answered the door, the officers knew they were at the wrong house. They were looking for a young woman that was in tears on the phone, not an elderly man. The police officers asked where I was and Carl's parents directed them to our house.

Between leaving Carl's parents' house and arriving at mine, these two officers, who happened to be friends of ours from The Taverne, realized who had placed the call. When they arrived at my front door, they immediately asked if Carl was there. I told them no. They gently guided me inside as they checked my condition and looked at me closely. I was shaking really bad so they started asking me what day it was and similar questions. They then did what I now know to be a part of their police training. They observed the scene and took mental notes of the condition of the room. After they had assessed both my condition and the condition of the room, they determined I didn't require medical attention then proceeded to ask me what happened. I told them I just wanted to document that Carl had hit me first because he was accusing me of hitting him first. I said I didn't want him to get arrested. They calmly told me that I didn't have a choice. In the State of Ohio, if one party reports being struck by another party and there was evidence it occurred, the State would press charges even if the victim chose not to. I remember trying to comprehend what they'd said, and kept repeating that I didn't want Carl to go to jail as I was trying to write my statement through the tears and the still-lingering confusion. Another odd fact I recall from that night was wishing I could type the statement because it would have been much faster and neater. The things that go through your mind in a traumatic situation are crazy. I really just wanted to get it over with because I was beginning to feel the pain from my beating.

After I painstakingly wrote every detail of what had happened on the multi-page carbonless paper form, my friends came out from behind their badges. They again explained to me that the law said if there was evidence of physical harm, which in my case there was, the State would press charges even if the victim didn't. That meant Carl had to be arrested.

As I processed what was happening, I again told them I just wanted to document the event because he tried to say I hit him first, and I would never do that. I realized how childish and unreasonable that must have sounded. They looked at me with a sadness reserved for a child that just doesn't understand as they explained it doesn't work that way. Officer Terry and Officer Lou, as they were known socially to us, were compassionate, supportive and brutally honest with me, which is what I needed at that moment. Their observation of my bruises and the overturned furniture told them this was more than a heated argument. They understood that for me to have called 911, this had to be bad. It was a Thursday evening, so Carl had to be arrested and processed for his first court appearance by 7:00 on Friday morning or he'd have to spend the weekend in jail.

Since Carl wasn't there and may or may not have known the procedures, I wanted to make sure he was booked in on time so he wouldn't have to spend the weekend in jail. These were times when naivety ruled my brain. I did not harbor bitterness toward him...yet. Terry told me they'd be looking for Carl all night, but in the event they didn't locate him, they repeated that he'd better show up to get booked in before 7:00 a.m. or he'd be in jail all weekend. They asked me if I had someplace to go and I told them I didn't want to drive anywhere. I knew in my heart there would be no more physical contact. I knew Carl knew it had been a mistake and he was probably as shaken up as I was. I promised myself I'd make sure Carl was at the jail in the morning if he returned home. Once the officers were convinced I was okay, they left. I was still in a state of confusion no matter how hard I tried to convince myself otherwise, so I went upstairs to our bedroom.

When I moved into the house years earlier, Carl's roommate had just moved out. He lived upstairs, Carl lived downstairs, and they shared the kitchen. Carl had kept his downstairs bedroom in tact after we married, with the idea that it would be our guest room. It turned out that he never felt at home upstairs, so anytime we had a fight, he slept in his old room. I knew I'd find him there if he made it home tonight.

As I crawled onto my bed and cried harder than I've ever cried in my life, my head pounded and my body ached from the crying and the beating. After I had released the pain and sadness that overcame me, I started to think about what had happened. I then realized I had customers to see the following day, and tried to figure out what to do. I owned my own nail business, so there was no calling in sick. My friend Rosie had just gotten her nail license and started to share my space to build her own clientele. She was the answer I needed, so I called her right away. Fortunately, she answered and listened to my account of what had happened. She asked me if I needed someplace to go, and I told her I'd be okay at home. I told her the best thing she could do for me was to show up for my customers tomorrow, because I had to take Carl to get booked into jail in the morning and I was really starting to hurt. Rosie saved my life that night. I'll never forget the feeling of comfort she gave me. Just knowing I had someone to come to my rescue in my darkest hour meant the world to me.

My marriage to Carl should never have happened, but when you're young and in love, there is no logic or reason. Had I listened to Jo or my mom on my wedding day I would have walked away from the whole thing, but I didn't. They both asked me if I was sure I wanted to go through with it. Jo even offered me her car keys. I was so desperate to be loved, I created this fantasy relationship that really didn't exist. In reality, Carl had to be drunk to open up to me. When he was sober, he was silent. I remember friends telling me he was shocked that as soon as we had a conversation about getting married, I had jumped into wedding planning mode. He told me that since I lived in his house for free, I had to buy my own ring. I thought that seemed reasonable in my highly logical mind, so my friend Ester and I went shopping downtown at the pawn shops looking for an antique ring. I found a great ring, and that solved that.

Between the pain and tears, I slept very little that night. I was worried about Carl. I was up with the sun because I knew I had to get him to the police station for booking. Even though he'd caused the worst night of my life, I still worried about him. My head was so sore from being pounded that I couldn't brush my hair. I did the best I could to appear normal, then headed downstairs. I found him sleeping in his downstairs bedroom and was relieved he made it home. I woke him up and told him what the officers said about getting booked in before 7:00. Even after a few hours of sleep he was still inebriated, so I said I'd drive him to the police station. He glared at me with a new found hatred as he got cleaned up and followed me to the car. The only words spoken on the two-mile drive were me saying that I'd pick him up if he'd call me when he was finished.

I continued to live in the house with Carl because I simply refused to leave. I hated the thought of the long commute from my parents to work, so I lived upstairs and he lived downstairs. When he realized I wasn't leaving, he began a crusade to poison everyone against me. He told our friends he caught me cheating, which wasn't true, and he went back to my family and told them I was still using cocaine, which also wasn't true. He was trying to turn everyone against me because I'd gotten him arrested. There were also a lot of other things going on in the background that I wasn't aware of. The beating, which I believed was fueled by my asking him to move to Florida, was actually fueled by a combination of many different things, one of those being that his relationship with our former bridesmaid was still very much alive.

During this time, I worked and stayed out of the bar. I didn't want to face the people that were going to judge me. I was trying to move on with my life and going back there would just be a step in the wrong direction. Besides, I knew everyone had heard only Carl's side of the story, and I'm sure it wasn't anywhere near the truth. There would be no loyalty to the wife who called the police on their beloved Carl.

Though we lived in the same house, we rarely saw each other. The next few months were filled with avoidance and awkwardness as the court date for Carl's domestic violence charges approached. I was left in the dark regarding the hearing because any paperwork that was delivered to the house for me was taken by Carl. I was never directly served a subpoena, so I wasn't able to attend the hearing. Carl never said anything about it, so I had no way of knowing what happened, and I didn't really care.

A LIGHT AT THE END
OF THE TUNNEL

I remained living upstairs in our house, as Macy had replaced me in
Carl's life downstairs. I continued to work at my nail salon and manage
my volleyball league on Monday through Thursday evenings. When
Carl first started to date me, he used to visit me at volleyball once in awhile,
but he wasn't much of a sports guy, so he never stuck around long enough
to meet anyone. It had now become my safe place away from him. This was
a completely different circle of friends for me than with Carl, so I wasn't
worried about scrutiny from people regarding our fight.

One of the brightest moments for me during this dark time was when
an old friend named Brent reached out to me. Brent and I met at my first
volleyball club years earlier and became fast friends. He helped me with
my leagues and taught me a lot about sports management to make my job
easier. He always sponsored a team in my leagues, no matter what they
were. To promote the venues I worked for, we created different leagues such
as wally ball (volleyball in a racquet ball court), water volleyball, and our
most popular, beach volleyball. Brent had heard through the grapevine
about Carl getting arrested and wanted to hear my side of the story, so he
invited me to dinner. Because I was still legally married, we didn't want
to risk being seen together, so we travelled forty-five minutes from home.
As we were escorted to our table, we looked up to see a fellow volleyball

player leaving the bar. Unbelievable! He was a mutual friend, so we swore him to secrecy then proceeded to our table.

It was an amazing night! Being with someone that actually wanted to spend time with me was a refreshing change. My last few relationships certainly didn't feed my soul and this evening definitely opened my eyes to that. We spoke about the downfall of my marriage, my drug addiction, and reducing my drinking. Brent appreciated my efforts to get better, and felt badly that I wasn't getting more support at home. We had the best conversations. They were about our mutual friends, funny stories, and everything we never had time to talk about at volleyball. It was the best night out I'd had in a long time. Brent's company offered me the solace I desperately needed to pull me out of the dark cave of depression I'd fallen into.

When he dropped me off, we sat in the car and talked for awhile. But, because I still lived in the house with Carl, we didn't want to continue talking too long and risk running into Carl as he came home from Macy's bar. Brent hesitantly leaned in to kiss me good night. He hadn't been sure if he should, but once our eyes locked, we both knew it was going to happen. The electricity we created in this kiss left us both yearning for more. I was at the point of saying to, "To Hell with my marriage, I want to kiss this man some more," but Brent ended the kiss and said it couldn't go any further until my divorce was final. I reluctantly left him and retreated to my upstairs bedroom with a smile on my face.

THE ADVENTURE OF A LIFETIME

Just a few days later, I received an invitation from two girlfriends planning an adventure to Florida. There was something about a custody battle and an ex-husband for one friend, and the other friend was going along for moral support. I didn't ask questions, I just said yes. It was the perfect opportunity to get me out of Ohio for a week. I agreed to drive because I had a convertible.

Becca, Sheri, and I completed the drive to Singer Island, Florida in only sixteen hours. We'd split the driving so everyone would be rested when we arrived in the early afternoon. I had never driven to Florida before, I'd only flown to Cape Canaveral, but this was a few hours south of there.

On the way to our motel, we stopped at an area Becca called Double Roads. She said we just had to see it. Double Roads was a short dirt road that was a section of Highway A1A. We parked and looked out and couldn't believe the incredible view of the ocean. The turquoise green water rolled onto a white sand beach and it was just breathtaking. We slid down the path toward the water and ran right into the waves. I was hooked.

After our late afternoon swim, we enjoyed the beach for awhile before heading to Singer Island to check into our motel, grab some drinks and find dinner. We drove south down US 1 to Highway A1A, which took us onto the island. We drove over a series of land and low bridges, and then through the woods past John D. MacArthur State Park. As we crossed the last flat bridge, the luxurious high rise condos came into view. There were a bunch of them lining the beach, and you could see bits of the Lake Worth Lagoon through the mangrove trees to our right. As we approached the curve taking you toward the causeway off the south end of the island, we found our motel. It was right on the beach. It was located right next to the Ocean Mall, which was a two-story strip mall. It had a 7-Eleven convenience store, Subway sandwich shop, a big two-story bar called Ocean's Eleven North, some offices and shops on the second story and a few other restaurants including Portofino's and The Green House.

After we checked in and unpacked for our week of fun in the sun, we headed to the bar at Ocean's Eleven North for a drink. We met the manager and bartender when we arrived. They told us they were all from somewhere else, specifically Youngstown, Ohio and Boston. They offered to buy us our first round to welcome us to the Sunshine State and we gladly accepted. Kenny, the manager asked us where we'd come from and how long we'd be in town. We told him we were all from Cleveland and that we planned to be there for a week. I asked about the club upstairs, and he explained to me that it was only open three nights a week and that it had a local cult following. The same crowd showed up each night and filled the place. We enjoyed a couple of drinks at the bar before Kenny offered to show us the club upstairs. As we approached the elevator, Becca and Sheri shoved me into the elevator with Kenny and went back to the bar. Apparently they'd seen something I hadn't…Kenny was interested in me.

When the elevator arrived at the top floor, Kenny proceeded to show me the club and the deck overlooking the ocean. We talked for awhile while we enjoyed the view. On the way back to the bar downstairs, he asked me if I'd like to go to dinner with him. I was pretty surprised that he was asking me out, but managed to accept without embarrassing myself.

On our dinner date, Kenny told me on the day we'd met, he'd been conspiring with Becca and Sheri to get me alone. My friends told him I was recently divorced and planning to relocate, so Kenny wanted to get to know me. We enjoyed a great dinner at Portofino's, then headed back to Ocean's for a nightcap. Kenny invited me to his apartment, which was right across the parking lot from Ocean's. I ended up spending most of the night there. We had a great time together, but something Kenny told me caused me concern because it was very unfamiliar to me. He told me he'd gotten several DUI's in Boston. He'd gotten so many that his license was revoked until at least 2008. It was currently 1995. I'd never met anyone that had their license revoked before, but it explained why he lived in the apartment right across from where he worked. From what he'd explained to me, his friends gave him rides when he needed to go off island, which wasn't too often. There was a grocery store right around the corner and a 7-Eleven in Ocean Mall, so that gave him everything he needed. I accepted it because he was making it work. He had a good job and a nice apartment that he shared with a surfer guy named JD. JD worked at another restaurant and surfed a lot, so he wasn't around much, but he seemed nice.

It had started raining heavily on the second day of our stay, so we just walked around all day in swim suits and flip flops because it was pretty much impossible to stay dry. Because it was the middle of summer it was extremely hot, so the rain kept us cool. While Kenny was at work, Sheri and I walked around the beach and the island. We spent time swimming and walking on the beach until the rain got too heavy, which was when we made our way to the bar. Becca was tending to the business she'd come to Florida to conduct, something about trying to get visitation with her daughter, so I gave her the car.

When the rain continued for the remainder of our vacation we decided to extend our stay, hoping the weather would improve and we'd get some real beach time. In the meantime, Becca learned seeing her daughter was going to be more complicated than she thought. She learned she could get nothing accomplished in our short time there. When we were out one night, she ended up meeting an older rich man who, after hearing her plight, said he was willing to help her, but it would take a few weeks. They became an item and she eventually told us she would be staying with him and not coming back to Ohio with us. Sheri and I stayed hoping the weather would get better. Our initial stay of a week turned into eight days, then nine, then ten and finally eleven. I remember looking at the sky and just seeing a big dark umbrella of clouds over our heads. When the weather still hadn't broken by day eleven, we decided it was time to throw in the beach towel and head home.

Sheri and I packed the car and stocked a cooler with Zima (the original alcoholic seltzer), Diet Coke, and sandwiches, then stopped in to Ocean's for one last round. Kenny asked me to join him upstairs for a few minutes.

He told me he'd really enjoyed our time together and told me he'd heard a rumor that I wanted to move to Florida. I told him I was thinking about it, mostly because he'd asked right then. He said he'd been looking for an excuse to evict JD, and if I was serious, I could be his roommate. Although we'd been having a romantic relationship, he promised I would officially have my own room, and we could see where it went. Knowing I would be relocating but was going to have my own room versus sharing a room with a man I'd just met made a big difference. If he remained a roommate with benefits, so be it. The rent was affordable and the apartment would be available in thirty days. It was all perfect. I could go home, tie up loose ends, and come back in a month. Never mind that I had no job, no savings, and wasn't yet divorced, I'd figure that out later.

Sheri and I made our way back to Ohio slowly but steadily. The rain didn't stop for almost the entire trip. Our defroster fan died somewhere in South Carolina, so we had to crack the windows in order to keep the windows from fogging up, then the wipers went on the blink shortly after that. They would only work on slow speed but we really needed high speed for the rain we were experiencing. The stress of driving with slow wipers and no defroster fan had taken its toll on both of us. By the time we pulled into the gas station just over the Ohio and West Virginia border, we both needed a drink. We filled up with gas, drove to the parking area and cracked two Zimas. The ice had all melted in the cooler, so they were piss warm, but we didn't care. They did the trick. We sat in the car drinking our warm Zimas and laughing our asses off. It was all we could do to keep our sanity.

NEW HORIZONS

*A*fter my first night back in my own bed, I woke up with a renewed sense of self. I had a plan, and I was amazed at how easily everything fell into place. I decided to have a house sale to sell everything I had left. I then arranged to move back in with my parents until I could leave for Florida in about a month. I talked to Rosie at work, and asked her if she'd be interested in buying me out of my nail business. She had been in talks with the owner of the salon and I knew he'd be willing to help her out, so we settled on a price and I turned over my equipment and client list to her the following week. My mom helped me with the house sale, which was a huge success. I sold almost everything. After the sale was over, I borrowed Carl's truck so I could move my bedroom set back to my parents. He said I could use the truck, but that he wasn't helping me move. The couple of friends that were supposed to show up to help me didn't. I wasn't surprised because that kind of thing always happens to me. So, once again I was on my own.

I methodically took the drawers out of the dressers, slid them down the stairs then loaded them into the truck. Next, I packed my boxes and bags. Then, all I had left was the mattress. The king-sized pillow-top mattress proved to be a challenge because it was a fat mattress I needed to move through a skinny stairwell with a low ceiling. The house was an old Craftsman-style house with rough sawn cedar siding inside, not the best for trying to slide a mattress against. Because I didn't have anyone to help me get it down, I tried to pull it down the stairs, then go back up to get it unstuck from the handrail and ceiling. It worked for the first few steps, but then it got wedged about halfway down. I tried everything to get it out, including running and jumping into it, but nothing worked. I was exhausted and defeated. I finally called my mom to see if she could help me. She said she'd be there soon. About an hour later, my brother and sister showed up. I couldn't believe it! They helped me get that mattress unstuck, but it took awhile. We then put it in my brother's truck and caravanned to my parents house.

I later learned that my mom called them both and told them to get their asses over to my house and help me move NOW! She was mad because they didn't volunteer to help me knowing what I'd gone through with Carl. I was grateful for their help because I was so exhausted after packing that truck myself, but they still looked at me like a coke addict even though I'd been clean for almost a year. That proved to me just how much Carl's visit to my family's home affected me. In their eyes, I would forever be a drug addict who probably caused her husband to beat her. I had no control over that, and was glad I was leaving for good. I later learned my sister remained friends with Carl and even hired him to do some home improvement work for her. I also heard he screwed her over and didn't finish the job. Now that's karma.

HEARTBREAK

*A*fter I got settled back at my parents' house, my friend Nita told me that Ed's Upper Deck in the town of Mantua (pronounced Manta-way), (the complete opposite direction from my parents' house than Solon had been) was hiring. She put in a good word for me, and they hired me for the last few weeks I'd be in Ohio. They knew it was only temporary but didn't care…short-term help was better than no help. I had a lot of fun working there during breakfast shifts on Sundays and a few nights during the week, and it helped me add to my traveling fund.

Kenny and I had been speaking on the phone almost daily since I got back from vacation. We had to keep the calls short because they were long distance and I was using my parents' phone. I couldn't wait to get out of Ohio and get back to Singer Island. I had sold most of my belongings and was counting the days until I could leave.

During the last month of living in the home where I grew up, I was able to attend my ten year high school reunion. I was excited because I hadn't seen my best friend Kelly for a long time. The reunion was set in a pole barn/barbecue restaurant in a rural part of the county. It was very rustic, just like where I'd grown up. It was funny to see people show up in heels and dresses when we were simply gathered on a concrete slab, with a volleyball court outside for entertainment. We had a lot of fun. As I listened to one of my friends tell me that a girl we went to school with had been hitting on her, I was shocked to learn she was gay. I had been friends with that girl for years, and I never had a clue. That was the beauty of growing up in such a rural place. Everyone nice was a friend, it didn't matter if they were gay, of a certain culture or religion. We were all just kids going to school together. There was a purity and naivety that came with growing up that I was blessed to experience, and I'm happy to say I still have a little of it.

Kelly was about eight months pregnant with her second son and her belly was huge. That didn't matter to her, she still got out and played volleyball with me. Kelly has always been the adventurous one, and that's why I love her so much. She drags me out of my shell and makes me experience things I might never have had the opportunity to otherwise.

About halfway through the event, a summertime thunderstorm rolled in. It was a bit concerning because we were in a metal-sided pole building with lightning striking right outside. Then, the power went out, and we couldn't leave because it was raining so heavily. We all hung out for a bit until it passed, then tromped through the mud to get out of there. I made sure to carry an aerial view postcard of Singer Island around with me showed everyone where I was moving to in ten days.

My departure date had finally arrived. The car was packed with almost everything I owned. I planned to leave around noon because some friends from Ed's were throwing me a going away party. It was a beautiful day, but I couldn't put the top down for all of the crap packed inside. The party started at 9:00 so we could share one last breakfast together.

I was excited and nervous as I walked into the restaurant. I knew this was going to be a permanent move because it was such a long way from home. Everyone was excited for me, and showed it by asking questions about where I was going and how I'd been able to swing it, so I told them the story of how my place to live manifested during my vacation, and finding a place to live was the hardest part of moving away. I could get a job anywhere, so that didn't concern me. I had enough money to live on until I found a job, so I wasn't worried. We spent our time reminiscing and enjoying each others' company.

As we were clearing the tables, I noticed Brent, my old friend from volleyball, walk in. I was very surprised and happy to see him. The last time I'd seen him was our dinner date after Carl had beaten me. It was really great to be around him. He has always been a calming presence around me because he is a beautiful soul. I really liked Brent, but he held true to saying he wouldn't date me as long as I was married. Unfortunately, I was still married.

Although I respected his decision to not get involved with me because I was still married, I wished things had turned out differently. He couldn't believe I was actually moving away and gave me a long hug as he told me he'd miss me. When we separated, he held my face in both of his hands as he pulled me in to kiss me good bye.

The kiss was tender, warm and sweet…and I didn't object to this kiss lasting much longer than it should have. After we parted, he continued to hold my face in his hands as he looked into my eyes and said, "I love you, Shelly."

It was a good thing he had a hold of me, because I almost collapsed.

After I got my footing back and realized what he'd said to me, I looked him straight in the eyes and told him, "I love you too, Brent. I've always loved you."

Thoughts were racing through my head, and my heart was aching, and as much as I wanted to stop everything and stay right there in his arms, I knew I had to leave. Brent opened my car door for me, and I reluctantly got in. I waved goodbye one last time before I burst into tears and drove away.

CAT PEE, A TICKET AND FIFTEEN HOURS TO GO

Singer Island, Florida was a sixteen hour drive from my parents' house in Auburn Township. That was, if I caught a good flow of traffic. After only an hour, my cat Thomas was angry that he was stuck in a cat carrier. Like me, he was a free spirit and was not happy being caged.

How Thomas and I met was serendipitous. It was my last day of work as a groom at Thistledown before leaving for Tampa, Florida in 1990. As the grooms from my friend Cindy's racing stable packed the last of their gear into their trucks, they could not catch this black and white fluffy kitten. One of their grooms had acquired two black and white kittens for the barn and named them Tom and Jerry. Jerry had already began his trek to Florida with the horses, but Tom wasn't willing to leave the barn. He and I had become fast friends. He liked to sit on my shoulder like a parrot while I walked my horses around the shed row each morning. That cat took to me like no other pet I'd ever had.

After the grooms got tired of chasing him, they asked me if I wanted him. I replied, "Absolutely!" Thomas, as he became known to me, became my soul mate and remained with me for most of his twelve-year life.

When I took Thomas to Florida that winter back in 1990, he was still a kitten so I just let him sleep on the passenger seat. Now that he was grown up and very independent, I feared if I didn't keep him in a carrier, there

111

was a risk of him jumping out of the car when we stopped. He howled his dissatisfaction with being locked up until I couldn't take it anymore. To save my sanity, I let him out of the carrier.

I was deep in thought as we travelled south down Interstate 271 when the realization of what was happening hit me. I was leaving everything I had ever known behind. I'd had a week-long affair that happened because my friends and I decided to visit Florida in the rainy season, where we spent almost the entire time in a bar. It had been raining for eleven days straight with no end in sight. As I was reliving the memory, a strange smell shook me free of my thoughts. It was the unmistakable smell of cat pee. No wonder Thomas was so vocal—he didn't want to pee in his house, so when I let him out he peed on the seat. Only fifteen more hours to go.

My distraction reflected in my driving. Before I could realize I was traveling way over the speed limit, I saw a state trooper behind me with his lights on. After he wrote me a nice little going away present, he told me to slow down and wished me well in my new home. There would be no warning for me. Trust me, I asked. Just over fifteen hours later I arrived at my new home just before my roommate/boyfriend's birthday.

It had been a long trip, even with my lead foot. I had been fortunate to get in line with a bunch of cars traveling about ninety miles per hour most of the way, and made it from outside of Cleveland to West Palm Beach in about sixteen hours. As I drove south on A1A past the high rises on the beach, I felt a strange sense of being home. I'd never felt that way before, and couldn't explain it. It was an inner peace. I made my way south until I found my new home perched atop a pizza place facing Ocean's Eleven North. This was the most urban setting I had ever lived in. I could actually walk to most places from my apartment, including the beach. This was going to be amazing!

As I pulled up to the curb in front of Kenny's apartment, a feeling of apprehension washed over me. I couldn't put my finger on it, so I ignored it. I attributed it to the exhaustion of my sixteen-hour drive and the excitement of a fresh start.

One thing I will remember vividly for the rest of my life was the blast of heat and humidity that hit me as I exited my car. It literally took my breath away. We didn't have that much humidity in Ohio, so this was something I'd never experienced before. When I visited a month ago it rained the entire time, so I missed out on that blast of hot air. I was excited to see Kenny as he made his way down from the apartment to meet me at the curb. He told me he hadn't evicted JD, so he and I would be sharing a room and a bed.

THE PARTY'S OVER

In celebration of Kenny's birthday, we were met by a group of fellow "in the biz" employees, a term given to restaurant, bar and casino workers. They were joining us at Ocean's after Kenny and I had dinner at Portofino's. We were also expecting crew members from a casino boat based out of the Port of Palm Beach to join us after their evening trip. By the time they got there, we were all ready for shots. Ocean's was the popular choice for those "in the biz" because it was open until 4:00 a.m. giving them the opportunity for a full night out after work.

We made our way through several shots and drinks while we played pool. It was a great group of people, and we had a lot of fun. I lasted as long as I could, but my batteries gave out just after 1:00 a.m. The birthday boy decided to close the bar. I was long since asleep by the time he got home in his advanced state of drunkenness.

Apparently, the crowd didn't do what they normally did, which was go to breakfast at Buddy's. Buddy's was a bar that was open very early for breakfast. It was located in the Sands Hotel, a couple of buildings south of our apartment. Thus, Kenny was hungry for Taco Bell when he walked in, saw my car keys on the counter and then made the biggest mistake of his life. He took those keys and headed for Taco Bell's twenty-four hour drive through on Northlake Boulevard.

When I met Kenny on vacation, he told me he'd been convicted of several DUIs in Boston, and that his license was revoked for a very long time. He said he hadn't driven in years and had adjusted because everything was within walking distance. It never occurred to me that I should hide my car keys, Kenny told me he had no desire to drive. This blind trust taught me a hard lesson that day. A really hard lesson.

Kenny took my car and drove to Taco Bell, where he successfully purchased his dinner/breakfast from the twenty-four hour drive through. He tore into his burrito as soon as he pulled away from the window. He also bought a Mexican pizza and nachos with a large Mountain Dew. He made it down Northlake Boulevard all the way to US 1, where he ran the red light traveling approximately eighty miles per hour.

As Kenny drove my Toyota Celica convertible through the intersection of Northlake and US 1, he T-boned a 1989 Oldsmobile Delta 88 so hard, it turned the car onto its side. My Celica landed on top of it. The crash ripped the bottom of my engine off and embedded my car's frame into the side of the Delta 88, where it came to rest. This happened while I was sound asleep in my bed. Both vehicle's occupants were transported to St Mary's trauma center and placed in intensive care. The driver of the Delta 88 was flown by trauma helicopter because they weren't sure he'd survive.

There was a strange ringing I heard that I thought was part of my dream. It persisted until it pulled me out of my very restful sleep. I noticed two things immediately. First, it was 10:48 a.m., and second, Kenny wasn't in bed next to me. I called out thinking he might be in the kitchen or living room, but heard nothing, so I stumbled out of bed to look for the cordless phone. I finally found it tucked into the Papasan chair and answered it. The caller said she was from Palm Beach County Sheriff's office, and asked me if I knew a man named Kenny Thomas. I told her he was my roommate, and then the deputy proceeded to tell me that he had been involved in a car accident and was in the intensive care unit at St. Mary's hospital.

Shocked but trying to compose myself so I could get the details right, I asked her where St. Mary's was located and explained that I'd just moved here. I took down the address of the hospital and thanked the deputy for her help. I quickly showered and grabbed some breakfast. As I approached the front door to head for the hospital, I reached for my keys which had been on the kitchen counter. They weren't there.

In that moment, a tremendous wave of fear washed over me, causing me to lose my breath. I realized Kenny had been in an accident in MY car. The realization of what happened caused me to have a panic attack. I almost passed out as an overwhelming feeling of dread consumed me.

The gravity of the situation became real very quickly. I had no idea how I was going to find the hospital, or even get there. Then, a second wave of panic washed over me as I realized I only had Kenny's phone number, not anyone else's. Although I met a bunch of people at the bar, I didn't know their last names, so I couldn't even look them up in the phone book.

After the room stopped spinning and the nausea passed, I snapped into secretary mode, which means I got my act together and tried to figure out my next move. I thought out loud, "How am I going to get to the hospital, how can I get a ride? Since I have no one's phone numbers, I guess I'll have to take a cab. Now, how do I find a cab?" After a few minutes, I found the Yellow Pages. I found a local cab company and called.

Shortly after, a nice older man in a 1975 Lincoln Town Car pulled up and asked me where I wanted to go. He had the comforting demeanor of a kindly grandfather, so I spilled my guts to him. He said he'd help me get to and from the hospital until Kenny got out. He was a very nice and comforting presence among the chaos I had just suffered.

After I learned how much the daily cab fare was going to be, I got concerned. I hadn't yet gotten a job and only had $1,600.00 to my name. I'd have to find a job quickly and figure out what to do about the car. Well, I actually wouldn't have to figure out what to do with the car, I'd have to call my dad because my car was on his insurance policy. That was a conversation I was not looking forward to having.

My dad had received threats of policy cancellation from Allstate a few times since I'd started driving. I wasn't a bad driver, I just maintained at least one ticket per year and suffered a brush or two with a few of the many deer that Ohio is known for. We have always had an overabundance of deer in Ohio. Then there was the time I was backing out of my friend's carport and ripped the front fender off my car, and the time my other car got stolen from the mall. Dad always managed to talk our agent into insuring me because they'd worked together for so many years. Notifying my dad of this accident was not something I looked forward to.

I was raised to respect my elders and listen to authority. In the state of shock I was experiencing, I had foolishly given my cell phone number to the deputy who called me. She added it to the accident report which meant it became public record, and was offered to the other party involved the crash.

Not long after I arrived at the hospital, the other driver's attorney started to call me. He was really rude when he asked me why I didn't report the car stolen. I explained that the accident happened while I was asleep and the deputies knew the car was taken without permission, so they said there was no need to file a stolen car report...but he relented. That man called me no less than five times over the next few days, each time with a new threat. I answered when the phone rang because I was afraid it may have been the hospital or sheriff's office calling. I finally had to call the sheriff's office to tell them about the attorney harassing me. They were very nice, and whatever they did made the calls stop.

As mentioned earlier, when I arrived in Florida I had only $1,600.00 to my name. I was already responsible for a car payment, and now I had additional charges for my cell phone and cab fare. Money was getting tight because I still had no job. I was getting nervous.

Kenny was in Intensive Care for a couple of days. I was allowed a short visit with him every morning. I looked for a job in the afternoons. I finally got the rental car provided by the insurance company, but I had to pay for the insurance coverage on the vehicle out of pocket. I was terrified of not having insurance after what had just happened so I paid for it with a credit card.

Kenny was scheduled to get out of the hospital, but he told me the deputies would be arresting him upon his release, and that I should start working on getting bail for him. I made a few calls to bail bondsmen and got the same answer from all of them—you had to be a resident of Florida for at least two months before you could bail someone out of jail. I had never dealt with anything like this before, so I was clueless. I didn't understand what bailing someone out of jail meant. I just did as I was told and made the calls. When I relayed the information to Kenny, he was pissed because I couldn't help him, which turned out to be a blessing in disguise.

Our apartment was located above a pizza shop owned by a guy from New York. He was a nice guy and reminded me of one of the characters from the Godfather because of his accent. He was standing out front when I got home from a job interview. Since he'd learned about the accident, he always asked for updates on Kenny. I greeted him, and when he asked about Kenny, I told him about the issues I was having with the bail bondsmen. He immediately told me not to worry about it, that he had a bail bondsman on retainer for his son and he'd call him for Kenny. All he needed was the date Kenny was arrested. Done and done!

In the meantime, I'd gotten a job at a new company just a few miles from home. The owner desperately needed a secretary and was willing to pay me a good wage. I started immediately. Everything now seemed to be falling into place. I had a job, Kenny's bail was arranged, and I had a rental car. I thanked the entire flock of guardian angels that had been helping me.

MANDATORY WHAT?

The day finally came when Kenny was released from the hospital. As expected, the sheriff's deputies arrested him immediately, and as promised, and our neighbor arranged for Kenny's bail. The bail bondsman even brought him home.

Kenny had only been home for a few days when we learned that Hurricane Erin was apparently headed our way. We watched the news and decided we'd stay put. We put tape on our windows in the pattern of an "X" because that's what people told us to do. Neither of us had ever experienced a hurricane, so we just followed the herd. We bought water, bread and peanut butter along with some Pop-Tarts. We thought that would be enough get us through a few days if the power went out.

I had asked my new boss if he planned to evacuate for the storm. He said, "What storm?" I laughed and told him I'd be in the next day as long as the weather wasn't too bad.

On July 31, we were awakened at five thirty in the morning by a sheriff's deputy pounding on our door. He told us Singer Island was under a mandatory evacuation order and we needed to leave. Kenny and I had no idea what was going on, so we packed our water, bread, peanut butter, and Pop-Tarts and jumped in the car. We thought if we went to Orlando we'd be safe and there were plenty of hotels where we could stay. All I could think about was the cost of the evacuation. Kenny hadn't been working and we had limited funds, but we did as we were told and left. Kenny's aunt lived in Vero Beach, which he said was on the way to Orlando, so we stopped in for a visit. She said she was planning to evacuate as well. We spent about an hour with her, then continued toward Orlando.

We found a reasonably priced motel and checked in. The storm was supposed to hit Singer Island the next day, so we watched the news in anticipation of the landfall. It made me sick that I let Kenny talk me into leaving Thomas at the apartment. He said Thomas would be fine because he'd hide in a closet if it got bad. I felt horribly guilty and prayed the storm wouldn't damage our apartment.

We were awakened during the darkness of the early morning by winds howling really loud. We turned on the TV to see what was happening and were happy to see that the storm had missed Singer Island, but unfortunately it was going to make landfall in Vero Beach. We hoped his aunt stuck to her plans to evacuate because it was her neighborhood that was in the crosshairs.

Hurricane Erin came ashore in Vero Beach right near Kenny's aunt's neighborhood. It continued on a northwest track right toward our motel. I remember the wind howling louder than it had been earlier when it woke us up. The motel eventually lost power. The sound of the wind howling constantly was horrible. It just wouldn't stop. It howled for hours. The rain was coming down so hard, it was sideways. It was also so heavy that we had a very limited view, but we did see a lot of debris flying around outside. Thank goodness we were on the third floor. At least we didn't worry about water coming in. I couldn't believe were were in the middle of a hurricane. I had only lived in Florida for about a month and had already experienced more craziness than I had my entire life.

After the storm subsided, we got out of town as quickly as we could. Since there was no power after the storm, having no air conditioning or running water was not something I wanted add to my already long list of experiences in Florida.

The ride home was eye opening. Although it was only a Category One storm, there was a lot of damage. We saw several billboards and trees down as we drove south down the Turnpike. We even saw some small buildings that had suffered what looked like tornado damage.

CALLING ALL ANGELS!

*A*fter we got back from Orlando, my parents arranged air fare for me to fly home, where my dad co-signed for me to lease a Honda Civic. Because I had to get back to my new job, I left for Florida as soon as the papers were signed and I thanked my parents profusely.

My boss had given me the time off in order to get my new car, but was very happy when I returned. The company was just starting out and he had a long list of things for me to do. I enjoyed helping build something that I could be a part of. It was nice to feel needed.

The first of the month was approaching, which meant rent would be due. When I got home from work, Kenny told me he was going to need more time to recover and wouldn't be returning to work immediately. He announced that I would be responsible for covering all of the rent and expenses if I wanted to continue living there. The problem was that was he wasn't trying to heal. He wasn't taking care of himself or doing his physical therapy, instead he was sitting on his ass and drinking all day. He had put me and my family through enough in the short time I'd known him, so I told him I couldn't afford to cover him. I had a higher car payment due to the new car, and unexpected bills thanks to his accident. I slammed the door as I walked out. At that moment, I realized he was never meant to be my boyfriend, he was just a stepping stone to help me get to Florida. Now, with the help of that powerful flock of angels I'd been working with, I had to find a new place to live.

I cleared my head on the walk to my new friend Deidre's apartment, which was around the corner in Palm Beach Shores. I hoped she was home as I knocked on the garden gate. I was relieved when she yelled a familiar, "It's open!"

Deidre and I met at Ocean's a couple of times on my vacation, and then again at Kenny's birthday party and a few times after. We'd connected immediately. She was a lot of fun and always made me feel welcome. She was the only girlfriend I'd made on the island. We'd gone off island a few times just for a change of scenery, which is where she got to know and trust me.

When Deidre saw the look on my face, she knew something was wrong. She told me to spill it. My explanation was followed by her mouthing WOW. After a minute of pondering what advice she could offer, she said, "Fuck him, move in with me."

I returned to the apartment to find my belongings on the patio in trash bags. I just laughed and shook my head as I flashed back to the last time this happened to me. I was just glad it wasn't my fault this time.

When I got back with my trash bags, we smoked a joint and shared a bottle of wine. Deidre lived in a one bedroom apartment with a daybed in the living room, so at least I had a real bed. She told me she could definitely use help covering the rent because living by the beach was not cheap. She said if it worked out between the two of us, we could find a larger place when her lease was up in a couple of months.

Deidre had moved to Florida from Memphis for her job a few months before I got to town. She worked for Shoney's in the technology department.

We lived in the one bedroom apartment for the remainder of her lease. I had also started to date a young man that was twenty-one. Billy was a local boy raised by an alcoholic father that lived in a nearby trailer park. He worked on the island and was a friend of Deidre's. Billy and I shared a joint one evening shortly after we met, and ended up talking for four hours. I found him very interesting. He was wise beyond his years, which wasn't surprising knowing his story. When he eventually asked me out on a date, I gladly accepted.

The insecurity I suffered after leaving my home and marriage, and additionally the conflicts with Kenny, was overwhelming. My self esteem had taken a huge hit after Kenny rejected me. I was trying to start a new life in Florida and it was kicking my ass. It seemed every time I'd get a little ahead of the game, something would knock me back. I was too young to understand what priorities I should have, so I partied. I worked hard at my office and played hard after work. My boss loved me because I was resourceful and learned quickly. He trusted me and continued to add responsibilities to my duties. Adding Billy to the picture also boosted my self esteem because he made me feel loved. I think he was as broken as I was.

Billy and I dated for the next few months and when Deidre and I found a larger condo to rent in Jupiter, he followed us. Deidre didn't mind because we put him to work when we needed a man to do things. He was very humble and appreciative, plus he got us weed. He didn't officially live with us, just stayed most of the time.

Deidre had begun to date a new man named Rod. Rod moved down for the winter from somewhere in Canada. He managed an event rental company and hired Billy to work for him through the winter. We had a lot of fun and spent many nights grilling on our patio in our new condo in the Bluffs.

I was on my way off of Singer Island for the last time as a resident, when I ran into the Godfather that owned the pizza shop above my apartment with Kenny. He asked if I'd seen Kenny and I told him I hadn't. He placed his hand on his chin as he shook his head side to side. He said, "The son of a bitch skipped bail on me." I didn't know what that meant but I knew it wasn't good. He asked me to let him know if I ran into Kenny and I assured him I would.

OPPORTUNITY OR CATASTROPHE

My job was going well. We were making money and getting products shipped out efficiently. My boss had put me in charge of the company because he had to return to Canada for awhile, for some reason. He was pretty quiet about what he was doing, but it didn't bother me because I didn't care.

The company was a business opportunity company, which meant we advertised the opportunity in newspapers around the country, and had salesmen hold seminars at local hotels and sell packages of display racks and toys to people. The package was designed so purchasers would consign their products to shops, airports, restaurants, convenience stores and similar places. They provided carousel racks along with the products and sold licensed Disney toys on the carousels. The company was called Carousel of Toys. I thought it was a great concept. I was in charge of setting up seminars with local venues and advertising in local newspapers. The sales manager arranged for the staff to travel, and I took care of the office. I got to meet with vendors and purchase the products we offered with the packages.

We also had to file for permits with the Federal Trade Commission and local authorities, which I handled. As our company grew, we maintained a second office for our sales staff. After my boss stepped out, he turned operations over to me and the amazing new secretary he hired.

Dee was just starting on her own after losing her husband. They'd had an amazing life together throughout his career in the military. She was born in Lake Park in the 1950's. Lake Park is across the Intracoastal waterway from Singer Island. She told me great stories from her days growing up on the beach. We thoroughly enjoyed each other, and her matter-of-fact personality matched mine well.

Dee had a lot of experience running a business and how the world worked. I did not. She got along with the boss enough to please him, but she didn't like him. She knew there was something shady going on, but kept her mouth shut about it until he went back to Canada. My boss was very good at what he did, which was creating opportunities. He eventually told me he had to return to Canada for an extended amount of time due to his visa expiring. He then told me I'd done such a good job for him, that he'd like to list me as president of the corporation and add me to the bank account so I could sign documents and checks in his absence. He said he'd help with any questions I had via telephone, but he was confident I could handle things. He acted like he was promoting me by handing the company over to me. I couldn't believe my luck! I was excited for this opportunity. This business opportunity.

I had worked hard for the company for over a year and learned a lot. My boss was a talented salesman and said everything I needed to hear to willingly put myself in that position, which released him from all liability because his name was removed. Dee knew something was up.

We filed the necessary paperwork with the state and the bank and just like that, I became the President of Carousel of Toys.

Dee had been looking into everything and realized the company wasn't all it was advertised to be. We had great success in selling the packages, but after the company had been transferred to me, the changes my boss made proved to Dee that she had been right—something was up.

Our pool of potential customers had been drying up. That was why my boss planned his exit. We had sold packages in the biggest cities around the country, but were limited as to the business we could conduct in smaller states due to strict laws. My boss had remained on the bank accounts and continued to receive a pay out for a month after we transferred everything as part of our agreement. He then restructured the packages to include less inventory to increase our profit margins.

Shortly after that, we began to get complaints from people regarding the lack of product on the initial orders. We also began to receive complaints from some of our existing customers. Some of the complaints were solved with business advice and suggestions for better locations, and some of them were smoothed over with free inventory. Meanwhile, the boss got upset with Dee because she spoke out about the misrepresentations he had built into the new sales pitch. He knew she was onto him, so he fired her.

To clarify the issues with this business opportunity, the sales staff overstated income potential and ease in which it could be achieved, and overstated how much inventory you'd receive with the initial order. The market had also been flooded with similar offerings from other companies, so getting the display racks into good locations was more challenging than advertised. When my boss left the business, he amended the sales pitch to a more aggressive version and greatly reduced the amount of inventory provided, which caused complaints and reduced sales. He knew this type of business had a limited lifespan, and this one was nearing it's end. Many business opportunities would hit the market hard, selling a bunch of packages, then hang around for a couple of months to present an air of legitimacy, then close their doors to avoid dealing with the complaints they knew would soon follow. I had no experience with this type of business, so I willingly walked right into the lion's den. I was left to deal with the complaints that were now coming in from the initial purchasers because they'd followed the plan and had been unsuccessful due to it being misrepresented.

Losing Dee left a huge hole in our operations, and I was floundering. I had another secretary who handled paperwork and phone calls, but she didn't have the business acumen that Dee had. Dee continued to help me from the outside, but it wasn't the same as having her expertise in the office. After she found a new job that demanded all of her time, she offered me guidance when she could, but she had to move on. I am grateful for everything she taught me in our time together and was happy to see her move on.

Shortly after Dee's departure, one of the first customers who had purchased a large package, somewhere in the neighborhood of $18,000.00, called me to lodge a complaint. She threatened to sue us, which was now me, because she felt shorted on product when she received her package. Even though the paperwork outlined everything she'd receive, not seeing the product and only having a stock list to refer to left her feeling shorted. She was also having challenges placing her product in stores because she was in St. Augustine, a huge tourist area, and most of the locations she'd hoped to get were already taken.

Even though it had been over six months since she'd purchased, I wanted to make her happy at any cost. I hadn't had any serious complaints up until now, and wanted to keep it that way. I told her she could come to my warehouse and take whatever she wanted. I wanted her to be happy and feel as though she received a satisfactory resolution.

Somewhere in the middle of all of this, I hired Billy to manage my warehouse. I desperately needed a second set of hands to help with shipping and inventory, and it just so happened his last job had just ended, so it worked out perfectly. I had to go back to Ohio for my divorce hearing and felt better about leaving knowing Billy would be there to keep an eye on things. I didn't look forward to seeing my soon-to-be ex, but I had no choice and had to be there. I wasn't sure what he'd try to pull after his domestic violence conviction.

Shortly after Billy had started, the lady that complained drove two hours from her home to our warehouse, as I had requested. When she arrived, I introduced her to Billy and instructed him to allow her to select any boxes she wanted and make sure they were loaded in her truck. Then, I left her alone so she could peruse the inventory in her own time. I didn't want her to feel like she was being watched, so I returned to the office.

A short while later, she came in to tell me she was finished. I reiterated that she could take anything she wanted, but she assured me that she was happy. I walked her back to her truck and noticed only about four boxes. I really wanted to make sure her complaint was resolved, so I insisted she take a couple more boxes. I wanted her to feel as though the long drive she took to get to us had been worth it. She ended up taking about six boxes of product in total. She, once again, assured me that she was happy and went on her way.

I was shocked when a month later, I received a letter from her attorney asking for a mediation regarding her purchase contract. What I later learned is she was a chronic complainer who rushed into decisions without thinking them through, then did everything she could to back out when things weren't going as she pictured. She didn't realize how much work running a business of this size would be, and regretted her purchase. I agreed to go to mediation with her.

Our date for mediation was set, and we even settled on a location half way between her home and our office so she wouldn't have to drive two hours to get to us. The proceedings began, and we were told we'd each have a chance to explain our side. The mediator began with the complainant. I listened intently as she explained her plight. When she was finished, I noticed she neglected to inform the mediator about her trip to my warehouse. She didn't mention anything about my attempts to resolve her complaint.

He asked her a few clarifying questions and then moved on to me. He had received documents from me prior to our meeting, so he began to ask me questions about the documents. Once he was happy with the information, he asked if there was anything else I wanted to add, so I told him about my previous attempt to resolve her complaint. I explained how she was given free rein to take anything she wanted from my warehouse. With raised eyebrows, he clarified that I allowed her to take anything she wanted, which I affirmed. He then looked at her and harshly told her he wasn't sure what she was expecting from the hearing, but in his opinion I had done everything I could to resolve her complaint. Case dismissed.

Meanwhile, back in Cleveland, I walked into the courthouse and saw my ex. He was alone and made no effort to communicate, so I didn't either. The judge asked a few questions, granted my petition to restore my maiden name and that was it. I was officially divorced.

I had driven up to save money. I was at a red light when my ex walked up to my window and slipped a small piece of paper inside. He said it was Jaime's number and he was in Fort Lauderdale if I needed anything. I intentionally let him see me throw the piece of paper out the window and watch it flutter down to the street. Jaime was our former coke dealer and I wasn't going to give my ex any reason to believe I wanted any contact with our old coke dealer. I drove away and that was the last time I ever saw him.

A TERRIBLE PAIN

I had been seeing the dentist for a crown that fell off. The dentist informed me that too much of the tooth had been broken off to hold a new crown, so he suggested I pull the tooth and get a dental implant. A dental implant is a bolt implanted into your jaw bone that protrudes through your gum, where a porcelain tooth is then screwed onto the top of the bolt. It was expensive, but I made good money so I agreed to move forward. In preparation for the implant, I had several sets of x-rays and scans and had taken pain medicine on and off from the time the tooth was pulled through the implant procedure, which spanned several months. I had also begun to suffer severe lower back pain and couldn't figure out why. I didn't injure myself, so it made no sense. I tried everything from stretching to pain medicine, but nothing worked. I'd visited my doctor, a chiropractor, and a masseuse. The pain continued for about a month, and no one could offer an explanation.

The pain got so bad at one point that I went to the emergency room. They couldn't find anything wrong, so they sent me home with orders to rest and use pain medication as needed. I was very frustrated because I didn't want to mask the pain, I wanted to know what was causing it.

After a week of more rest and pain medicine as needed, I still had this terrible pain. What made matters worse was that the pain was now at a level I would call excruciating. It had gotten much worse since my emergency room visit, and I just couldn't take it any more, so I returned to the emergency room. They weren't as busy that day so I felt like the doctor was able to assess me more thoroughly than on my last visit. I explained that I'd had ultrasounds, x-rays, and examinations, and no one could offer a solution. The pain had grown worse, and I really needed help.

The doctor asked if I was pregnant, to which I replied, "Absolutely not." I had been on birth control pills for over ten years. The doctor then asked what had been going on medically, so I told him I had been undergoing preparation for a dental implant. I'd been given antibiotics for the oral surgery I had the week before, and was to continue taking them for a few more days.

I noticed the doctor's light bulb come on as he listened to my situation. He then ordered an ultrasound for me. I was confused because I'd already had one, but he seemed to have an idea. At that point, I was willing to do anything if it would relieve this pain. When I arrived in ultrasound, I was pretty shocked when the technician told me she was going to do a transvaginal ultrasound. She explained the procedure, and then we began. Transvaginal ultrasounds are performed with a wand-like device. It is inserted into the vagina and allows the technician to see the organs inside of the pelvis. I knew I hadn't had one of those yet, so I consented.

It wasn't long after she began the ultrasound that she very cheerfully said, "Congratulations, you're pregnant!"

I couldn't see my face, but I could see hers. When she saw the look of utter terror on my face, she said, "Are we not excited about this?" She got her answer as I burst into tears and blurted out a resounding "No!" Her bedside manner was impeccable. She immediately shifted gears and gently asked why. As I sobbed on her table, I told her I'd been on painkillers, antibiotics, had numerous x-rays and scans done and also had been on birth control pills, and had been steadily for more than ten years. I would never proceed with this pregnancy just because of all of that. This poor baby had no chance of being born healthy, and I knew at that moment that I would have to terminate the pregnancy. Her professionalism was amazing as she soothed me and helped me recover from the shock and tears.

When I returned to the ER, I was further educated on my situation and released. I had to be realistic, and made the decision to have an abortion. I suspected Billy wouldn't support my decision because he couldn't grasp all that was happening, and I was correct.

Billy cried when I told him. He was only twenty-two years old and actually thought keeping the baby was a good idea. His reaction was very different than I assumed it would be. I never thought it would affect him so deeply. I did my best to explain the reasons for my decision and hoped he would be able to accept them, but I could tell that something had changed in him.

After my procedure, I took a few days off to heal both physically and mentally. They had used a twilight anesthesia for the procedure. I have a stronger resistance to anesthesia than most people, so during the procedure I could still feel all of the pain and hear all the sounds and voices of those present in the room. It was a horribly painful procedure. I really needed much more than the few days I took, but I just wasn't able to miss any more work. This was another one of those situations where I knew my flock of guardian angels were with me. They gave me the strength to do what I had to do, and then process what had happened. Something like that is never an easy situation, but you do the best you can with what you have to work with. It definitely made me stronger. I also never told my parents. I wasn't sure if they ever wanted grandchildren, and I wasn't willing to break their hearts if they did. Like all of the other hurdles I'd encountered in my new journey, I knew this was something I was going to have to handle on my own.

A NEW FAMILY

O ur lease was coming to an end on the condo Deidre and I rented. I couldn't believe it had already been a year. So much had happened. I knew I wanted to try to buy a house while I had the income to be able to qualify for a loan, so I went house hunting. This was another situation where the stars aligned and pieces fell into place perfectly. The house I fell in love with was close to work and in a great neighborhood called North Palm Beach. It was a three bedroom/two bathroom home on a corner lot with a huge Ruby Red grapefruit tree, a huge avocado tree, and a medium sized Honeybell orange tree. It was like heaven. It also had new carpet and paint, and was exactly what I needed. I wanted to put in an offer, but the real estate agent said they were expecting another offer and that I should offer full price if I wanted to be guaranteed to get the house, so I did.

After jumping through many hoops with a mortgage lender, including asking my accountant to provide everything needed to the mortgage broker to help me get the loan, I got the house. I was so confused during the transaction that I had no idea what was going on. I kept getting calls from title companies, the mortgage broker, processors, and the real estate agent. My agent was not very good at explaining the process of buying a home for the first time to me. I would never forget that.

After a lot of drama and trauma, I was finally able to get the keys to my new home. Billy and I moved in what furniture we had, and were thankful for friends of his who gave us their old living room and dining room sets. We were lucky to find people that were willing to help us like that.

Then, Billy had a brilliant idea that we needed a puppy. We already had Thomas the cat, but Billy wanted a dog. I had no objection, and thought it would ease the pain of the abortion for him, so we stopped by a pet store one night after dinner. As soon as I walked in the door, I was immediately drawn to an open top pen full of wood shavings. That display stuck out to me as if it were illuminated by a bright golden light shining down on it. Curled up in the corner was a small black Chow Chow puppy. She was absolutely adorable. She had been born on February 29, 1996, leap year. She was quiet and sweet, and once she was in my hands, I couldn't put her down. I had to have her, so I filled out the credit application to purchase her, and we took her home.

The pet store offered a free medical checkup at the vet's office down the street, so I made the appointment and took her in. They said she was in excellent health, which made me feel better. I had only recently learned about puppy mills, and hoped that wasn't where she came from. She was AKC (American Kennel Club) registered, so I thought that added some credence to her story, but you just never know.

I was excited to learn the vet's office offered dog obedience classes for both owners and their dogs to attend together. The trainer, Debbie from Ace Dog Training, would teach our entire class how to train our dogs and practice with us for an hour each week. It only cost ten dollars per week, so I gladly signed up. My parents raised me to discipline animals to get them to obey, but I wanted to learn a better way with my new puppy. Her AKC registered name was going to be Pee Wee's Black Coral, Cory for short, and she was perfect. She and Thomas got along great, which made me very happy.

Billy was a bit jealous because he wanted the puppy to bond with him and instead she'd really bonded with me, so I let him talk me into heading back to the puppy store to see if the little black male Chow Chow we had noticed when we bought Cory was still there. He was, so I bought him for Billy. We named him Brandon. The pet store said he was Cory's brother.

I enrolled Billy in training class with Brandon, and Debbie taught us both how to properly train our two dogs.

THIEVES IN THE NIGHT

*A*fter I made the decision to run Carousel of Toys legitimately, the sales staff left. They knew there was no commission to be made if I switched tactics. I was happy, because it gave me a reason to close the second location. We had a healthy bank account, and I wanted to expand on selling products instead of the business opportunity.

We were located in an industrial complex in Riviera Beach off of I-95. The location was remote, and offered excellent proximity for re-entry to the Interstate for fleeing thieves. Since we'd opened up, we'd been robbed twice. The first time, they pried the door away from the deadbolt to gain entry, but were scared away too quickly to take a lot of merchandise. The second time, they smashed the window with a hammer and bled all over the place before taking my computers and a bunch of merchandise. In the latter case, the police were able to get a description of the U-Haul truck they were driving from the business owner next door. He heard the glass break and had time to get identifying markings off the truck, then called the sheriff's office. The deputies got them stopped on I-95 shortly after, and then called me at 2:00 a.m. asking me to report to the side of the Interstate to identify my belongings. These burglars had been coming up from Miami to rob us. They were arrested and prosecuted. They actually served time in jail. I had been getting notices that I was entitled to $1,500.00 in restitution to cover the cost of replacing my front door, and I foolishly thought I'd actually get it. I eventually received notice that the burglar who was supposed to pay me the restitution had been released from jail. A few days after that, I received a notification from his attorney that he'd filed bankruptcy and I wouldn't be getting that restitution I'd been promised. He had an attorney but couldn't afford to pay me back for breaking my door. What a world we live in.

That robbery was the last straw. I decided to move so we could open a true retail store to supplement our wholesale income stream. I found a great location on US 1, in a strip plaza with an antique store and a bike shop. Cartoon Corner was the name of my new retail store in Lake Park, Florida. We set up the front half of our space as a retail store, and the back was our office and storage area. We had enough room to keep sufficient stock and to pack and ship orders for our customers.

END OF THE LEASH

Billy and I had never fully recovered from the trauma of the abortion. After we moved into the house and got the dogs, he began to act like an entitled little kid. He whined when he didn't get what he wanted, blew through three different jobs because they weren't making him happy, and killed what little of our relationship that was left.

Billy came from a broken home and was raised by his alcoholic father. His father was a nice man, but he had horribly succumbed to his demons. We tried to help him financially a couple of times, but it never worked. I even bought him a car and he was supposed to make low payments to me, but defaulted. Billy had been driving the car because he really liked it, so I gave it to him. His poverty mentality really took its toll on our relationship. Once I started to make good money, Billy acted like a rock star wanting to buy everything he saw, then disposed of it because it wasn't new and shiny any more.

I decided our time together was over. Unfortunately, because Billy was so poverty-minded, I had to put out even more money if I wanted to get rid of him. I had to help him get an apartment, pay his security deposit and give him furniture. I didn't care, I just wanted him gone.

Right after he left, my parents decided they wanted to come and visit for the winter. They had met Billy when I took him home to Cleveland one Christmas, but they didn't like him. They saw in him what I couldn't, and it wasn't good. Because they didn't like him, they wouldn't come to visit me. Once he was gone, they came down for the entire winter. Among other things, they helped me build a shed, fix my fence and build some shelves in my house. It was great to have them around. They gave me a sense of comfort from home that I'd desperately missed. It was during that first visit that I realized how much different they were when they were around only me, and not my sister and me. We had a great time exploring and shopping. They helped me buy a new bedroom set from a cool rattan store called Sheribel's, and my mom and I explored every store we could find. We had a blast.

We were out in the back yard one day when Brandon, Billy's dog, began to give me problems. He'd become a bit belligerent after Billy had left and wasn't responding to me very well at obedience class. Brandon and I definitely shared alpha personalities, and when I tried to get him to listen he snapped at me. I was so shaken I exploded with anger and started to hit him with my shoe. That just made things worse, so I grabbed his collar and shoved him into the dog crate in the house. He got so angry that he started to snarl at me and act like he was going to attack me. My dad said that he shouldn't be acting like that, so I should leave him in the crate. Our interaction shook me so badly that I was afraid to ever let him out of the crate again. I wanted to euthanize him, so I called animal control and asked if they would help me, but they said they could only help if he'd actually bitten me, which he hadn't. I was at my wit's end and so shaken I didn't know what to do. Looking back, I should have remained calm and corrected him as Debbie had taught me, but that unfortunately I didn't. I exploded, causing him to explode, then I got scared when he didn't back down. I was so wrong, it hurt my heart to know what I'd done, but there was no going back.

I called Billy and told him if he wanted Brandon, he had to come pick him up after work or I was going to have him put to sleep. He told me he'd be there, and showed up as promised. I gave him all of Brandon's things and wished them well. It felt good to know Brandon would be with Billy, who loved him like nothing he'd ever had. I wish I'd have let Billy take him when he left.

GOING OUT OF BUSINESS

*M*y parents stayed through early spring, then headed home. My dad had helped me complete all of the projects I'd asked for and more, but was eager to get home and return to his own life. He had to get his taxes done and prepare to plant his garden. They'd stayed about three months, and we were all ready to return to our own lives and routines.

Meanwhile, the store was failing badly. I learned a lot about what to do and what not to do during the time we were opened. The type of retail surrounding us did not afford us the amount of foot traffic I'd needed. It wasn't the type of plaza that encouraged browsing. People visiting stores there came specifically for that store, and we were unknown so few people randomly walked in.

I'd attempted advertising and promoting the store by donating toys to Christmas toy drives to no avail. I cut my pay and medical insurance to help, but it just wasn't enough. There just wasn't enough business to sustain our existence any more.

Before we were able to fulfill our one year lease, I came to the realization that it was time to close our doors. We offered a liquidation sale to our customers, shipped their orders, and walked away.

When I cut my pay I picked up a part-time job as a waitress at a local bar to supplement my income. As it happened, Deidre and I were sitting in a booth having drinks one evening when I got the wild idea to ask the waitress if they were hiring. She said they were, and introduced me to the owner. He interviewed me right there and hired me on the spot to work part-time on busy nights for dinner. I thanked him for the opportunity and returned to my table with Deidre, where we laughed about how I was back "in the biz" just like that!

NEW ADVENTURES

When I closed the doors to the store, I found myself repeating something I'd done earlier in my life. I left my corporate job and asked my boss at the bar for a full-time position, just like I'd done when I left Creative Graphics and went to work at The Taverne.

After my part-time trial, my boss offered me a full-time day shift position with occasional dinner shifts as needed. I worked Monday through Friday, and loved it. The problem was, I had purchased my home a year prior when I was making a lot more money. Because I was self employed, I was given a very high 13% interest rate. I took it because I was afraid I'd never get the opportunity to buy a house again, and I really wanted that house. I just had a hard time affording my car, insurance, mortgage and necessities. I knew I had to find something that paid more, but this would hold me over until that happened.

One afternoon after we'd finished our shifts, I was sitting at the bar having a beer with my co-workers. We used to have a few beers after work and enjoy some Happy Hour appetizers before going home. I wanted to grab a bite of something different that night and asked if anyone wanted to go somewhere with me, but there were no takers. My best friend and fellow waiter, Michael told me to wait before I left. He was up to something, but I wasn't sure what. He walked over to a table and was talking to Jerry, one of our evening regulars.

A few minutes later, both men walked up to my barstool and Michael officially introduced us. He said Jerry was also hungry, and suggested the two of us grab some dinner. Jerry was a bit older and good looking, well dressed and very likable. He reminded me of actor Pierce Brosnan. I couldn't believe someone like him would want to go to dinner with me. What I did not know is that Jerry had been asking Michael about me from the first time he saw me, and Michael was just waiting for the right time to fix us up. After we were properly introduced, Jerry looked at me with an adorable crooked smile and said, "I'm hungry, you're hungry. Let's go eat." So we did!

Jerry took me to dinner to a place I'd never been. It was inside a country club, and the staff knew him by name. I was impressed. This place had the air of a beautiful old library with dark wood paneling and ambient lighting. We sat at the hand-carved bar and Jerry ordered us a bottle of merlot—my favorite. I wasn't sure if we both liked the same wine or a little bird named Michael had filled him in, but I didn't care. It was the first time in my life I'd been to dinner with a man who enjoyed wine!

Jerry was a skilled conversationalist. He was engaging, interesting, and funny. He told me he was a partner in a jewelry store that serviced high-end clientele. He made regular trips to New York to attend auctions for gemstones. I was fascinated because I'd never known anyone in the jewelry business. It was very interesting to learn how it all worked.

When he asked me about myself, I had such a high level of comfort with him that I spilled everything. He listened intently, and with no judgement. I told him about moving to Florida, my divorce, being in the process of closing my business, and looking for a secretarial job. He told me he was in the process of getting separated, and had two young sons. He and his wife were concerned with the well-being of the boys, so they were taking it slowly. Then, he talked about a separate business venture he was working on. Jerry and his business partner were opening an Irish pub in Key West. They wanted it as authentic as possible, so he had been traveling to and from Ireland to arrange work visas for people to staff the pub. It was going to be located right across from Jimmy Buffet's Margaritaville restaurant on Duval Street.

Jerry and I learned a lot about each other, and enjoyed an amazing dinner while knocking back three bottles of merlot. It was such a magical evening, I'll never forget it. We drank Matanzas Creek merlot, which became my new favorite wine. As we finished the last bottle the bartender told us he had to close. We had spent three and a half hours sitting at the bar and talking. Jerry insisted on picking up the tab, for which I was grateful. As we walked to his car, he said he enjoyed our conversation and asked if we could do it again. I could hardly wait.

Although I'd never noticed Jerry while we were sitting at the bar, he certainly captured my interest after our shared dinner. We were as different as night and day, but there was definitely a connection. For the first time in my life, I wasn't chasing after someone begging for their attention. Jerry fed my soul. He was open and real with me, and didn't hold anything back. If I did something silly, he called me on it, and vice versa. We grew to be close over the next few months. My boss wasn't happy about our relationship though because he and his wife were friends with Jerry and his wife. My boss considered Jerry to be cheating on her, even though they were separated. I guess he thought there was a chance they'd reconcile, but I certainly didn't get that impression from Jerry. He had gotten his own apartment, so I saw no harm in having a relationship with him.

Our normal dates were downtown West Palm Beach for dinner at either ZaZu or Sforza's on Clematis Street. ZaZu had the best leg of lamb in the world and we'd split one for dinner and enjoy two or three bottles of merlot. We always sat at the bar, which was fine with me because being a waitress myself, I wouldn't want a couple taking up a table in my section for three hours. Plus Jerry knew all of the bartenders and they always took excellent care of us.

We never spoke of any commitment to each other, we just spent time together when we could. Jerry was in the middle of his divorce, running his jewelry business, and now the bar in Key West, so he had a lot of balls in the air. He didn't need to add me to the list. And truth be told, it didn't really bother me that we had no commitment. He had made it clear to me that if I needed anything, he'd be there for me, and he proved it time and time again.

Jerry had sponsored a young man from Ireland named Connor, who began working at the country club restaurant in Jupiter, where we had our first dinner together. I was in my late twenties at that time, and Connor was just a couple of years younger than I was. Jerry took great care of Connor, and in return he was very loyal to Jerry. We tended to visit Connor at work when we weren't dining downtown. I got to know him pretty well, and he treated me with kindness and respect. Connor was also instructed to assist me in any way I needed if Jerry wasn't around. It made me feel very special to know Jerry was looking out for me.

As we spent more time together, Jerry introduced me to his sons. They came over to my house one afternoon for a visit, and then we all went out on Jerry's boat. His youngest son was just four years old and really bonded quickly with me. By the end of the day, he was on my lap and chattering endlessly to me. His older son was six, and you could tell he was daddy's boy. He was glued to Jerry's side the entire day. He loved to mimic Jerry's actions and it was adorable. It was a great day. It was very obvious to me that it was a test to see how the boys would react to me, and I was pleased we all got along so well. I was secretly hoping our relationship would grow after that, because now Jerry knew he could trust me with being around his boys.

Not long after that, I was offered a temporary position at a golf organization, in their trade show department called Expo Services. I was going to be the Assistant to the Director of Expo Services. This organization was pretty prestigious, and liked to work with new employees on a temporary basis before hiring them. It was a pretty smart move, since they could release you with a simple phone call if you didn't fit their mold. I was happy for the opportunity.

I was to be part of an eleven person team that existed solely to put on two of the largest golf trade shows in the world. One would be held in Orlando, and the other in Las Vegas. My boss was in charge of setting up contracts with hotels for all attendees and staff of our organization, securing temporary staffing for the shows, setting up shuttle services, and other events such as dinners and award ceremonies. She had a strong personality and got things done. We fit together very well, and she decided to offer me a full time position.

Jerry had been away for awhile, and recently returned home. I had just come home from the grocery store on a Saturday afternoon when he pulled into my driveway in a brand new Porsche 911 convertible. He was so excited! It was nice to know I was the first person he wanted to share his excitement with. He acted like a little boy with a brand new toy. He was showing me how to put the top up and down, the amazing stereo system, and then showed me the sticker. When I saw the sticker price of that car, I almost had a heart attack. That car cost him almost as much as my house had cost me. I just stood there with my mouth hanging open until he finally told me to put my groceries away and get in so we could grab some drinks.

Jerry asked if I knew how to drive a stick shift, to which I replied, "Come on, I grew up in the country, of course I can drive a stick." He let me drive to dinner. It was an incredible car. It had a six-speed manual transmission, and I had it up to seventy miles per hour by only third gear. All I could think about, as we roared down Alternate A1A toward downtown, was Julia Roberts in *Pretty Woman* being absolutely correct when she said, "These babies corner like they're on rails."

We headed to ZaZu and found a couple of seats at the bar. We followed our normal routine and enjoyed three bottles of merlot and dinner over the next three hours. Neither of us had issues holding our liquor back then, but something was definitely off with Jerry. He was slurring, which he never did. He asked me to drive home, which he never did.

When we got back to my house, Jerry came inside and spent the night, which he also never did. As we were about to fall asleep, he whispered, "I love you, you know." I had been longing to hear that, even though I knew we'd never be any more than we were right then. By the time I whispered back to him that I loved him too, he was sound asleep.

That was the first night of many we'd spend together, and I really enjoyed it. Jerry then bought two brand new jet skis, and kept them at PGA Marina, where he kept his boat. When he wasn't around, he'd let me take the jet skis out with Deidre. That was a summer I'll never forget.

TWO TRIPS

Since Jerry was in the middle of his busy season with the jewelry store, Deidre and I decided we wanted to go to Key West to see his new pub. When we told him of our decision, Jerry handed me a wad of cash and told us the only condition tied to it was that we had to spend it all. We were definitely up for the challenge, so we booked our stay at the Holiday Inn La Concha on Duval Street. It just so happened we chose the weekend of the Ernest Hemingway Days festival, and fortunately we got a room due to a cancellation. When things like that happen, you just know everything's going to work out perfectly.

Deidre and I experienced Key West in a whole new way that weekend, we were right in the middle of Duval Street and didn't use our car once. Deidre also invited her friend Ann and her husband Bo to join us. Ann and Deidre worked at the same company, and when the company relocated its headquarters to West Palm Beach, Ann only had to report to the office once a month, so she and her husband decided to move to Big Pine Key because it was worth the commute. Ann and Bo and showed us Key West from a local's perspective, which is the best way to see it. We had an amazing time with them, and vowed to visit again very soon.

Deidre and I got home from Key West on Monday morning. Tuesday nights were the big night out on Clematis Street in downtown West Palm, called Clematis by Night, so we decided to go after work. Deidre said she'd meet me down there, since she had an errand to do after work. Her errand was to pick up some "party favors" for us. She had gotten a vial of Ketamine from a friend of hers. She told me it was a cat tranquilizer. She said her friends tried it, and it was awesome so she put a few drops into each of our glasses of wine as we sat at a bistro table on the sidewalk in front of ZaZu. We thought we'd just hang out there until we figured out what effect it would have on us.

About twenty minutes later, I began to feel super drunk, like room-spinning drunk. I was telling Deidre how I felt, and she was even worse than I was. She had difficulty forming words. All she could do was laugh, which in turn made me laugh. After we sat there for what felt like an hour laughing, we decided we were done drinking and needed to head home. Thank goodness for my ability to metabolize drugs and alcohol faster than most people, because of it, I was able to recover and function enough to get us moving.

By the time we walked to Deidre's car, I realized she was in no condition to get behind the wheel, so I got in and drove her home. I figured I would drive her home and then call Jerry, who I knew was either with Connor or at the bar.

Jerry returned my message while I was driving Deidre home. He said he was in the middle of a card game and couldn't leave, so he sent me a taxi to Deidre's house so I could go back and retrieve my car from downtown. I was thankful for that, because there was no way I was leaving a convertible downtown overnight.

MERRY CHRISTMAS
FROM THE FBI

For Christmas that year, Jerry gave me a beautiful diamond tennis bracelet, a twenty-four karat gold chain with a coin pendant, and a pair of diamond earrings that were more than a half karat each. I couldn't believe it. Once again, Jerry shocked me. I'd never had such beautiful things before, and felt incredibly grateful to have him in my life. He teased me, saying that he knew I was secretly hoping for a ring, but that couldn't happen.

It was not long after that Christmas when one day I was trying to pay for my groceries with my debit card, but for some reason it wouldn't work. I knew I had more than enough money in my account, so I couldn't figure out why it wasn't working. I tried again, then again. No luck. The cashier said it was showing declined. I was about to panic when she suggested I try the ATM machine and see if that would work. I did. My card didn't work there either, and to make matters worse, the machine kept my card. Now I panicked.

By the time I got home, there was a Federal Express package at my door. It was from the Federal Trade Commission. When I opened it and read the very official looking letter, it said my assets had been seized. Apparently, some of the customers of my old business had filed complaints, which initiated an investigation by the FBI. While they were investigating, they seized all of my assets and I would have no access to my bank account or credit cards. I had no idea what all of this meant, so I called Jerry and Deidre. They were both older than I was and had much more life experience, so they were the two I turned to. They both arrived within a half hour and each took a look at the letter. I told them about what happened at the grocery store and how the ATM machine kept my card.

Jerry knew exactly what to do. He asked me if I had any checks outstanding, and I burst into tears when I realized my mortgage payment hadn't yet cleared. Jerry looked at Deidre as he handed her enough to cover it in cash. He told her to write a check for my mortgage payment and overnight it to the mortgage company for me. He then handed me a handful of $100 bills and said that should tide me over until we got this settled. He said I should call a lawyer before I spoke to anyone so I didn't incriminate myself, but after I explained what actually happened, he said I should be okay to call the investigator first to see what he had to say.

The next day I called the FBI agent whose name was on the letter. He asked me a few questions to confirm my identity, then explained what had happened. The complaints were against my old boss and the lead salesman, but since my boss had me put on the corporation as the President, they were looking at me. The agent said they'd been trying to track down my boss, but had no luck. As he explained everything, he asked if I'd be willing to cooperate with their investigation. I asked a few initial questions that popped into my head, and after I was told what was going to happen, I agreed to fully cooperate with them because I had nothing to hide.

I'd tried to run the business legitimately but made no money, and that's what I told them. They told me their main goal was to locate my boss. They asked me his name, and I told them. They then told me he was using a different last name, so they wanted to send me a photograph to be sure we were talking about the same man. I happened to be on my lunch break at work, so I gave them my fax number. As I stood by the fax machine awaiting the arrival of the photograph, I felt my jaw drop as my old boss' photo began to creep out of the fax machine. It was a full eight by eleven inch photo of him. I couldn't believe this was really happening.

I immediately called the agent back to confirm the photo was actually my boss. He thanked me and advised me what to expect next. They knew I wasn't the person they were after, and if I agreed to testify against my former boss should they catch him, I was off the hook. They were releasing my assets that day, and my only obligation other than to testify if necessary, was to keep them informed of my whereabouts for the next five years. I thought that was very reasonable and quickly agreed.

JERRY'S TURN

Coming into the next summer, I began to see less and less of Jerry. If I'd call him, he'd answer but the answer was very elusive. I'd run into Connor and asked him how Jerry was doing. I said I hadn't seen him in a few weeks, and Connor just looked down and shook his head. I could tell he didn't want to risk sharing anything he shouldn't with me, so I told him I was just worried and wanted to make sure he was okay. Connor said he had been spending a lot of time in Key West, and he'd started using body building steroids and wasn't himself. For some reason, he started working out and was trying to build muscle quickly. I attributed it to the end of his divorce approaching and a mid-life crisis. He was now in his late forties, so it made sense.

Deidre and I decided to go to Clematis by Night the following Tuesday. There were a bunch of us, so we sat at a big table. From where we were sitting, I was able to see the bar at ZaZu. I immediately spotted Jerry sitting at the bar. There was a moment of excitement, before a moment of shock as I noticed who he was with. Seated very close to him and looking very comfortable was a semi-attractive blonde that looked a bit younger than me. Even though we never had a commitment, it still shocked me. As Deidre noticed the look on my face she turned around to see what I was gaping at and then said rather loudly, "That son of a bitch!"

We had enjoyed a few wines before we saw Jerry, and Deidre was feeling no pain. Before I could stop her (although I secretly didn't want to stop her) she made her way to Jerry and the blonde and asked him to step away so they could speak privately. After he stepped away from his date, Deidre quietly but effectively read him the riot act. I could see him squirming due to the uncomfortable circumstances of her conversation with him, then he explained something to her, and she nodded and walked back toward us and he returned to his date.

Upon her return to our table, she explained that the young lady was Fiona, from Ireland. She was the manager of his pub in Key West. That explained a lot.

A couple of weeks later, Jerry walked back into my life. I was sitting on my couch reading a book when he walked in the front door. I wasn't sure what to say or how to act, so I just sat there. He smiled at me with the same smile he offered the first night we went to dinner years earlier, the one that melted my heart. Then he began to pace back and forth while he was trying to figure out how to say whatever he'd come to say. As I studied him, I could tell something was wrong…really wrong, and I just knew in my gut that it had nothing to do with Fiona.

I waited very impatiently for Jerry to start explaining. He took a really deep breath as he continued to pace, then told me he was under investigation by the FBI. I looked at him skeptically, and he returned a look that told me he wasn't lying. Jerry was scared. He said he wanted to protect me, so he'd been staying away. He had recently found out he'd been under surveillance for a few weeks, and said he didn't want to get me dragged into another investigation. I believed him. Now I knew why he was acting this way. After what I'd gone through with my investigation, which I was sure was nothing compared to what he was under investigation for, I fully understood. He was desperate for a voice of reason to help him find his way out of the thick fog that enveloped him, if only for a short while. That's why he showed up at my house. We really did love each other, but we were at two very different places in our lives. There was no way, as much as I didn't want to admit it, that things between us could ever work. But right now, in this moment, I didn't care about any of that. I stood up and hugged him. He melted into me, and for the first time in our relationship, I was the one offering strength.

Although Jerry and I were never meant to last, our time together had served us well. We provided each other with love and support when each of us needed it most, but Jerry's life had turned into a very complicated situation. As if the impending divorce, his children, me, Fiona, and the bar in Key West weren't enough, adding the FBI investigation that stretched on for almost two years broke Jerry. The last time I saw him, I was at the Waterway Cafe, a restaurant/bar near my house. It was about a month after he stopped by my house to tell me that he was under investigation. He left the Porsche parked under the portico and came running in the bar looking for me. Fiona was in the passenger seat. He was in a frenzied state as he rushed over and asked me if I knew where he could get some blow. I hadn't done coke since I left Ohio, and the fact that he asked me showed how desperate he was to find it. I told him I did not know where he could get some blow and gave him a look of disapproval. He gave me a quick kiss on the cheek and squeezed my arm before he ran back to the car and left. Jerry always drank a lot, but he was good at it. He also ate well and took good care of himself...until Fiona had shown up. I just knew Fiona was responsible for the frenzied state he'd been in when he came to me asking about that nasty drug that had turned my life upside-down not so long ago.

Jerry was eventually arrested, convicted, and placed in federal prison. By the time the investigation got really serious, and the court dates happened, it had been over a year since we'd been in contact. I followed his story in the Palm Beach Post as they reported on the progress of the trial. He eventually turned state's evidence on his boss and was given a reduced sentence. Jerry's ex-wife had taken the boys and moved back with her family up north. Someone with influence was able to help them arrange Jerry's relocation so he was able to serve out the remainder of his sentence near his his boys. Jerry will always hold a special place in my heart. I am thankful for the time I felt protected under Jerry's love, and grateful for the time we had together.

MAGICAL HOLIDAYS

I spent the remainder of the summer and fall single and alone. Jerry's absence in my life left a big hole, and I was terribly lonely. Dee invited me to her boat for Monday night dinner parties, and tried to fix me up with a captain she knew, but it didn't work out. He invited me over for grilled chicken legs then played a how-to porn video for our entertainment. So much for blind dates.

Not long after that, I was thrilled to learn Jo (my Hairdresser Extraordinaire) and her boyfriend, Bill (my old friend from The Taverne) were moving down to Miami. Then I learned my friend Rik, (my first boyfriend's best friend) was moving to Orlando around the same time. Another synchronistic event occurred when we were able to coordinate Bill and Jo's moving company to transport Rik's numerous Marshall guitar amps to Florida for him, since they wouldn't fit in his car. The moves happened because Bill had been offered a job transfer to Miami when his company was bought out, and Rik wanted to grow his entertainment business in a nicer climate. All at once, I had three great friends that would live less than two hours from me, which really helped my loneliness subside.

Bill's new position had him traveling to South America frequently, so that gave Jo and me the opportunity to hang out together. It was great to have my friend and her talent back. Once the movers were close, Rik followed me down to Miami to meet them. Jo knew how desperately I'd missed her doing my hair, so she planned to give me a trim and highlights that weekend. Bill and Jo moved into Jo's sister's rental condo after she'd bought a house, another synchronistic event because the timing worked out so perfectly. The rental was in Coconut Grove, which is also known as "The Grove." The Grove is a great entertainment area that was packed on weekends. Our favorite place to hang out became a bar/restaurant called Señor Frog's. They had great food, a big bar and music and dancing. It wasn't long before Frog's was The Grove's version of our beloved Taverne in Ohio.

It was a great weekend catching up with all of my new old friends. When I returned to the office sporting my new haircut and color, Jo's talents did not go unnoticed. Several of my co-workers asked who did my hair, which gave me a great idea. If I could get enough people looking for a great hairdresser together, we could have Jo come to my house and have hair parties. Four or five customers could justify her travel, and it would help her make some extra money.

It was much easier to get a group of ladies together for the hair parties than I thought it would be. For our first gathering, each person brought something to share, from food to wine. We ended up with five plus me and had a great time. As word spread, Jo's Palm Beach County clientele grew. Our crowd had gotten so large, there were times when she ran out of time to do my hair at the party, so she did it the next day. I was happy it worked out so well and that I could help my friend get off to a good start in her new home state.

Bill was scheduled to be out of town for the early part of December, which was when my company Christmas party was being held, so I asked Jo to be my plus one. Since we already had a hair party scheduled for later in the month, this was going to be just a social visit.

The Events Department had been holding back on announcing where the party was being held, so we found out when we got the invitations. When I read the location was to be at the Mar-A-Lago Club in Palm Beach, I couldn't believe it. Our previous parties had been at hotels, granted nice hotels, but nothing this exclusive. It was quite a nice surprise. The event was to be a ninety-minute cocktail reception in the pool area. When we learned what it cost, we weren't surprised it was only for ninety minutes!

The party was on Saturday night, and Jo arrived on Friday so we could spend the entire weekend together. I worried about finding something appropriate to wear, since everything I had at the time was office attire, and she told me not to worry, that she had the perfect dress for me to wear. Jo was right, she loaned me the greatest dress I'd ever worn. It was black velvet, off the shoulders, and the length was just above the knee. When I tried it on, it fit like it had been tailored just for me. Between the dress and the new hair, I felt like a princess going to the ball.

Saturday night had finally arrived, and the drive to Palm Beach at Christmas time was beautiful. There were lights everywhere, and decorations adorned every sign and street light. We oohed and aahed all the way through town and past the mansions on the beach until we finally reached our destination. Once we figured out which gate to use, the guard verified we were on the list, then directed us to the valet. As we stepped out of the car, we were awestruck. We just couldn't believe we were actually there. We were ushered into the grand foyer, where we mingled with my co-workers as we waited our turn to be professionally photographed in front of a huge Christmas tree. We then made our way to the pool area, where we were allowed to explore a few of the surrounding rooms. The rooms were impeccably furnished with the antiques placed there by Marjorie Merriweather Post, who had Mar-A-Lago built between 1924-1927. We were told when Donald Trump purchased the property in 1985, he purchased all of the furnishings and kept everything in tact. It was truly a gift to be able to visit this beautiful piece of Palm Beach history. We then enjoyed hors d'oeuvres and cocktails while we toasted to a Merry Christmas and Successful and Happy New Year. Once our ninety minutes were up, we headed to Waterway Cafe with a few of my co-workers for a night cap.

THE PAST RETURNS

It was New Year's Eve Eve, 1998 (aka: January 30). Jo was back at my house for the last hair party of the year. She wanted to make sure everyone looked their best for their New Year's Eve celebrations. Bill's job had him out of town until the next day, so Jo scheduled the hair party planning to spend the night, then head home to spend the holiday with Bill. The ladies that got their hair done later in the afternoon were still with us as we enjoyed a pre-holiday buffet and talked about our magical evening at Mar-A-Lago. As we waited for Steph's color to cure, Jo started on my highlights. She was just about finished applying my color and the foils when we heard a knock at the front door. When I opened the door, I couldn't believe I saw another Ohioan, my brother's best friend William, standing there. My brother had told me William was moving to Florida, but he didn't say when or where. I certainly never thought I'd see him that soon. I invited him in, introduced him to Jo and Steph, and got him a beer. I knew he'd have one. William was always up for a beer.

My history with William began with a short love affair when I was twenty and he was sixteen. William was a very charismatic young man, and he had a crush on me from the day we met during his freshman year in high school. I say that with confidence because he told me. William used to come to our house and beg me to go to the prom with him. He told me how much he loved me and wanted to marry me. I told him freshmen weren't allowed to go to the prom, so that got me off the hook for that year. As for the marriage proposal, I just ignored it.

A couple of years later, my parents and brother were out of town so I had the house to myself. I decided to have a few friends over instead of going out. Money was tight, and having friends over afforded me the opportunity to save some. William, his brother, and their best friend, along with one of my friends were all hanging out drinking beer and playing cards. William was a seasoned drinker at sixteen, so he fit right in with the older crowd. As the night wore on, and the crowd thinned. William hung back. After just the two of us remained, we ended up in bed together. He didn't have a hard time convincing me, because I'd had a lot of beers and I did like him. It was our age difference that presented the problem.

The second time we hooked up occurred under similar circumstances about a year later. When I moved out of my parents' house shortly after that, our random hook ups ended. That was when I moved in with my co-worker from Kicks Night Club, and William eventually fell deeply in love with a young lady that soon became his fiancé.

Shortly after their engagement, they learned she had some form of reproductive cancer. It was a very aggressive form of the disease that took her within a year. The couple never got to have their wedding because she got so sick so quickly. They were both around twenty-three years old when she passed. William really struggled with her death, and had a hard time trying to regain control of his life. He never took the time to grieve, he just kept himself busy to avoid dealing with the pain of losing her. He tried to find relief in the bottom of a bottle. Once she knew she was dying, she encouraged William to date and move on with his life because she didn't want him sitting beside her bed waiting for her to die. He refused at first, but eventually ran back into the arms of his former high school girlfriend, Jessica. Jessica was a great girl, but not a very good match for William, and their on again, off again relationship proved it.

Back at the hair party, William filled us in on what had been going on in his life more recently. He had been working for his stepfather, JC who ran a construction company that installed electrical poles in Ohio. When the company offered JC the opportunity to relocate to South Florida, he took it. He also offered William the opportunity to relocate to Florida with the company, and William took it. He would be an electric lineman apprentice, which is a really great paying union job with a great future. William and JC rented an apartment in Hypoluxo, about thirty minutes south of me. They arrived on December 26 so they could open their new office just after the New Year's holiday.

Not too long after William arrived at my house, his mother called him on his cell phone. His side of the conversation was very evasive, but I heard him say he was at a friend's house and wouldn't be back to the apartment until late. She ended up calling twice more to ask the same question over the next couple of hours. I asked William what was going on, and he finally explained that his mother had just arrived from Ohio, and she brought Jessica with her.

William confessed to us that he'd taken the job in Florida to get away from his past, which included Jessica. He realized they were on two very different paths. She wanted a career and kids, and he didn't. So, instead of being honest with her, he evaded telling her the truth. He assumed she'd get the hint when he told her he was moving to Florida. He even started a fight with her so they'd part on bad terms.

William's mother arrived at the apartment earlier that day with Jessica in tow. He was pissed, so he evaded conversation with them and left. He didn't say where or why he was going, he just left. Now, he was in my kitchen.

William continued telling us that when he learned of his opportunity to relocate to Florida, he stopped by my parents' house to say goodbye. On his way out the door, he asked my brother Randy what I was up to and where I lived. Randy told him I lived in North Palm Beach and that I was working as a secretary...and yes, I was single. William got my number and address from Randy before he left. When I heard that part of his story, I remembered that he has always been very adept at planning his future steps, so he was never without an escape plan because William is a true survivor.

When William needed to get away from his mother and Jessica, he headed to my house. He knew he'd be welcome and it was a great place to "hide." Of course I was happy to see him, because I hadn't dated anyone since Jerry, and the blind date Dee set me up on. Seeing William at my front door was like getting a late Christmas gift, until I learned about Jessica. I know he would have spent the night with me if I would have allowed it, but I made it clear that he needed to handle the situation with Jessica before anything happened between us. He promised, and left my house just after midnight.

At three o'clock the next day, William was once again on my doorstep. I invited him in and asked him what happened. He said he officially ended his relationship with Jessica, and all parties were in agreement that it was over. His mother was on her way the airport to drop her off. He then asked me if I had plans for New Year's Eve, to which I replied, "I do now."

My friend Jack's band *Up Next* was playing, and I couldn't wait to see them. They played almost every weekend and I loved watching them perform. Jack plays a rendition of *Scenes from an Italian Restaurant* by Billy Joel that is my favorite.

William waited for me to finish getting ready, and then we headed to the Waterway. We planned to grab a bite at the bar instead of trying to get a table for dinner. Flynn, the best bartender ever, had saved me a couple of seats next to the dance floor. He always took good care of me. I usually went there alone, so he always made sure I had a seat at the bar and kept my purse behind the bar so I could get up and dance without worrying about it.

William and I had a great time, and he spent the night. We spent New Year's day together watching old movies and shared a traditional dinner of pork roast, which is said to bring good luck in the New Year.

William began his new job the next day, and I returned to the office. I'd been working with my team for a little over a year now. When we returned from the holiday, we learned our department, Expo Services, was being sold. The organization wanted to focus on membership, tournaments, and merchandising, so they decided to outsource the trade shows. There would be months of due diligence, but the bottom line was that my team would eventually be split up. We would learn our individual fates later in the year. Until then, we were ordered to conduct business as usual, which was difficult knowing the changes that were coming.

CH, CH, CHA, CHANGES

O ur first trade show of the year took place in late January, which meant we hit the ground running right after New Year's day. We would depart for Orlando two weeks before the show, and return a few days after it concluded.

My co-workers and I had good relations with our exhibitors and vendors, so the show went off without a hitch, as usual. I will say that knowing about the potential sale dramatically affected many people's good moods though. After we got back, there was a meeting with the entire team and the upper management staff. They broke the news to us that the sale would be going through, and that we were to continue to work on the next show, set in the fall, until we either received our offer of employment with the new firm, or didn't.

It wasn't long before the invitations were extended to our executives, which wasn't a surprise. Then, the next level supervisors were either offered positions or not, so some would be staying with the organization in other roles. There were three admins on our team, Sarah, Andi, and me. Andi left the company to start a family, Sarah was invited to join the new company, and I was not. Because I was so new to the team and had little experience in the field, my boss knew it wasn't likely I'd be invited to the new company, but she didn't tell me right away. I later learned she worked behind the scenes to secure a position for me with the Merchandising department. She wasn't willing to work for the new company even though they offered her a position, but she took care of me on her way out the door.

Moving to the new team was going to be challenging. I was excited to be staying where I'd built a home for the past couple of years, but it just wouldn't be the same. My old team worked really hard, but we also had a lot of fun on the road. We'd work as much as 100 hours per week, but it was always gratifying. We had good relationships with the contacts in both towns where our shows were held. We accomplished some pretty awesome feats with only eleven people because everyone knew their job and did it well. There wasn't a single person on that team that didn't pull their weight and more.

When I began my new position with Merchandising, I was told I was going to be my new boss' personal assistant. She was a lady who'd been in merchandising for over thirty years. She was now in her mid-sixties and slowing down a bit, but remained one of the foremost experts in event merchandising in the country.

When we travelled to events, she constructed a small 20,000 square foot department store that averaged more income during the two weeks it was operational than some brick-and-mortar department stores earned in an entire year. She knew how to set up the merchandise for optimal sales and customer flow. She was truly a genius. Aside from my boss, there were two other ladies in the department at our office. The two handled the administrative duties relating to the point-of-sale system and inventory. They had conditioned our boss to work on her own, mostly due to their lack of willingness to help her. When she got the opportunity to add me to her team, she was thrilled.

I quickly learned who ran the show in our department, and it wasn't our boss. The two admins basically bullied this soft-spoken woman into catering to their whims. She did it to keep them happy because she didn't want to be bothered with the drama. When I learned one of the ladies asked for our boss to pay for her mother-in-law to fly to her house to take care of her forty-year-old husband and seventeen-year-old son while she was on the road, I was shocked. Then, the other admin asked her to pay to board her dog while we were away, because apparently her husband couldn't manage the dog on his own in her absence. I couldn't believe these people had the audacity to ask for such things, when they both knew that travel was a big part of their jobs. I was even further repulsed when I found out my boss accommodated their requests.

As our first impending trip together grew closer, I was anxious to help my boss prepare. Whether it was picking up her dry cleaning or booking air fare, I did it. I wanted to make her life as easy as possible. It was the least I could do after she'd been treated so poorly by my co-workers.

Our accommodations were arranged, and we would be using loaner cars from Oldsmobile, one of the event sponsors. I was to get a van when we arrived so I could continue to assist my boss with errands. That was the first issue with my co-workers. Even though they weren't arriving until a week after I'd been there, they were upset because I was assigned a vehicle and they weren't. I had also been assigned private accommodations, and they were made to share. Two strikes against me.

Aside from their angst with having been assigned a car and private accommodations, all went well for the first week on site. I was to be there for a total of eighteen days. On alternating years, our team hosted two events within three months, and this was that year. When I returned home, I'd have a two week period of working at the office to tie up loose ends from this event, then I'd be back on the road for the second event, where I'd stay for another eighteen days. It was a crushing schedule, but I thrived on pressure at that state of my career, so I looked forward to it.

As I entered my second week on the road, I was expecting a trunk full of credentials for our merchandisers and pricing documents for all of the merchandise. It was to have been sent by my co-worker from the office back home, but it hadn't arrived. When I called her at the office to find out where it was, I was told it had shipped. However, when I spoke to my friend Faith, whose cubicle was right next to my co-worker's, she said the trunk was sitting on the floor. My heart sank as I realized what was happening. My co-worker (the one with the mother-in-law flying in) wanted to hand out the credentials to the executives herself, and expected them to wait for her arrival a week after the practice rounds started. Apparently that had worked in the past, but I'd just learned that some of the high-level executives had arrived early and wanted to watch practice rounds, but they couldn't since their credentials were in that trunk. My experience with my new boss and how she was manipulated by my co-workers had already shown me that going to her for help wasn't a good idea, so I got creative.

I visited other departments within our organization asking how I could obtain alternate credentials for these folks. They were willing to trade credentials for clothing samples from my department. Our vendors constantly provided us with event-specific outerwear, sunglasses, shoes, and other various golf items, which were kept in our office trailer. Our sample collection was highly coveted and accessible only by our team, which included me. I gathered up some jackets and shirts and returned to barter. I was able to obtain exactly what I needed to fulfill the requests I'd been given earlier, in exchange for just a few samples. Mission accomplished.

William and I spoke every night when I returned to my room, which was usually around nine. He became very concerned after I described what had been happening. Although I was thriving in my job duties, the stress I was under was causing me some physical issues. I had been suffering acid reflux so badly that I was vomiting acid. I had to have my doctor call in a prescription of Prilosec for me because it wasn't yet available over the counter, and at that time, I didn't realize how much diet played a part in my symptoms. So, between the prescription and some over-the-counter products, I was able to keep the raging symptoms somewhat under control. I was also struggling mentally with the fact that I had been betrayed by my co-workers, when all I was trying to do was my job. My presence at this event was in no way compromising either of my teammates' positions and mostly allowed our boss to have some much needed help, so I was at a loss to comprehend why they were fighting me so much. Instead of them being grateful that our boss had someone else she could rely on for menial tasks, they were jealous. Because I am not a jealous person, it was difficult for me to understand why they were working against me. All I was trying to do was be a part of the team and contribute whatever I could to help our cause, so I was confused by the sabotage.

After I returned home from the trip, William voiced his concern because he knew I was scheduled to take the second trip soon. I was mentally broken from defending myself against my coworkers, and knowing my family history, he understood why it had affected me so much. I fell in love with him all over again when he told me if I needed to quit, I should do it. He said no job was worth sacrificing my health.

After I got home, I had a couple of days off before I had to return to the office. As soon as I got in, I believe I knew things were about to change, but

I didn't want to admit it. I began to work on my expense report and event summary paperwork. When my boss arrived, I asked her if I could talk to her for a few minutes. I explained what had happened the road and how I was constantly fighting to get anything accomplished. I was hoping she'd talk to my coworkers in my defense, but that didn't happen. She told me that we would have to work it out amongst ourselves, and that she wasn't getting involved. I felt very betrayed. The emotions I experienced took me back to my childhood, when my parents would leave me to fend for myself against Tina. I left her office and headed to Human Resources. I'd spoken to them earlier about the issues with one of my co-workers, and they just said I should just give it time. They said that just to get rid of me because they were afraid of my co-worker and my co-worker knew that, which is why she acted so horribly. They acted surprised that our issues hadn't worked themselves out during the trip. As I left their office defeated, my body was vibrating. My intuition was screaming at me to end this. I told her I was going to take care of the issue on my own. I'd be turning in my letter of resignation. I turned and walked out. As I made my way back to my desk, I constructed the letter of resignation in my head. I would thank my boss for the opportunity to stay within the organization, but had realized on that last trip that I was not going to be allowed to perform the duties for which I'd been hired. I would explain the sabotage that I was subjected to by my co-workers was unacceptable, and I did not deserve to be treated that way. Satisfied with the imagined content of the letter, I'd get it written, finish my paperwork from the trip then turn it in.

Just as I printed and signed my letter, my two co-workers showed up at my desk, as if they'd planned the attack on me. They were asking me questions about point-of-sale issues that I had no knowledge of, as if they were trying to accuse me of neglecting my duties. I asked them which of the two of them taught me to handle the items they were speaking of, and they had no answer. I told them I'd dealt with enough of their abuse and that they could figure it out on their own because I was quitting. Their actions at that moment cemented my decision to walk out.

I had planned to complete my paperwork before I left because I wasn't trying to dump my work on anyone, but their power game drove me to do it sooner than later. Once the words came out of my mouth, it set a whole new set of events in motion. I walked into my boss' office and found her on the phone, I assumed with HR. I gave her my letter as she was finishing up with the call. I explained that I should not have to fight just to do my job, and that I refused to be treated so poorly with no support from her or HR.

I could tell by the look on her face that she was not happy, but did her best to stay neutral. I walked back to my desk to finish my paperwork when the lady from HR appeared and said I'd have to leave the building immediately. I told her I was just trying to finish my report from the trip, but she didn't care, so I didn't either. I stopped working on my paperwork, packed the few personal items I had on my desk, and walked out. I really hated leaving work undone, but I had no choice. Apparently, they thought I'd try to sabotage their computer system or something, which really hurt because I never did anything but work my ass off for that organization, and had I given two weeks' notice, that wouldn't have happened. That indicated to me that something more serious was going on behind the scenes.

Leaving that situation was forced on me because there were better things ahead for me. I know that now. I was only just beginning to understand that sometimes things just aren't meant to be, so the Universe will force you to change your path, whether you like it or not. Whatever the reason, I felt the tremendous weight I had been carrying since I'd been placed in this controversial environment, lift off as soon as I left the building.

The experience of going through the buyout and being placed somewhere I wasn't wanted was unpleasant, but it taught me a lot. I was proud of the work I had done. The experience of going from that team of eleven, that complimented and appreciated each other, to a team of four led by a self-centered and conniving witch, had been a huge shock to me. Just when I began to feel like I fit in, the rug was pulled out from under me. That shake up was one of the reasons Faith and I became such close friends. Faith was the one who told me the missing trunk wasn't actually missing when I was on site. We met shortly after I started working with my original team. We bonded immediately because of our similar personalities and personal struggles. We were both struggling financially, and worked together to better our situations. She had my back when I was on the road, and alerted me to the scandal going on in our department. She's that friend that would create an alibi and help you bury the body.

THE BITCH IS BACK

I had been living in Florida for about three years when I learned my sister Tina was moving down. She had employed a job recruiter and, through them had secured a job with a famous golfer in nearby Jupiter. I had no idea why she wanted to move near me, and I was horrified at the thought. I just knew my parents would guilt me into helping her out, and that she would lean on me for everything. This was right before William moved down, so I was essentially single.

Just as I'd expected, she latched onto me expecting me to show her the way. I avoided her as much as possible, but she and my parents were masters of manipulating me into helping her out no matter what. I really didn't want to be around her because I simply didn't like her, but I wanted to respect my parents' wishes.

This was the late nineties, which was around the time we could afford dial-up Internet and home computers. I had acquired a personal computer when I closed down my business, so I learned about chat rooms. I enjoyed talking to people from other places and learning about them. I'd sit down at my computer after dinner with a glass of wine and find a chat room with an interesting conversation taking place. One night, I found a chat room talking about strange song lyrics, so I joined in. Before we knew it, we were singing through typing the strange lyrics together. I think that's where "LOL" was created. We had so much fun, I'll never forget that group.

Tina used the Internet to sign up for online dating sites. She was constantly looking for a mate, so she signed up for both Match.com and e-Harmony, although she preferred Match.com because she didn't want to spend the amount of time required to fill out a proper profile for e-Harmony. She felt her time was much too valuable to be wasted on details like that.

Despite Tina's resistance to dedicate a sufficient amount of time to create her profile, Tina eventually met a man that she liked. He was just her style…shallow, pretentious, and excessively tall. Tina stood five feet, eleven and a three quarters inches tall, and was sure to make sure everyone knew that. She would never think of dating anyone that wasn't at least a few inches taller than she was…she had an image to uphold, after all. Not surprisingly, I found him to be just as obnoxious as she was. The more I got to know him, the more I didn't like him…but they were perfect for each other.

Thankfully, as Tina's relationship with Mr. Wonderful grew, she drifted in and out of my life. The couple bought a huge house they couldn't afford, but it fit their need to keep up appearances. My parents, who had previously either stayed with me or in a hotel for their winter stays, jumped on the opportunity to spend the winter with their favorite daughter in her big new house. They got a huge wake-up call as to where they stood with their little princess and her new beau when he accused them of stealing from him, and Tina did little to defend them. Mr. Wonderful owned a vending business and had buckets of quarters in his office. My parents felt the need to earn their keep, so my mom would clean inside and my dad would work outside. Because my mom was vacuuming all of the rooms upstairs, Mr. Wonderful assumed she was stealing quarters from his buckets. My parents may have been many things, but they would never they steal from anyone. I was appalled at hearing this accusation. Of course, their favorite daughter did nothing to defend her doting parents against these irrational accusations. It made me sick, but they stayed right there with her.

For Valentine's Day that year, they got engaged. He came from a large Italian family from New York, and Tina was in all her glory trying to impress them. Because his family was naturally very close, Tina created this illusion that our family was as well. Unfortunately because of that, she asked me to be the maid of honor for her wedding. But, the real reason she asked me was because she had no other friends that would work hard on her behalf. I really didn't want to do it because I had enough going on in my life, but she begged…and my mom begged…and my dad guilted me into it, so I felt I had no choice.

SOMETHING NEW

After I left my job, William encouraged me to stay home and be a housewife. He said he made enough to support us, so I should take some time off and enjoy myself. I tried. I cooked, did crafts, and spent time with my dog on long walks, and rode my bike, but I soon realized that being a housewife during that stage of my life just wasn't for me.

Right before I contacted my former employment agency, I got an out of the blue call from Dee, the former secretary from my failed toy business. She was working at a mortgage bank that was looking for an admin, and thought of me. I told her I'd love to interview for the position. When I did, I was offered the position before I left the building…and just like that, I had a new job. I knew nothing about the mortgage industry, but for what I would be doing, I would learn enough by just doing my job.

My new boss, although very nice, was very indecisive. She suffered from paralysis by analysis much of the time, which made us a great pair. All she had to do was tell me what she was trying to accomplish, and then I would present her with a solution. This job, although menial, allowed me to be creative while solving problems, which was greatly satisfying and without having the kinds of pressure I'd had in the past from owning my own business or while at my last job.

One of the conditions of my accepting the position was that I needed time off shortly after my start date. I requested a week for our honeymoon.

William and I were actually getting married right before his birthday in mid-October, and just like in my first marriage, I solicited the proposal. I, once again, got caught up in the moment and suggested it. And yes, there was alcohol consumption involved. Poor William, who was also day drinking with me, went along with it. I believe we were both on the same page; we'd both been through failed relationships, but because of our history together, we felt like getting married so quickly after our relationship began would be okay. This is how it happened...

William had re-entered my life just before New Year's Day, and we'd become a committed couple pretty quickly. It was now August, and we'd travelled to Ohio for William's brother's wedding. William's father and brother still lived two houses down from my family (where we stayed), so everyone was in close proximity for the pre-wedding gatherings. We had been day drinking at William's father's house with the rest of the wedding party the day before the ceremony. I got really caught up in the emotions of the whole wedding experience, which caused me to whisper in William's ear that we should pretend we had eloped over the summer. He looked at me with confusion, but after he saw how desperately I needed to show my family that I was in a good place, he went along with it. I wanted to convince my parents so badly that I wasn't the screw up they'd thought I was, that I was willing to drag William into this crazy stunt. We were both the black sheep of our families, and even though we were both highly intelligent and resourceful, we would never be able to shed their labels of us. I thought showing our families we were starting a life together would change their opinions of us.

So, we told everyone we'd gotten married on a whim at the courthouse earlier in the summer. We told them we planned to have an official wedding in October for anyone that wanted to attend, so as soon as we got home from Ohio, we began to make plans. I know everything happens for a reason, but I also know that sometimes we try to create our own destiny out of desperation or loneliness. Looking back, it really wasn't the best way to approach marrying someone, especially someone as special as William, but because I was desperately seeking solutions to whatever problems I thought I needed to fix, we rushed into it.

A STORMY START

The events of the night before our wedding still remain vivid in my memory. At our home in North Palm Beach, there was a motorhome parked in the front yard to house out-of-town guests. I was fortunate to have made some amazing friends in Florida. Dee and her boyfriend were so kind, they allowed me to borrow their motorhome so I could house extra friends from Ohio for my wedding. That was not an easy feat, and it took a lot of work to bring it to fruition. Other friends helped me with errands, assembling bouquets, party favors and throwing parties. My new friends helped me more than I appreciated at the time, but some realizations just don't reveal themselves to you right away. This was definitely one of those situations.

Hurricane Irene decided to make landfall near our home the night before our wedding. With Hurricane Irene's arrival came a lot of damage, not only to our property, but also to our plans. The wedding was to be aboard a sixty-one foot sport fishing boat captained by my good friend, Captain Ray. We were to go out of Palm Beach Inlet just past the reef, where we'd be married by Ray. We would then offer our thanks to Mother Ocean with a gift of seashell and flower leis we'd made. We would "take the plunge" by jumping off the tuna tower of the boat holding hands. Finally, we'd travel back to the dock then meet everyone at the Waterway Cafe to enjoy the sounds of our favorite band, *Up Next*. Dinner was being catered by Waterway and would be set up as a buffet in the bar/dance floor area.

Waterway was our favorite place to listen to live music and hang out, so it was a fitting location for our reception. The celebration would wrap up with us getting all of our guests back to their respective accommodations.

We planned to leave for Jacksonville the following morning, where we would watch our beloved Cleveland Browns take on the Jacksonville Jaguars. One of our wedding gifts had been a pair of club seats for that game. We were both very excited because the Browns had just returned to the NFL after the former team had been relocated to Baltimore. We couldn't wait to see them live again…it had been a long time. Jacksonville was as close as to our home that the team would play, so we planned to spend a few days in Jacksonville and St. Augustine then jet off to the Bahamas to enjoy a timeshare week that my friend Deidre had given us as a wedding gift.

When we selected October for our wedding, we never thought we'd have to deal with a hurricane. That year, the named storms had only reached the letter H, so it hadn't been a busy season. When Hurricane Irene showed up the night before our big event, it was most unexpected. The storm seemed to come out of nowhere and caused just enough havoc to put us in a tailspin. I had worked hard planning our elaborate but small wedding, and then having everything fall apart the morning of the wedding horrified me. Our power was out. A tree had fallen on the roof of our car, smashing the windows out and allowing the rain to pour in. A tornado struck the Waterway Cafe and separated the floating tiki bar from the restaurant, in the process tearing out their water supply lines. The restaurant was unable to open for business until the water lines could be repaired, which wouldn't be for at least a few days. Our giant Jell-o shot wedding cake liquified without refrigeration due to the power outage. Captain Ray called early the next morning to tell me that Sailfish Marina, where the boat was docked, had sustained enough damage to close the facility, which meant we couldn't access the docks or his boat.

That was the bad news. The good news was that as the day progressed, we fortunately were spared the total loss of our wedding by Divine intervention that allowed everything to fall into place for us. The restaurant had already prepared our wedding food and had kept it cold with their generators. They were kind enough to donate all of the food to us, and had arranged for the wedding to be held across the river at Panama

Hattie's. Dee and her boyfriend, also a boat captain, donated the use of their boat for the ceremony, and as captains also, agreed to officiate the ceremony. Unfortunately, their boat wasn't able to leave the dock, but it was conveniently located across the street from the Waterway Cafe in Soverel Harbor Marina.

We weren't able to attend the Browns game due to the car being damaged and also having to deal with storm clean up. Fortunately, our friends' generous gift of the motor home in our front yard was protected and suffered no damage, but ironically our car that was crushed was parked right in front of it.

Our wedding turned out to be an unforgettable affair. After we got married, we "took the plunge" from the bow of motor vessel *Day's End* among the storm debris. We then migrated to Panama Hattie's where Waterway Cafe had arranged our substitute venue. There was an amazing reggae band playing, and they stepped into the role of a wedding band flawlessly. Waterway had made so much food, we had plenty to share with everyone in the bar. Everyone had an amazing evening.

After things settled down, I wrote a lengthy letter (complete with photos of the wedding and car damage) to the Jacksonville Jaguars, explaining what had happened. I thought it wouldn't hurt to ask if they might send us some bleacher seats for the following year. I was excited when I received a Federal Express envelope from them just days later, that included a nice letter sympathizing with our plight, as well as a pair of club-level seats for the following year's Browns/Jaguars matchup in Jacksonville. We were overwhelmed by their generosity, and I will always have a soft spot in my heart for that team.

Although our wedding plans were turned completely upside down, what occurred as a result of the hurricane worked out for the best. It taught us to just roll with the punches, which was easy with a lot of help from our friends.

MOVING SOUTH

William and I lived at my home in North Palm Beach for the first year of our marriage. Shortly after we got married, he applied for a job at BellSouth, our telephone company. Because of the experience he gained working with JC at his electric pole installation company, he passed the entrance test without an issue. William is also intelligent, articulate and has a very strong work ethic, which insured him the job. He attended his training to climb utility poles, then was assigned to work out of the Delray Beach yard, which was about twenty-three miles south of us. He loved his job, but the combination of working an outdoor job in Florida's grueling heat, and also having to deal with home maintenance took its toll on him. He convinced me that we should sell the house and move south, into an apartment that was closer to his job and required no maintenance. I agreed because home maintenance is an ongoing project, and I was getting a bit overwhelmed with it too. We made a deal with Twila, a co-worker and friend, to let her assume our mortgage until she could get one on her own, which wouldn't be for another year. Twila had filed bankruptcy and wouldn't be able to qualify for a mortgage until it cleared. This was a great opportunity for us because we'd make a nice profit when she got her own mortgage, and we didn't have to go through a home inspection, pay real estate commissions or negotiate anything. It allowed us to get out, and her to get in, easily.

At about the same time we were moving out of our house, the mortgage bank where I had been working was undergoing a lot of changes. There were a lot of personnel shifts and restructuring in the department. I saw the writing on the wall, and chose to leave. It wasn't worth dealing with the backstabbing that was going on amongst those that used to be trusted coworkers.

William and I moved into a brand new rental apartment at Via Lugano apartments in Boynton Beach. We'd made a lot of new friends between William's job and joining both the VFW and American Legion veterans' organizations, and were now free of the responsibilities of owning a home. We enjoyed the first six months there until our new neighbors moved in.

Our new neighbors were four young men sharing a two bedroom apartment. They lived like they were in a college dorm. They were loud, inconsiderate and made my life a living Hell. They were so loud, I couldn't sleep, so I decided to visit the leasing manager to see if there was anything they could do to help us. Because it was a new complex that was still under construction, they had a waiting list for units, so they let us out of our lease. We then moved into William's mother's winter home in Delray Beach. It is an adorable little cottage, and because she and her husband were living and working from home in Ohio, it worked out well. We'd stay there until we could find a home to purchase.

A few months later, we bought half of a duplex in western Delray Beach and started remodeling it. It was in rough shape because the elderly couple that had lived there were very sick and couldn't maintain it. We were fortunate because we had the luxury of working it while not having to live there, which allowed us to take our time and do everything properly. It was an absolute mess, but it would be great when it was finished. It gave us the privacy of a house with a garage, but also the convenience of not having yard work, and we loved it.

Because the remodel was going to cost a good amount of money, I decided to look for a new job close to our new home. It didn't take me long to find one in Boca Raton, just south of where we now lived. The company imported curio and relic firearms from all over the world. The vice president needed a new assistant, and they felt that I fit the bill. The company had a strange dynamic, but the generous pay helped me overlook it. The strange dynamic was that it was run by four siblings, three brothers and a sister, whose parents had started the company. When they retired, the parents left it to their children, but only four of their five children chose to work there. They were all nice individually, but when you put them in a room together, it was sibling rivalry at its best, and I knew why the fifth sibling elected to work elsewhere. My desk was in a large cubicle shared with the file clerk. We were surrounded on three sides by walls full of files. The two of us got along great, and she'd been there for many years so she taught me the ropes. My position was pretty simple. My boss would show up, I'd present him with any files that had received return correspondence, and he'd reply. His job was to secure new purchases of weapons from various sources all over the world. We corresponded with numerous countries and people looking for old caches of war weapons or other military surplus. I had a lot of down time at this job, because from the time my boss arrived and through lunch, I would just be waiting for him to read through the new correspondence and formulate a reply. Once he did, he'd sit down next to my desk and dictate replies to various pieces of correspondence. I'd prepare the correspondence and present it to him for his approval, then send it. My boss worked from 10:00 a.m. to 6:00 p.m., so those were my hours as well. I used to play on the Internet in my down time there. I say all of that to say this…there was a time where my sister was trying to get back into my good graces. Once she knew I was at a job where I had time on the Internet, she began to correspond with me via instant messaging. We'd been messaging for awhile because it allowed us to keep in touch between our tasks discreetly and much more easily than risking being overheard on a phone call. She began messaging me one day and telling me about a fight with her husband. I listened to her plight and offered her some advice to stop fighting with him and listen to him. She was always looking for drama, and I was constantly trying to diffuse it.

William and I had also been trying to work through some things. This was just after the plane crashes of 9/11 into the World Trade Center, Pentagon, and a Pennsylvania field. William had been drinking more and more since we'd moved into our new home. We even went to a marriage counselor to see if we could try to figure out what was happening. I really felt like he was still suffering from the loss of his young fiancé, and couldn't move forward. He seemed to keep trying to push forward, but until he dealt with the loss and went through the grieving process properly, he'd continue to struggle. I tried so hard to help him, but I just couldn't get through. He seemed to be haunted by a ghost that he was unable to let go of. It was almost as if he felt that hanging onto his grief was mandatory.

Because I was harboring my own struggles with William, I related to Tina's pain as she described her situation to me. She really seemed to be listening to my advice so I used the opportunity to address some things between us. I think the mutual troubles we were going through made me feel like I needed my sister, and I hoped this could be an opportunity to develop a better relationship with her. I happened to be alone in the office at the time, so I took advantage of the privacy and poured my heart out to her. I told specifically what she had done to hurt me over the years, and that I didn't understand why she was so abusive to me. I told her I didn't understand how she expected me to stay around her after being treated that way. I named a lot of situations in the recent past that had negatively affected me hoping to get through to her. I really felt in my heart she would listen. She seemed to, so I continued laying my heart on the line to her. She claimed she didn't remember a lot of the things I was referring to, but that she felt badly for acting that way. I really thought it was a positive interaction between us, and hoped it would heal our broken relationship. I thought it would be nice if we could have each other to lean on.

DEATH SENTENCE

Tina later disclosed to me that her husband had been diagnosed with anal cancer. After the initial shock, I felt it was fitting that an asshole would be suffering from cancer of the body part that he was. There were many negative interactions between the two of us over the previous years that brought me to this conclusion, but the worst thing he ever did to me took place on our family cruise in 2004. This was the only vacation my entire family would have together during our adult lives. It was a cruise going out of Port of Miami to Puerto Rico, St. Thomas, and St. Martin. My parents and brother had never been on a cruise, so it was a big deal. It was also special because my brother Randy was able to get an entire week off of work, which was rare, so we were excited to have everyone together.

My mom and I were in our room having a conversation, when Tina's husband barged in and started to yell about how I ruined his vacation. My travel agent was trying to get us a great rate, so she booked us as quickly as she could. Because she didn't know who was who, she put all of the men in one room and all of the women in the other. This caused a bit of an issue with his room key not opening his door, then it pissed him off more because his room charges were mixed up and he didn't know how to fix it. He wanted me to go to the front desk and straighten it out because he refused to stand in line. I explained that I wouldn't be able to help him because they would need his identification and credit card to make the

178

change. Once he absorbed that bit of information, he then stood over me and pointed his finger in my face while yelling that he was better than me. He told me I was worthless and useless, and that he was better than I would ever be. He did all of this right in front of my mom. He wasn't man enough to respect my mom and speak to me privately. I didn't care what he thought or said about me, but to say something like that in the presence of my mom was lower than low. That little stunt cemented his status as an asshole.

Tina eventually began the long and arduous journey of trying to help her husband overcome his cancer. They tried all of the things the doctors suggested, but due to his negative mindset and lack of true desire to make a big change in his life, he eventually succumbed. It took a little over a year for the cancer to spread throughout his organs. Toward the end, my parents came back to help Tina with him because he insisted that he wanted to remain at home. But, once the cancer compromised the liver's ability to filter toxins out of his system, he got mean and physically violent with my mom and Tina. He tried to push them both into a wall, which ended his stay at home. The Angels of Hospice accompanied him to his final destination without any more pain or suffering.

As expected, it really took a toll on Tina, and left her strapped with debt and many choices to make. She made some bad decisions that she paid for over the next few years. She was too worried about money to do the right thing. She learned the hard way that we reap what we sow.

ANOTHER ENDING BEGINS

*W*illiam and I were really struggling in our marriage. He wanted to be away from me as much as I from him. We had developed some sort of animosity toward each other, from what I now deem as lack of communication. He was suffering from his grief, and I was suffering from missing my husband. When he got home from work every night, he'd start drinking beer right away. A six pack a night became a twelve pack a night over the next few months. Our marriage counselor diagnosed his drinking as a symptom of covering something up, but we couldn't get him to admit what it was, so our downward spiral continued.

My parents had been down to help Tina with her husband, and when he passed they stayed until after the funeral. Of course, Tina was so wrapped up in appearances, that she spent way too much money on the funeral, just to impress his family. It was quite a circus. It proved to me that the old Tina was still in there, even after suffering such a devastating loss.

After the dust settled and the asshole was in the ground, my parents were getting ready to head home to Ohio. Our American Legion was hosting a weekend bus trip going from our Post in Delray Beach to Key West. We would stop at various American Legion Posts along the way, spend two nights in Key West, and then travel back home on Sunday. We also revisited the Posts we'd stopped at on the way down, on our way home. William elected not to go, so I took my mom.

The bus trip was a blast. We packed sandwiches and cocktails for the ride and because my mom didn't drink and I didn't need to drink that early, we were deemed the bus bartenders.

We stopped at American Legion Posts in Homestead, Key Largo, Marathon, and Key West. At each stop we were greeted by the full regalia of officers and regulars. We made a lot of new friends and caught up with some old friends. But when we got to Marathon, we were greeted by all of the officers and a Post full of people who welcomed us with open arms. It was at that Post where I made two new friends who would end up changing the course of my life.

After a fun-filled two hour pit stop, we left Marathon and proceeded to Key West for our last stop. We had a great time with those members, then headed to our motel. We spent our two days in Key West, which allowed my mom to see a place she'd never been. My friends Ann and Bo, who I'd met years earlier with Deidre, met us at the motel on their Harleys. We hopped on and proceeded to see Key West in a way we never could have imagined. Seeing my mom on the back of Bo's Harley was something I never thought I'd see, and it was awesome! We both had a great time with Ann and Bo. I got to see my mom as a friend for the first time in my life.

My mom had known something was up with William and me when he declined a drinking trip. She loved William like a son, but she also knew his drinking was out of control. She'd known him since he was fourteen, and had seen him go through a few tailspins over the years. She never came out and said it, but I could see her silent approval as I carried on a conversation with a new male friend I'd made back in Marathon. He and I had a great conversation, and I laughed more than I had in a very long time. It was refreshing. There may have been just a little bit of flirting mixed in with the conversation, but I didn't care.

We enjoyed two great nights in Key West. Our itinerary had us visiting the same posts we'd visited on the way down, so we headed to the Key West Post shortly after check out. We hung out there for a bit, then headed back to Marathon. I was secretly hoping for another opportunity to talk with my new friend. Much to my delight, he was there. Apparently, the members we'd met on the way down had enjoyed our visit so much they decided to hold a luncheon in our honor. It was put on by the SALs, or the Sons of the American Legion. Back then, they were a branch of American Legion membership that was reserved for non-military men who were relatives of veterans, or a men's auxiliary. In Marathon, the SALs were very active and had a large membership. Their luncheon was much appreciated, and a testament to their dedication to their Post.

We spent a few hours there and made more new friends. We also saw the same bartender as on our original visit. I learned her name was Marla. She was around the same age as me, and I welcomed the opportunity to spend a little time with her. She warned me that my new friend was married and liked to flirt. I didn't mind, I just enjoyed our conversation.

Marla told me she was looking for a roommate so she could leave her boyfriend. She didn't want to break up with him until she could secure a new place to live. At that time, I had no intention of moving there, so I wondered why it came up in our conversation. I chalked it up to her needing someone close in age to talk to, but later figured out that everything happens for a reason.

When we returned from our trip, my parents headed home to Ohio and I returned to working Sundays at the VFW for breakfast shifts and bartending in the afternoons at the American Legion. I still worked full time during the week at the arms dealer.

William had always enjoyed spending Sundays at the VFW for breakfast while I waitressed, and then continuing on to the American Legion for lunch while I bartended. He would spend the day with our friends and watch the NASCAR race or whatever other sports event was on. Because the breakfasts served at the VFW were rather large, he'd eat there in the morning, and then we'd eat together on the way home. The Legion bar closed at 6:00 p.m. on Sundays, and we'd usually grab a bite to eat on the way home, but on one particular afternoon, he decided to head home around 3:00 p.m. He'd been pretty drunk when he left, so I thought he'd just go home and pass out. I never thought he'd continue drink once he got home.

Our friend Dave, who was a Vietnam veteran, ran the kitchen at the VFW. After he finished his prep work for the day and cleaned up, he'd usually make his way over to the Legion for a drink or two before we closed. Since William was gone when Dave arrived, he asked me if I'd like to grab some dinner with him after I closed. Considering William was probably already asleep, I agreed.

Dave and I grabbed some Mexican food, spent our dinner bitching about the characters in the VFW and Legion, and parted ways. I brought a meal home for William just in case he was awake. If he wasn't, Mexican made great leftovers.

As I pulled into the driveway and started up the front walk, I realized William was sitting in the front screen porch, almost like an angry parent waiting for their teenager who's late for curfew. I held up the bag and told him Dave and I grabbed some Mexican and that I brought him dinner. He didn't say anything, and just sat there smoking a cigarette in the dark of our porch. As I opened the screen door, he, in his very drunken state, said, "Are you sleeping with Dave now?" The thought of that made me laugh because I thought he was joking. Dave was almost thirty years older me, and he dated one of my good friends. The thought of it was insane. We were just friends that grabbed a bite to eat together.

William was so drunk that he was paranoid. I told him Dave and I just had dinner, and walked past him into the house. After I put the food in the refrigerator and walked back toward the hallway, William had this really distant look in his eyes as he got in my face, wrapped his fingers around my throat, and pushed me against the wall. Then, he gritted his teeth and put his face really close to mine and spat out his next words, "He can have you." It was awful. Seeing the man I loved so dearly in such a state was heartbreaking, but being handled like this by William was even worse. I ran into the guest bedroom and locked the door. I wasn't going to let William's anger lead him to doing anything more physical to me than he'd already done, and although I never thought it would be possible, I wasn't going to be on the bad side of a beating again.

EVERYTHING HAPPENS
FOR A REASON

One night turned into one month of living in the guest bedroom. And when I tell you I was living in the guest bedroom, I mean I was living my entire life, with the exception of cooking dinner and bathroom time, in the guest bedroom. William had begun stopping for drinks after work every night. Since I worked until 6:00 p.m., by the time I'd get home he'd either be passed out on the couch or still at the bar. The few times we did cross paths, he was very cold to me. He wouldn't look me in the eye, and no matter what I said to try to convince him I had not been unfaithful, it didn't work. He truly believed I had slept with Dave.

William's new pattern of behavior meant I had time to move all of my belongings out of the master bedroom and into the guest room without him being there. I knew we'd reached the point of no return, and that room contained too many memories of us. Fortunately, the guest room housed our home office and computer, so I had easy access to the Internet. Since I'd already been through this scenario once in my life, I knew what came next…I had to get out.

There had been some strange things happening at my job as well. The secretary of my boss' brother had been out of town for a week, so I was handling her correspondence as well as my own. On the day she returned, I welcomed her back and set the pile of her boss' files on her desk. I know how chaotic it is returning from vacation, so I didn't want to keep her after I said hello, so I just walked out.

I returned to my desk and began shuffling through my files. I didn't realize that what I had done really pissed her off, but for some reason it did. She began to huff around the office, and I could hear her venting to our co-workers, but I couldn't decipher what she was saying, and I really didn't care. I tried to avoid office gossip. The next thing I knew, she stuck her head into my cubicle just enough to say, "You'd better watch your back," then she slapped my cubicle wall twice to emphasize her point, and left. I had no idea why I needed to watch my back, but I started to get flashbacks of my old job in merchandising and the bullies who worked there. I decided right then and there that I wasn't going to be treated that way again, and it was time to leave.

My boss hadn't arrived yet, so I asked to see the president of the company. He was a very nice older man that had stayed on at the request of my boss' parents after they retired. I suspect it was to keep the peace among the siblings. He welcomed me into his office, and though I wasn't sure what I was going to say, I walked in and sat down. Before I knew it, a story about William getting a transfer to Pensacola in the next thirty days flowed flawlessly out of my mouth. I then told him I was sorry to leave, but I wanted to give them as much notice as possible. I couldn't believe that I was quitting a job before I had another one, but my intuition made me walk in there and tell that story. It was as if I wasn't even speaking, like the words were forming without me knowing what was going to be said.

Since I had never gotten very close to anyone at work, it was a believable story. No one knew what I was going through, and it was just easier to make up a story like that and blame my departure on William's job. I knew in my heart that I'd find somewhere to go within a month because that's what always happened for me, and I felt better knowing I'd given notice so they could work on replacing me.

EVERYTHING DID HAPPEN
FOR A REASON

*A*fter the night of being pinned against the wall by the throat, and seeing what it was doing to William, I stopped drinking. I needed an exit strategy, and had to save my money. Besides, William had begun to frequent our former hangouts without me, and I knew what that meant. The rumor mill was running at full capacity, and he was the one providing the fuel. During all of that time, there was just one person, my friend Linda, who cared to hear my side of the story. She was the only one that ever reached out.

As I pondered where to go next, I remembered Marla, the bartender at the Legion Post in Marathon, telling me about wanting to leave her boyfriend and find a roommate. I really liked the vibe there, so I searched the Internet for information on living in Marathon. I learned the *Key Noter* was the main newspaper in town and that it had an online edition, so I began to regularly check the classifieds for a job. I didn't have Marla's telephone number, so I called the Legion, aka: the Post, and asked to speak to her. Fortunately, she was there and we had a nice conversation. We exchanged numbers, and I told her I'd keep her posted on my job search. She said she'd start looking at what was available so we'd have a sense of rent costs if I got a job and could get down there. Our conversation gave me a positive feeling about things working out for me in Marathon.

A couple of weeks later, I noticed an ad for an administrative assistant/

bookkeeper for a dive instructor training facility and dive shop. I wasn't an official bookkeeper, but I had enough accounting experience to warrant a closer look. I called the number and asked to speak to Bob, whose name was in the ad. Bob answered shortly after, and I learned he was anxious to find a replacement for his former admin, who'd left suddenly and without warning. We had a long and positive conversation, and he asked how soon I could come in for an in-person interview. We scheduled it for the end of the week so I could make proper arrangements with my job at the arms dealer. I also notified my bartender friend from the Legion, who advised me she'd found a few potential places that we could afford. I called Ann and Bo in Big Pine Key and asked if I could stay with them for the weekend, since I'd be driving down for a job interview. They were thrilled to offer me a place as long as I needed! Things were finally starting to fall into place, and just in time because there was this bird that was living in the top of the palm tree right outside my bedroom window and he was loud. Every morning before I needed to be awake, I was awakened by his loud calls. It was almost as if he were trying to drive me out, so I wanted to do everything in my power to help him.

My appointment was for 9:00 a.m., so I left around 5:00 a.m. to ensure I'd get there on time. I knew Miami traffic would be a bear in the morning, and wanted to sneak through there before rush hour hit.

My plan worked, and I arrived around 8:00. I had time to grab some coffee and breakfast at the Stuffed Pig before my meeting. The Stuffed Pig is a cute little pink building right on the corner of US 1 and 35th St. Gulf (the streets in Marathon are all referred to based on which side of US 1 they're on, Ocean or Gulf). They serve some great dishes and seemed to be a popular spot for both locals and tourists. It gave me a chance to relax after the long drive and get ready for my interview.

The fact that I was interviewing for a job at a dive shop and dive instructor training center left me unsure as to what to wear. As I entered the dive shop in my casual suit, I immediately noticed the error in my judgement. The employees were wearing dive shop tee shirts, shorts and flip flops. The owner, with whom I was interviewing, had on a Hawaiian shirt and khakis, much different from the skirt and jacket with low-heeled pumps I was sporting. He smiled when he noticed how uncomfortable I was, but I could tell he appreciated my efforts. He invited me to his small office in the back of the shop and offered me a seat. I noticed another desk in his office, and he explained that would be where the admin would sit. Due to limited space and the duties of the position, it was the best option. He then proceeded to explain what he was looking for, and asked me to describe why I was trying to relocate, and then he asked about my previous experience. He shared the history of the facility, and how he'd acquired it from the founder. Hall's had an amazing history and was very well respected in the diving industry. Not only was it a working dive shop, but they offered dive instructor training and several additional diving modalities. It was an accredited vocational education provider. It was like no place I'd ever seen before. After hearing how Bob had started with nothing and created the highly-respected training center it was now, I just knew I wanted to be a part of it. I listened with interest as Bob shared the story of Hall's Diving Center that began almost thirty years prior and two locations ago. He shared with me some of the accomplishments of his facility, such as placing graduates with NASA to work in the weightless environment necessary for astronaut training, and with cruise lines and live aboard dive boats, as well as placing rescue and recovery divers around the US and the Caribbean. Being a diver myself, it was an interesting prospect to earn a living diving, but due to my upbringing and growing up in Ohio, it never occurred to me as an option.

After about an hour, I was offered the job. The pay was generous, so I was excited to accept. Bob asked if I could start immediately, as in right then! Since I didn't have anything else on my calendar, I told him I'd be happy to stay for the rest of the day.

At the conclusion of my first day of work, I headed to the Legion for a drink. I called William to tell him I'd found a job and had already worked my first day. Since it was after 5:00 p.m., he was already into his first six pack. He got silent for a second, then came back with, "If you don't come home right now, I'm going to kill your cat." I wasn't sure if he actually would or not at that point, so I paid my bill and hastily exited the Post. I notified Ann and Bo that I would be back on Sunday night for work Monday morning, and they told me to do what I needed to do. I began the four-hour drive home to save Thomas from potential tragedy.

When I arrived home, William was well into a twelve pack. He was belligerent and had broken my prized paper nautilus shell, as well as the glass on one of my paintings after he ripped it off the wall. I retrieved Thomas and we slept together locked in the guest room.

I'd notified Marla that I was ready to commit to a lease with her, and she was able to get the keys for our new home over the weekend. Back then, things in Marathon were really simple and informal. The real estate agent gave her the keys and told her to just have me stop by the office when I got there to sign the papers and pay my portion of the fees. Marla had gathered a few of the ladies from the Post and cleaned the place up after the exterminator had bombed it for palmetto bugs. When I arrived on Sunday afternoon, they'd gotten a good bit of the cleaning done, and I thanked them profusely. I had a great feeling about my future in Marathon, and let out a huge sigh of relief for the first time in a couple of months.

Getting out of my marriage to William just about killed me. He did everything in his power to hurt me upon my departure, and our struggles continued on for the good part of a year. I think part of it was because he couldn't believe I would leave him, and another part of it was because he was the one being left. That only happened to William when his fiancé died.

Whatever the belief was that he created in his mind, he turned into a monster toward me, and I just wanted to get away. Even if you removed the physical act he'd committed against me, the fact that I couldn't change his mind about suspecting me of sleeping with Dave really haunted me.

I left for Marathon the next morning with enough clothes for the week, and my cat. I'd come back the next weekend to get the rest of my things with a U-Haul. Half way to Marathon, I went to make a call and learned that William had terminated my cell phone service. We were on a family plan through his employer, so it was easy for him to do. I called customer service (because even if the service is inactive, they still let you call customer service), and they informed me that he'd cancelled my service. I asked them what I could do, stating I was a victim of domestic violence (with the hope that would help), and they directed me to stop at a local retail store and they'd help me reactivate my service.

When I arrived at the cell phone retailer, they advised me I'd have to put a $750.00 deposit down to start new service, but I could keep my phone number. I pulled out one of our joint credit cards to pay the deposit, and my service was restored in my name only. I couldn't believe he'd lower himself to do something like that, but he and his pride were hurt, so I should have expected it. In my experience, dissolving a relationship gets uglier as time goes on. Even if it begins on a cordial note, it never ends that way. The tremendous amount of pain caused by a failure of this magnitude grows as the idea of the relationship ending becomes real. It happened in my first divorce, and it seemed the second would be no different.

These thoughts became reality when I arrived at a gas station and tried to use one of our joint credit cards, and discovered it also didn't work. I had learned on the first go around to never be caught unprepared and to never fully depend on anyone. I have always maintained my own credit cards and a small bank account since then. I fueled up with my own credit card and continued on my way. I realized my departure from our marriage was going to be a lot harder than I'd anticipated.

William and I had built some great friendships and had some amazing times at the VFW and American Legion, but those times also allowed our differences to be amplified and brought to light. Those experiences forced me to see that our time together was not meant to last forever. Our relationship was integral to get us through the lessons we needed to learn so we could move forward separately.

After all of the turmoil with the cell phone and credit cards, I finally arrived in Marathon and stopped by the real estate office to sign my lease and drop off my check. As I left the office and headed to my new home, I finally felt free. I knew I wasn't completely free yet, I just knew that the hardest part...the departure...was behind me.

LOOSE ENDS

My new roommate and I got along great, work was going well, and I was having a blast. I'd made a lot of new friends in my new home and had an active social life. William and I eventually began to speak on the phone, and he kept begging me to come back. I told him that wasn't going to happen and that I wanted out of our marriage. He had broken my trust and there was no going back from that. I told him I just wanted out, and agreed to leave him the house and the bills if he'd just let me go. Based on when I'd left, I knew what our bills were and what the value of our newly remodeled house was. It didn't matter if he decided to keep it or sell it, he'd come out ahead. That was, if he'd stick to paying off our remodeling debt (which was on zero-interest offers) and live within a fairly liberal budget. But, he didn't. In my absence, he'd been spending way more time in the bars, causing a huge deficit in that budget.

William continued to call me regularly, usually late at night after he'd been drinking, and I tried to gently convince him that I really did love him but wasn't willing to live under the conditions which he'd created. I didn't trust him to change, and I was not coming back. I prepared and filed our divorce papers myself to save money. When we went in front of the judge (for which I had to travel back to Palm Beach County), he asked me why I didn't want half of William's pension. I was apparently entitled to it because he'd started that job after we'd gotten married. I explained to the judge that I didn't feel that our three-and-a-half year marriage warranted me asking for half of a pension that he would have to work twenty-five years to earn. He looked surprised, but granted our dissolution of marriage, with William getting the house and credit card debt, and me walking away only keeping his last name. I kept his last name, which was Evans, for two reasons. One because I'd been Drezinski long enough and William's last name was shorter and easier to spell, and two because I really still loved him. I wasn't quite ready to let go of the name I was so proud to have shared just yet.

BE MY GUEST

*W*hen I got back from divorce court, Marla asked if I minded if her daughter and year old grandson came to visit from Tampa. Marla hadn't seen her grandson since just after he was born, so she was really excited for the chance to see him without driving to Tampa. She told me her daughter was in her early twenties and worked as a topless dancer. I told her I didn't mind, and was actually kind of excited to meet her because I thought she'd be interesting to talk to. I'd never met a dancer before, and had so many questions.

When I met Marla's daughter and her son, I liked them immediately. The baby was really calm and content, and her daughter was interesting to talk to. All was well until the week turned into two weeks, then a month. As Marla announced the extensions of their stay, I just went with it. I was getting a bit pissed off that they weren't cleaning up after themselves, but I kept my mouth shut. I could see the extension in their stay began to concern Marla, and knew there was more to the story than was being shared. I just stayed away from home as much as possible, hoping they'd work it out.

When I learned the daughter got a job in Key West as a dancer, I became concerned. She finally told us she lost her apartment in Tampa and was starting over. That was a definite shock to me. Now we were all crammed into a 550 square foot double-wide with two bedrooms and two bathrooms. The daughter and her baby had been sleeping on our sofa bed, which was now permanently opened since the newness of their visit had worn off. The baby had grown more active and was causing total chaos in our small space. Apparently, Marla had never taught her daughter to clean up after herself, and we were constantly out of dishes because they were always dirty in the sink. My cat had resigned himself to living under my bed or in my bathroom window, whichever was further away from that baby. That baby, or possibly his mother, had been breaking anything they touched, and grandma was oblivious to the extreme discomfort that moving her family into our small space was causing me.

Don't get me wrong, I liked the daughter and found her to be an interesting young lady to talk to, but living with both a baby and his young mother who had no compunction about cleaning up after herself or her child, got really old after a month. I did my best to tolerate it knowing they were in a tight spot, but after she started telling me how much money she was making working in Key West, yet she never offered to contribute anything to our household, I decided it was time to reevaluate my living situation. Marla didn't care that her daughter caused me constant grief in my home. She did nothing to clean up after her or offset the impact she had on our lives. However, when my sister, brother-in-law, Jo and Bill came down to spend two nights at our house for my birthday, Marla was constantly bitching about everything. Whether it was us talking when we got home from dinner or my guests sleeping on our sofa bed, she made it known that she was not happy about being inconvenienced, so I quickly learned about the double standard that existed when it came to guests. So after over a month and a half of her guests, I decided to let her daughter take over my portion of the rent.

Our real estate agent wasn't surprised to see me. She told me she couldn't believe I'd lasted as long as I did. I just smiled and told her apparently it was just a stepping stone to get me to Marathon. She told me there was a one bedroom house next to the Gulf for rent, and the door was unlocked so I should go take a look. I went to the address she gave me and walked in the front door. I quickly discovered two things: One, no one in Marathon locked their doors, and Two, I had to be at the wrong house. I was certain the rent I was quoted was not for a waterfront house with a swimming pool and slide going into the Gulf. Thankfully, no one was home and I didn't scare the bejesus out of some poor soul by walking into their house unannounced. I made my way back to the real estate office and told her there must be a mistake, and that there was no way the house I had just walked into was available for what I could afford. She doubted me at first, but when I described the slide going into the Gulf, she realized she'd given me the wrong address. Once again, I headed out to look at my future home. This time, I was sent down a different street, and as soon as I saw it, I knew I was home.

It just so happened we were at the beginning of the month, so I signed the lease and told Marla I'd be leaving immediately. I told her it was nothing personal, but that her daughter and grandson needed her and they should have the opportunity to be together without me being in the mix. I really didn't care if she liked it or not, because I didn't sign up to live with a family of three.

HELLO, GOODBYE

*A*s soon as word got out that I was officially single, my friends at the Legion wasted no time in trying to fix me up. Marathon, at that time, was a town of less than 10,000 people, and most of them were married. When fresh meat moved to town, it didn't take long for the lions to pounce. Marathon, at that time, was like Alaska…the number of single men greatly outweighed the number of single women. People were trying to convince me to date their brother-in-law, son, grandson, or friend. All of that demand did wonders for my self esteem, but the problem was compatibility. These men were all nice people, but very few felt like a good fit for me.

One night while at the Legion, Marla pointed out a man that had been playing pool and asked me if I'd like to meet him. She said he was in the Coast Guard and worked in Key West, but lived in Marathon. She said she tried to date him but he wasn't interested in marrying her, and she was looking for a man to take care of her. I liked the look of him so she introduced us. He then asked me if I'd like to join him in a game of pool, so I did. I liked him immediately. He was intelligent, witty, and funny. After a few games of pool, he invited me to dinner at his favorite restaurant, The Cracked Conch, where we shared great food, great conversation, and a night cap. We began to spend time together here and there, and eventually started dating. He wanted to make sure I was independent and not looking for a husband.

About a month later, Tina invited me to her house because our friends Doug and Michelle from Pittsburgh were going to be in town. I planned to drive up on Friday after work and come home on Sunday night. Since Tina had met Tim when she was in Marathon for my birthday, I asked her if I could invite him. She said that would be great, so I asked him to join me. He said he couldn't because he was scheduled to work, so I drove up alone on Friday after work.

On Saturday morning, I was swimming in the pool when I heard the doorbell. I couldn't believe it when Tina escorted Tim to the back patio. He drove all the way up to West Palm Beach just to spend time with me. I was even happier when he said he planned to stay the night, and we could drive home together the following day. We had a great time and I hadn't laughed so much in a very long time. We went on a dinner adventure and listened to tales of Michelle trying to figure out how to use the automated airline kiosks that became a part of our lives after 9/11. She said she felt like she'd won at the slot machine when all the lights and sirens went off because she selected the option that said she'd let someone else pack her suitcase! Doug and Michelle are two of the funniest people I've ever met, and I love them both dearly.

Things were going well with Tim, but not moving too quickly. He made sure to not let us get too close. There were no exchanges of keys, and when I spent the night at his house, I had to leave when he left for work at 5:00 a.m., which wasn't very much fun after a night of drinking. But, I did get to see some of the most amazing starry skies I'd ever seen from his driveway as he kissed me good bye.

Then, one day he just disappeared. I hadn't heard from him in over two weeks. I asked our friends if anyone had heard from him, and they said they hadn't. He never mentioned any type of deployment to me, so I assumed the worst, that he was avoiding me. I thought it was really strange that he didn't return my calls or even answer his Nextel radio when I'd chirp him...he had always eventually answered. I just thought I'd done something to mess things up, so when an opportunity presented itself, I took it.

There was a charter boat captain that I'd made friends with who had rugged good looks and a job that was exotic to me, so when he asked me out to dinner, I accepted. Captain Tom actually cooked me dinner at his house, which I later learned was due to his lack of money. But, to his credit, it was the best steak I'd ever had. He was about nine years older than me, but he had a cool job and was a great cook, so I decided to give it a try.

We'd been together almost every day since that dinner, and ended up at my house in bed on a Sunday afternoon following a bout of day drinking that started at the Legion with breakfast. We'd just dozed off when my Nextel radio chirped. It was the long-lost Tim. He'd resurfaced at quite an inopportune moment. I answered the chirp and he acted like we'd only spoken a day or so ago. I was very confused and in a rather precarious spot, so I just told him the truth. I said since I hadn't heard from him in so long and because he hadn't answered my calls or chirps, I assumed he wanted to end things, so I was dating Tom Jeffries. He was rather surprised when he learned who had taken his place, but because I still had stars in my eyes for my new beau, I couldn't imagine why. It would take me about a year to catch on.

HOOK, LINE, AND SINKER

Captain Tom was different from anyone I'd ever dated. He had an exciting job and was a great conversationalist…as long as you got him before too many vodka and pineapple juices. The stories he shared with me spoke of an exotic past. He grew up in Washington state, and his sister had a wolf as a pet. He then had the opportunity as a young carpenter to live in Japan for three years and build homes there. He learned a lot of complex construction as he built homes and pagoda-like structures. In Marathon, Tom worked as a charter boat captain aboard the *Bounty Hunter*. He'd been the captain of that boat for ten years and had a great reputation for always catching fish. He had built a loyal clientele because he knew the waters of Marathon and where to find the fish at any time of year.

Tom lived in a rented duplex not far from my house. On my first visit there, I was shocked at the rough condition of the place. Tom explained that his landlord was a recent widow who was struggling to maintain the property. She offered Tom a discount on his rent in exchange for working on the place. His excuse for the condition was that he'd been working on the outside of the house and hadn't yet begun to refurbish the inside. His undependable truck looked as bad as it ran. This was fitting from what I'd learned from the short time I'd lived in Marathon. The town was full of working people who weren't concerned with appearances. I learned quickly that life in Marathon resembled life in Ohio more than it did in Palm

Beach County, which seemed to require you to properly dress and put on make up just to go to the store. It was a nice change.

Tom and I got along really well. Unlike me, he wasn't one to spend every night after work in the Legion, so I took that as a good thing. We started to spend our time together outside of the bar, so I saved a lot of money. During stone crab and lobster season Tom cooked for us because we got free lobster, stone crab claws, and fish from his best friend, Dooley, who was a commercial fisherman. He was another interesting character…a bit rough around the edges, but a teddy bear on the inside.

During off season, Dooley asked Tom if he'd like to earn a few bucks by helping him assemble traps. His business partner was sick and couldn't work, so he was in a pinch and needed an extra set of hands. Tom said he'd help, and was shocked when I asked if I could join them. I wanted to give back to the man that gave us literally hundreds of dollars in free seafood. They were both surprised that I'd volunteered, but I told them I grew up on a farm and wasn't afraid of hard work. Besides, it was exciting to be able to learn about commercial fishing.

When we arrived at the trap yard, the amount of work before us was a bit daunting, but we hit the ground running. There were only three of us to assemble hundreds of stone crab traps, which included using a cordless drill to attach a tag to each trap, then screw the sides, top, and bottom together, then someone else inserted the concrete bottoms to weight each trap. The styrofoam buoy balls had already been branded with their fishing license number and painted their color scheme, so we just had to thread them onto the line and attach them to the trap. It was a lot of hard work, and I must say that I have never worked as hard as I did that weekend, but it was a great opportunity to do something different that I will never forget. Working so hard to do so much work in such a short time really opened my eyes to just how hard commercial fishermen work to provide seafood for us. They will always hold my highest respect.

As Tom and I grew closer, we decided to move in together. I asked him to move in with me because it was my house. I wasn't going to give up my home in case things didn't work out. Besides, my house was waterfront, on a half acre with lots of huge trees and way off US 1. Tom's duplex was only a couple houses off US 1 so you could hear the traffic, it was not as nice and had no yard. After he moved in, Tom told me his landlord had asked him to vacate because he had been behind on his rent and commitment to complete the repairs he'd promised. I probably should have seen that as a red flag, but I was too busy trying to fix him to notice.

A few months after we moved in together, one of the brothers who owned *Bounty Hunter* got sick. They discussed selling the boat, which would render Tom jobless, so he was concerned. They offered to sell it to him, but he didn't have the means or ability to own such a business. He knew he could work with his friend on the commercial fishing boat and make decent money, but it wasn't his first choice. He was not very excited to have to work that hard.

Just two weeks after Tom was notified of the impending sale by his employer, he got a call from Del, a longtime charter customer. Del had just purchased a local dive shop and wanted to add a fishing charter boat to the business. Del and his wife had been vacationing in Marathon for years. They'd visit in both the winter and the summer, just so Del could experience all seasons of the fishing Marathon had to offer. He knew how talented Tom was was as a captain, so he asked him what it would take to get him away from *Bounty Hunter*. Tom named his price, and Del hired him immediately. Problem solved.

Del's new business was called *Captain Hook's* and the new charter boat was christened *Miss Hook*. Word of the new charter boat in town spread quickly, which meant the calendar started to fill. *Miss Hook* was booked every weekend for the next three months, and a few days each week.

Working on a new type of boat presented a few challenges for Tom. His previous boat (*Bounty Hunter*) didn't have an elevated bridge, so running charters by himself presented no problems if Tom had to assist with bringing in a fish. He was able to both run the boat and help the customers with their catches because they were in close proximity. However, the new boat, *Miss Hook*, had an elevated bridge, which meant Tom would have to climb down to assist customers with their fish. This presented challenges in situations where he had to get to a customer quickly. This challenge prompted Tom to ask me if I'd like to learn how to be a first mate for the weekend trips. He had been using Del as a mate during the week, but Del was a little older and didn't want to work every charter. Since the business was just starting out, they couldn't afford to pay me, so I just worked for tips. Tom was a great teacher, and I learned very quickly how to rig ballyhoo and run the outriggers. I began to work on the boat in the spring, so we fished primarily for dolphin (also known as Mahi Mahi) and tuna. If the weather was too bad to travel the thirty-four miles to our good fishing grounds, we'd fish closer to home on reefs for grouper and various types of snapper. This was another amazing opportunity for me to learn something I never thought I'd have get to to experience, and I loved every minute of it.

FISH ON!

The charter business had been going strong for a few months when Del was contacted by a television show called *Fishing the Florida Keys*. They wanted to charter *Miss Hook* to fish for dolphin and tuna in April, which was a bit early in the year for those species, but Del didn't want to pass up such a great opportunity to advertise his new business, so he booked the trip. The best time to fish for dolphin and tuna is when the waters are warmest, which is late May through November, but when filming television shows they worry more about their own schedules and not those of the fish.

On the morning of filming, we left the dock a bit late because the bait boat was having difficulty catching enough bait for us (because it was off season!) We needed as much live bait as we could get because we were fishing so early in the season. Fortunately, everything worked out for us. We got really lucky and caught a very small dolphin on the way out of the channel, but it was enough to satisfy the producer, which was all that mattered. We then had a long period of inactivity, which allowed us to get acquainted with our hosts, who were great guys. We were traveling out to the Humps, an area about thirty-four miles from our dock, that offered us the best opportunity to find tuna so early in the year. We eventually found a school of small black fin tuna and managed to hook quite a few, thanks to all of the live bait we'd brought.

When the producer was satisfied with the amount of footage we'd gathered, we headed back to the dock to clean our catch. Although our bounty wasn't as plentiful as it would have been if we could have waited just one more month, we'd caught enough to create the show. Del was kind enough to order me a copy of the show on VHS tape, which is still one of my most treasured possessions.

All of this happened right in the middle of Tom moving in with me. After the chaos of the busy schedule and filming of the show, we were able to find some down time and get settled. Our normal weekend routine took us to the Legion after charters where we'd have a few cocktails after the charter, then we'd head home to cook any fish the charter customers shared with us. As we settled into our lives together, we wanted to spend more time at home than out, so we started to grow vegetables in container gardens, and even added a washer and dryer to our home. Tom's friend Dooley was also a plumber, so he added the piping, and he and Tom built a really nice shed around the machines on the side of the house. We had a nice view of the Gulf, a nice large yard where we built a fire pit, and now a garden. It was our own little piece of paradise.

PARADISE LOST

What we didn't know, because the real estate agent never told me when I moved in, was that we were allotted a specific dollar for water and were responsible to pay any overage. Because our rental home was a duplex, the owners kept the bills in their name, and the real estate agent was supposed to bill us each month. We'd been there for over a year and had never been told about the water bills or asked to sign a new lease, so we just continued to pay our rent and live there.

It was about three months past the expiration of our lease when I learned the owners of the house got a divorce and the wife got the house. The real estate agent called me and said the owner was coming to town and was mad because I hadn't signed a new lease. I told them I'd be happy to sign a new lease, but because the owner had been receiving exorbitant water bills, and the real estate agent hadn't been collecting the overage from me, she said she wanted to inspect the property before allowing me to sign a new lease. When I had met the owners the previous year, she and her husband seemed really nice, so I wasn't concerned. I had been taking good care of her home and was confident she'd find no reason not to renew my lease.

I received a phone call from my real estate agent telling me the owner had arrived and was furious. I asked why, because I had only improved her house, but apparently we'd been parking on her septic tank drain field, which was right in front of the house. Because it was a gravel area in front of the house, we assumed it was the driveway. Things just went down hill from there and her visit turned into a real shitstorm. She was also furious that we hadn't paid a water bill, and wouldn't accept that fact that the real estate agent never mentioned it, or that there was no mention of it in the lease. The real estate agent knew she messed up and felt really bad about the oversight, so she paid the overages out of her own pocket in an attempt to keep the peace. The landlord was also mad about the washer and dryer being installed without permission, but once we told her they were professionally installed, she said she'd reimburse us for the wood we purchased for the surround and we could leave it up. Unfortunately, I trusted Tom to gather receipts for her, and he thought it would be appropriate to charge her for a power tool he purchased. Of course, that caused more anger, so she told us we had to remove everything and restore the house to original condition, so we did. She then had an issue with ceiling fans we installed, so we took them down and re-installed her original light fixtures. When I tried to tell her that the stove shocked you when you were standing on the terrazzo floor with bare feet, she told me I was crazy, but it really did. I had to stand on a rubber mat so I didn't get shocked. She then found issue with our container gardens, which she thought looked "trashy," and she was pissed that we planted aloe vera plants around trees in the front yard, so we pulled them out and took them with us. Once we completed her list, we couldn't get out of there fast enough. She had apparently had a terrible divorce (or I might say that her husband had a good divorce), because she was angry and hateful. This person was nothing like the nice lady I'd met previously.

CREATING A MONSTER

Our home search only lasted a few days. We learned our friends from the Legion were the managers of a fifty-five and over trailer park in Grassy Key, just north of town. They had been looking for a new tenant for an apartment, and were excited to offer it to us. They said the apartments welcomed all ages because they were on a separate parcel. These apartments were a row of four units that consisted of old travel trailers from the sixties, lined up end to end with additions built off of each unit's side to create a spacious living area. The trailer bodies served as the bedrooms and bathrooms. Whoever built these homes was very creative and resourceful. The rent was much cheaper than we'd been paying, so we quickly accepted their offer and began to move in. We were lucky to be right on the Gulf of Mexico again.

Once we settled in, we enjoyed sitting out front with our neighbors. One evening as we were enjoying some cocktails, it began to rain. As we scrambled inside, we all shared the same thought…we needed a covered patio. That way, we could sit outside and enjoy the rain without getting soaked. Tom's eyes lit up as the idea came to light. That night, we all shared ideas to create the perfect outdoor space. We asked for permission from our landlords, who approved our idea as long as it didn't cost them anything, which we were willing to do. Not long after, Tom built an amazing huge overhang with a clear fiberglass roof. It extended across the front of the entire building, which was three apartments. For a few hundred dollars, we were able to double our living area. Once the patio was built, all of our neighbors gathered there for evening cocktails, Sunday potluck dinners, and any other occasion we could dream up. We had picnic tables just outside the patio, and a full array of patio furniture under cover. I loved our new gathering place because everyone was comfortable at our house. It also gave us the opportunity to share with our neighbors. We had some seniors in our community that were struggling financially, so we always tried to help when we could.

My habit of being a fixer who loves to take care of people blinded me to things I should have noticed earlier. Since Tom and I were always entertaining, I made sure our liquor cabinet and refrigerator were always well stocked. I never paid attention to how much vodka we went through, because we often shared with our neighbors. When the supply got low, I'd stop at the liquor store on the way home. Our local liquor store offered name brands at great prices, so keeping everything stocked wasn't expensive.

For some reason, I became aware that we had been going through a lot more vodka than normal. I started to make a mental note of how often we'd run low, and found it was definitely more than it had been in the past. As I began to drink less, I started to watch more. Tom would pour drinks that were almost all vodka and very little juice. He was drinking almost a half of a 1.75 liter bottle of vodka every two nights. It had taken me almost a full year to figure out why Tim, my former boyfriend, was so shocked when I told him that I started dating Tom. He had known Tom was an alcoholic, but I had no idea. Until now, I knew nothing about alcoholics.

Once the problem was evident to me, I began to talk to friends and understand what I was up against. Kathy and Ed were our neighbors who wintered in Grassy Key from Michigan. Once we got to know each other, they adopted me. I spent a lot of time with them, and they taught me a lot. We became so close, they showed me where their secret stash of a couple of thousand dollars was hidden. When I asked them why they thought I'd need it, they warned me about the unpredictability of living with an alcoholic. I began to get scared and couldn't comprehend how this loving man I'd spent so much time with could be hiding this monster.

Kathy and Ed taught me about how alcoholics lie to cover the disease, and I began to put the pieces of this puzzle of a relationship together. I recalled when we had been on vacation in St. Martin, and Tom would get so drunk during the afternoon that he wouldn't want to go to dinner, so I often went alone. I mistakenly attributed it to him being somewhere new and overdoing it. I also eventually figured out why his former boss from *Bounty Hunter* tried to warn me that Tom was lying to me about a few different things, but Tom convinced me that the boss was the problem, so I sided with Tom. There were so many stories that I reflected back on and realized they were all lies, that it blew my mind. Tom had become so good at telling his lies, that he actually believed them himself.

The final straw came one Sunday evening after our weekly potluck dinner. As the crowd thinned, Kathy and Ed stayed for our usual night cap. We had all just refilled our glasses and were walking back out to the patio, when Tom flipped out. He went into a rage because he thought Ed had taken a swing at him, when all Ed had done was hold the door open for Tom. Tom was extremely inebriated, and was screaming and yelling and trying to swing at Ed, who was much larger and stronger, and not nearly as drunk. Ed patiently directed Tom back into the apartment to sit down on the couch. Tom continued ranting and raving, but stayed sitting on the couch because he was too drunk to get up after his outburst.

I was not going to tolerate anyone trying to hit anyone else, so I called the sheriff. Two deputies showed up about fifteen minutes later and took statements from all of us while Tom remained on the couch inside. The deputies asked Ed if he wanted to press charges because Tom tried to hit him, and he said he didn't want to. Tom was then charged with public intoxication and placed under arrest. The deputies handcuffed him and placed him in the back of the patrol car, then walked back over to let us know what was going on. Tom then started to kick out the back window of the patrol car, so the deputies pulled him out and placed leg shackles on him so he couldn't kick the window out. That added a charge of resisting arrest to his court docket. They told me it was a good thing I'd called because he was acting so violently, then left to take him to jail. The next morning, the jail called to get more information, and the deputy told me that in his drunken rage, Tom beat the jail door with his bare hands and actually dented the plate around the lock. They were surprised he didn't break his hand. That added yet another charge of destruction of public property to his court docket. I'm still not sure how that happened, but

I knew I wouldn't be bailing him out, and I certainly wasn't going to be waiting for him when he got home.

Fortunately, Tom was held without bail for a little over a week because of the additional charges levied when he damaged county property. That gave me time to find a new place to live. There was a trailer that had been for sale just a few rows away from the apartment and near Kathy and Ed's trailer. Thankfully, my brother is a saver, so he was able to loan me the money to purchase the trailer. I was able to move in before Tom got out of jail.

I received a pretty intensive education in the field of alcoholism that year. That was when I made a promise to myself that I would never bail anyone out of jail if they were arrested for being intoxicated. It was safer for both them and me to let them spend the night in jail. I'd be there after their morning court appearance. It was also hard believe I was starting over yet again, but I guess it was meant to be. Everything fell together flawlessly to get me out of my relationship with Tom and into my own place. Thank you to my angels and also to my amazing baby brother.

"PRECIOUS" COMMODITY

My boss had been struggling to find a new boat captain that was willing to work the hours required at our facility, when he came across a candidate that seemed a bit over qualified. At that time, we had two semi-retired captains that were looking to delve deeper into their retirements. When we got the resume of the new prospect, we both questioned why someone of that caliber would want to work on a dive boat in the Keys, when he'd been running high-end dinner cruises in Washington DC and Maryland. The ships he had been operating were between 80' and 110' long and fully staffed. We both suspected he was running from something, but that isn't always easy to uncover. Bob called his references, past and present employers, and everyone offered glowing references. His background uncovered nothing obvious, so he was offered an in-person interview. His name was Mike, and he was handsome and funny. Like I had done, he showed up for his in-person interview in a suit. Bob immediately looked at me when he saw Mike's attire and we both smiled.

Mike was around my age and was obviously well educated and mannered. He aced his interview and was offered the position. Since he would be relocating, he was offered a dormitory room to rent temporarily. He was excited to join our crew, and made arrangements to start work the following week. He had temporarily relocated to his parents' home in Yankeetown, which is on the west coast of Florida in Levy County.

Yankeetown is just south of the Big Bend area of the west coast, in a sleepy little town that abutted the Gulf of Mexico and Withlacoochie River. Mike told me he had been born and raised there, but he certainly didn't remind me of a small town Florida boy.

Mike meshed with students and crew very well but as we spent more time with him, you could tell he had the mentality of a frat boy. He was great at trying to schmooze the boss, but Bob saw right through him. He just let Mike believe he'd accomplished something. Bob didn't care about personalities, he just wanted a good captain, and Mike was definitely a good captain. Mike told great stories of his time running dinner cruise ships in Maryland and DC, but blamed his relocation to the Keys on being burned out. It always seemed like there was more to the story that he wasn't sharing…yet.

As we got to know each other, Mike encouraged me to come out of the shell I had crawled into after I left Tom. We became good friends and spent a lot of time together. Because we were close in age, we hit it off pretty well. I enjoyed how much he made me laugh. Mike also had the guts to tell me to my face how much I had let my personal standards decline. My parents had also pointed it out, but I resisted hearing what they thought because I was still happy at that time. Now that I was hearing it from an outsider, I decided to work on returning to my old self.

I had tried to save Tom because that's what I do…I am a fixer. But in my fight to save him, I had sacrificed myself. I no longer cared what I looked like, and I'd been drinking and smoking a lot more than when I'd met him. I stopped making an effort to better my appearance. I was always clean, but could definitely have done more. Mike was straight with me. He showed me what I'd let happen, and encouraged me to return to my earlier standards. He showed me that I could have fun without drinking, and urged me to try it. I tried non-alcoholic beer and laid off the vodka. It was refreshing to not feel like crap after a night of going out.

As Mike revealed more about himself to me, I began to understand why he'd run away from DC. He was a fun-loving guy that just couldn't hit the brakes…exactly the thing he'd been preaching to me about. Once he got on a roll, whether it was drinking, gambling or doing drugs, it turned into an all-out bender. His parents attempted to curb this behavior by severely limiting his finances, but that didn't always work. When people get around a Good-Time Charlie type of person, they'll buy them drinks just to keep up the fun. Mike was the spoiled, screw-up, and only son of a wealthy couple. He had been given the best education (George Washington University) for his field. But when his personal demons tarnished his attempts at excelling in that field, his parents resorted to his love of boats. They polished him to captain large yachts and ships, with the hope that he would find his way. Mike also wasn't able to handle the everyday responsibilities of menial things like paying bills, so his parents had only given him a Chevron credit card for gas. His rent was directly paid by the family accountant, and he was required to use his earnings for everything else. Mike was excited to learn that Chevron sold beer, and it wasn't long before he was using his Chevron credit card to fund our outings. That lasted for one billing cycle because his parents, who were closely monitoring his spending, put an end to that by lowering the credit line on that card. Boy, was he pissed. That was when I decided to give him a nickname…"Precious." I felt the name totally fit his persona and personal challenges. Mike loved his new nickname, but he made me promise not to divulge the real reason the name was given to him.

Back in Grassy Key, I'd settled into my little trailer nicely. I'd hired my friend Captain Al to build a kitchen island for more counter space, and to do some other minor repairs. My trailer had been sitting vacant for about two years when I bought it, so there were some maintenance issues that needed to be addressed. Captain Al was talented enough to build an entire house, so he was the best man for the job. He did all of our handyman work at Hall's, so I new he would be able to fix everything that needed to be fixed.

My new home was located one row south of Kathy and Ed's trailer, which was two rows south of Tom's apartment. Because I'd been hanging out with Precious after work, I rarely got home before dark. I hadn't been around the trailer park as much as I had been in the past, so I wasn't aware of what had been going on with Tom.

One afternoon I'd gotten home earlier than normal and caught up with Kathy and Ed. I was excited to show them the work Captain Al had gotten done on my trailer, so I invited them over for a beer. They told me they'd seen Tom walking around the park after dark, which he'd never before, so they started watching him. They saw him walk across the park to my trailer, where he'd just stand quietly outside of my window. I often slept with my bedroom window open in the winter because we got a nice cool breeze off of the Gulf of Mexico. Although I wasn't afraid of Tom, I was afraid of him starting trouble as he'd done when he was arrested. I knew if he was walking around after dark, he was definitely drunk because he'd never do anything like that while he was sober.

Once Precious found out about Tom's stalking behavior, he jumped into super hero mode. He was going to save me from my ex, whether I needed him to or not. He insisted I had to get out of that trailer park and further away from Tom. I told him I'd purchased my trailer and I was staying. It was one of the few places I could afford on my own. I thought that was the end of it, but Precious was so wrapped up in saving me that he actually created a false romantic relationship with me. It wasn't a good idea, but I chose not to see it at the time. I got stars in my eyes that such a "great guy" was interested in being romantically involved with me. But in reality, he was just a prettier version of Tom. He had better teeth, better clothes, and wasn't living at that level just above survival where Tom lived.

My decision to be star-struck at Precious wanting a relationship with me was based purely on loneliness. I didn't listen to my intuition, and I fell hook, line, and sinker for him. Since we were at my house when he found out about Tom's stalking behavior, he insisted on staying with me that night. Precious wasn't aware that I had a cat, and he was allergic to cats, so he ended up having to leave in the middle of the night. Of course I was disappointed, so I attempted to wipe down the entire trailer and found the cat a new home. Although he wasn't sure it was going to work, he made another attempt to spend the night. He apologized profusely, but he ended up having to leave shortly after he got there again. This time, though, he asked me to come with him to his house, so I did.

Precious had moved into a large house on Summerland Key with two roommates. He had the entire downstairs, which was a living room, bedroom and bathroom. He shared the upstairs kitchen with his roommates. Once we spent a couple of nights there, he said I needed to move in with him, so on our first day off, we packed my friend's truck with what we needed and headed west. Once we got there and unpacked, something didn't feel right. I tried to ignore it and enjoy the adventure, but it felt like I was an unwanted guest in someone's parents house. I began to have flashbacks to my first roommate, the one that wanted me to move in because he wanted a replacement for his mother, then told me he was getting back with his old girlfriend. My intuition had been trying to tell me not to move down there, but I was so swept up in the excitement of it all that I ignored it. It didn't take long for me to realize that Precious just wanted the same thing my first roommate did, a companion, except he was using Tom as an excuse to get to get it.

Our "romance" fizzled out quickly. Precious started acting like a brother to me instead of a boyfriend. Then, he always wanted to stay away from the house, which I thought was strange. I'd brought my patio set down so we could sit next to the canal and enjoy it, but we never spent any time there. I eventually learned Precious' roommates wanted only him as a roommate, not him AND me. I also learned it wasn't anything personal, they just didn't want their boss' personal assistant living with them. I understood. I also didn't like hiding our relationship from Bob, who had a strict policy against employee fraternization. I borrowed my friend's truck again, packed my stuff and headed east. Once I learned how Precious avoided telling me the truth, it became evident that he was more like Tom that I hoped.

My patio chairs were made of aluminum, so they were light weight. We stacked them together and put them on the top of the pile of things in the back of the truck then tied them down with some clothesline. I know it wasn't the most secure way to tie them down, but it was all that we had. Precious was behind me in the Camry. The Camry was Precious' grad school graduation present and it had been through a lot, and it looked like it had been through a lot. We always drove it to Key West because we didn't care if it got dented, no one would be able to tell.

As I reached the top of the hump of the Seven-Mile Bridge, a gust of wind lifted my poorly secured stack of chairs up and off of the truck, and placed them on the road. As I looked in the rear view mirror, the entire event unfolded right before my eyes as if it were happening in slow motion. This gave me plenty of time to process what was happening and notice Precious' reaction, which caused me to burst out laughing. This is what I saw...he was following me, the chairs took flight and landed on the road, his eyes opened really wide, then I saw his hands on the steering wheel quickly turn to the left which maneuvered the Camry around the chairs with great precision, then the car returned to the travel lane and continued on. It was quite comical to see it all happen in such an orderly fashion. I immediately pulled to the side of the road, and as he drove by he yelled out the passenger window to me, "Throw them in the drink!" He then continued over the bridge without stopping. I was pissed that he didn't stop to help, and I was absolutely not going to throw anything off the bridge, so I walked back to collect them. I threw them back onto the truck and re-tied them. Once we got back to my place, I asked him why he didn't stop to help. That was when I learned one last hold out of information from Precious.

Precious told me something I was shocked to hear. He said he didn't want to risk having a cop stop to speak with us and have to answer any questions. When I asked him why, he told me a story about how he used to take prescription sleeping pills that sometimes caused him to sleep walk and not remember it. He always took more than he was prescribed because that was his personality. One night after taking four of them, Precious woke up, got into his car, and drove to a bar where he started a fight with someone. The police were called. He then tried to fight with the officer, and Precious was arrested for battery on a law enforcement officer. His parents had to step in with their high-priced attorney to save his ass. The attorney was able to get the charges reduced if Precious agreed to enter a rehab program, which he did. He never took those pills again. His conviction resulted in him being labeled as someone that should be approached with caution if encountered by law enforcement. He was afraid if a police officer encountered him, they'd see his charges and label him as a trouble maker, which is not something you want in a small town like Marathon. I told him I understood, but secretly couldn't believe he'd actually tried to fight with a cop and had no memory of it. I'd never heard anything like that. It was then I realized people with money have way more problems than having money is worth. I forgave him for not stopping to help me with the chairs.

Precious and I drifted apart after I moved back home. I saw less of him at work, and the roommates (who also worked with us) began telling me about the wild parties he had been throwing at their house. They told me he would get really drunk and act crazy. They really thought he was going off the deep end. That explained why I hadn't heard from him. Although I missed our adventures, I knew it was for the best. He really wasn't good for me, and I didn't like trying to hide our relationship from my boss. I was naive enough to think he didn't know what was going on.

About a month later, I was getting ready to leave work at Hall's when Precious stuck his head in my office and told me that he missed me. I told him I missed him too, then he asked me if I wanted to run down to Key West. It was a Tuesday and I had nothing better to do, so I agreed. We left right from work, both sporting our Hall's tee shirts, so we looked like tourists, which would be perfect. We dropped my car off at his house then took the Camry to Key West. Precious was in a particularly jovial mood that afternoon, and had me laughing hysterically as soon as I got in the car. This was going to be a great adventure, and I was excited. Because we both had to work the next day, I warned Precious we had to keep it under control, but when you mixed Precious with Key West, you never knew what could happen.

Once we got into town, he parked near the wharf and we made our way to the waterfront. He noticed a sunset cruise about to depart, so he grabbed my hand and dragged me to the ticket booth. It was a dinner cruise, and since we hadn't eaten the timing was perfect. I slapped the credit card down and secured our tickets. Precious promised to pay me back on pay day, so I wasn't going to let his lack of funds stand in the way of our fun. The cruise was a blast with great drinks, good food, and a beautiful sunset. They had a really good reggae band playing, which definitely elevated our already great moods. After the cruise we stopped by a few of the local watering holes…Sloppy Joe's, Captain Tony's, and Hog's Breath. By then we were pretty drunk, and it was past midnight, so we decided to start trying to find the car. That was an adventure in itself because we really couldn't remember where it was.

During our search, we came across one of Precious' roommates, who was also our co-worker. He told us he'd pissed of the girl he'd ridden down with, so he was now stranded. We told him if he helped us find the car, we'd gladly give him a ride home. The remainder of the car search is fuzzy, but we did eventually find it. It was, amazingly, right where we'd left it. I knew I was our best chance of getting home in one piece, but I needed some food to offset all we had to drink. We pulled into the McDonald's drive through on our way off the island. When we saw that chicken sandwiches and double cheeseburgers were on sale, we ordered six of each.

We raved about how those were the best sandwiches we'd ever eaten as we wolfed them down.

Precious' roommate had gotten a little handsy on the ride home, and I was too tired to stop him. I just found it funny that he was so drunk he thought I'd sleep with him. Precious just sat in the back seat laughing at my predicament. He was so drunk, Precious and I had to practically carry him into the house. We got him upstairs and put him in his bed. He still kept asking me to stay with him. I told him I was leaving and headed downstairs to get as much sleep as I could.

The alarm clock rang at 6:00 a.m., which came way too quickly. Since I normally didn't start work until 9:00, I got up and drove home so I could get a little more sleep. I'd need it to get rid of my residual buzz. The boys weren't so lucky...they had to be at work at 7:00 a.m. to get the boat ready for a dive trip. I felt bad for them, but I did warn Precious not to overdo it.

When I arrived to work, I looked a bit tired but nothing like the two of them. Precious caught me in the back hallway and started to giggle. I looked at him quizzically and he asked me if I'd found the manatee. I asked him, "What manatee?" He busted out laughing as he said, "The manatee that was feeding in my car. There is lettuce EVERYWHERE! It's in the visors, for God's sake! There's so much lettuce in there I may have enough for lunch when we get back!" He then asked me if I got the license plate number of the truck that hit him and if I found the dog that shit in his mouth. I shook my head and smiled as I continued to my desk. I really loved my job.

MY NEXT CHAPTER

The Tuesday night Key West trip marked the end of my pseudo relationship with Precious. He resumed his bachelor life with the boys in Summerland Key, and I made my way back to the American Legion. Now that the drama of my break up with Tom and having him arrested had blown over, I felt comfortable going back.

There was a bartender named Nita at the Legion who seemed to always be at odds with the clique, but had reached out to me when I wasn't around them. She was a just couple of years older than me, but she had become a widow a few years before we'd met. She lived in a waterfront travel trailer that was right in town. She and her husband had a comfortable retirement fund, but his late in life illness and ultimate passing had just about wiped it all out. She kept his car, their boat and their vacation home in Marathon, which was where she decided to live after he died. Nita was a survivor who had raised a great son on her own, and she didn't take shit from anyone. That's what I liked most about her.

When we met, Nita was at the end of their savings and had to return to work. In addition to bartending at the Legion, she bartended at the Elks Lodge, and cleaned vacation rentals. Nita eventually hired me to help her clean, which allowed me to get back on my feet after burying myself in debt by living with Tom. We had a lot of fun together and became quite close.

One night, I was headed to the Legion, so I gave her a call. I knew it was her night off so I wanted to see if she'd join me. I desperately needed a girl's night out. Thankfully, she answered immediately. She said in her well known matter of fact tone, "It's about time you got your shit together. Let's get a drink and go see Freddie." I was thrilled that she was in the mood to go see Freddie. Freddie Bye is an iconic musician in Marathon and has played there for years. He leads the house band at a bar called the Brass Monkey, affectionately known as the Monkey, which is where we were headed. We always had a blast there, and it was conveniently located in the plaza next to her trailer park. I picked her up on my way to the Legion, where we started the evening with Happy Hour and eventually made our way to the Monkey to see Freddie.

Nita and I had been known to always have a good time together, except for two nights, one of which earned her the nickname "Tumbles." On that night, we had been at the Legion for happy hour. Nita had a good head start over me. She had stopped there for lunch after she'd finished cleaning and never left. Since she was still in her cleaning clothes, we had to stop at her house so she could change before we went to see Freddie. As she made her way down the front steps, her flip flop got stuck and she took a dive. Fortunately, she put her hand out before her face hit the bricks. Unfortunately, the bricks she fell on sliced her hand. She got up, dusted herself off, and proceeded to head to the car. Her son and I noticed the blood pouring from her hand and I said, "Hold on Tumbles, you're bleeding!" Nita had a nasty gash on the fatty part of the palm of her hand. Never being one to let anything interfere in her fun, she told us she was fine and we needed to get going. There was no way this was going to be okay without a good cleaning and hand wrap, so we talked her into letting us fix her up. It was during the cleaning and bandaging that her son started laughing as he recalled me calling her "Tumbles." Although Nita wasn't particularly fond of the nickname, we decided it fit perfectly and began using it regularly.

The second night of misadventure occurred when Tumbles was at the end of a relationship with a young man that she kept around strictly to help her maintain her boat. They'd gotten in a fight at her place one night after drinking. He went onto the boat and grabbed a hammer and went after her with it, so she ran into the house and called the sheriff's office. He was taken to jail, but unfortunately so was she.

It turned out that the Georgia State Police had a warrant out for Nita's arrest from eighteen years earlier, and they were willing to extradite her. She had taken her ex-boyfriend's truck to get away from him after a big fight, and he reported it stolen. A few days later, she dropped the truck off at the bank where its loan had originated. Although the bank processed the vehicle back into their possession, they never told the police it had been recovered, therefore the warrant remained active in the system. When she called the sheriff's office on that fateful night, they ran her driver license to complete their report. Because car theft is a felony, Nita was booked into jail that night in her in her pajamas and flip flops with no glasses, and worse yet, no cigarettes. She was held for four days in Key West while Georgia figured out the warrant should have been removed from the system years earlier. Upon her release, she was able to catch a ride home from Key West with my former beau, Tim the Coastie. Nita was fit to be tied for about three days after that. Being hauled off to jail without cigarettes will do that to you.

Fortunately, her son and I were able to cover for her at her jobs so there were no repercussions. She returned home and life resumed...and her warrant for arrest was now cleared.

Back to our night out, Nita and I proceeded to the Legion and Monkey as planned. As usual, Freddie was glad to see us and played my favorite song "Sweet Home Alabama" as soon as we walked in. It was great to be back.

When Nita and I returned to our seats at the bar after dancing, there was a familiar face next to me. It was my ex Tom's former neighbor. I remembered that he was in the Coast Guard, but I couldn't remember his name. He smiled at me then said hello to Nita, so apparently they knew each other. He then reintroduced himself to me. That was it...Greg. It was coming back to me. Greg's mother lived in the other half of my ex's duplex, and Greg lived in the big house across the street.

Nita knew Greg before I did, and she liked him better than Tom (the one that turned out to be an alcoholic), but less than Tim (the other Coastie I'd dated briefly). Since Tim had moved on after I told him I was dating Tom, Nita knew there would be no happy reconciliation with Tim, so she gave me the secret look of approval. She knew I needed a man in my life, and if I didn't end up with Greg, she'd have to endure my forlorn mood until I met someone else. Greg remained with us for the rest of the night and even bought our drinks. I enjoyed our conversation. He was well spoken and we shared similar interests. I think what sealed the deal was when he joined Nita and me on the dance floor...and held his own! That night turned into a dinner invitation, which turned into more dinner invitations. I eventually spent a couple of nights at Greg's house, but because he had custody of his seven year old son every other weekend, I only stayed over when his son wasn't there. I wanted to make sure we were getting along before we introduced a child into the mix.

Nita and I were at the Monkey a few weeks later when she told me that although she liked Greg, he wouldn't have been her first choice for me. I knew who she'd hoped I'd end up with, but that was no longer an option. Tim had been dating someone else for a few months.

I noticed the door open, looked up and saw Greg walk in. He spotted us immediately and came over to join us. I was surprised to see him, but he said his son had to stay with his mom this weekend so he was free. He just found out so he thought he'd try to run into me. I was really happy things had worked out that way. Nita seemed to be running on empty and was happy to have an out so she could go home early. Nita turned me over to Greg and told us she was going to bed. Greg smiled and placed his hand on my thigh and gave me an affectionate squeeze. He then whispered in my ear, "I know you need to hear this so I'm going to tell you...I love you." My heart warmed when I heard the words come out of his mouth. It was exciting. Greg was someone I respected and could see a future with. When Tom had said those words in the past, it felt like he loved me because he needed me. When Greg said them, it felt different. I'm not sure how to describe it, but it felt better. I returned the sentiment, but secretly wondered what he meant by telling me, "I know you need to hear this..."

Greg and I had been dating for about three months when he asked me to move in with him. He had grown tired of traveling all the way north to Grassy Key to my house, and sold me on the downside of being so far out of town. He also didn't like being at my place because it was too close to my ex, who was Greg's former neighbor. Greg's house was pretty big and had a great yard. It didn't take much effort on his part to persuade me to shorten my commute and be able to get my dog back because I would now have a yard, so I said I would. I decided to hang onto my trailer for the time being because I wanted to make sure things would work out. I was really excited to get my dog Cory back from Tina. She and her husband had been fostering my Chow Chow since I didn't want to leave her in the trailer alone for extended amounts of time. Tina and her husband enjoyed spending time with Cory and I think she actually softened his heart, so it had been a mutually beneficial fostering.

Of course, having Cory back was awesome. I'd really missed her. Greg had a seven year old son that visited every other weekend, so I also became a step mom. I enjoyed my new life. I spent a lot of time taking the little boy on adventures around town. We'd take Cory to the park, ride bikes and explore the woods near our house. We had a lot of fun together.

I learned that Greg had been married twice, which was fine because I had been married twice as well. He had two sons, the oldest from his first marriage, had just graduated high school and lived in St. Petersburg, Florida with his mom. The seven year old was from his second marriage, and he and his mom lived in Big Pine Key. Greg told me his older son had asked if he could come stay with Greg. Greg asked me, and of course I said it would be fine. Greg thought is ex-wife was pushing him out since he'd graduated, but no one would admit that.

About two weeks later, Greg, jr. showed up on our doorstep with his belongings in trash bags. I wasn't sure what to think, and didn't want to judge, but it was definitely a challenge. Junior, as we affectionately called him, turned out to be a big teddy bear. The problem was that his mother didn't teach him anything. He had never had a job, a cell phone, a bank account, or a credit card. He had no idea how to do anything for himself such as shop, cook, or manage his finances. He was very good at sitting on the side of his bed and playing video games, however. I realized I'd be taking on the burden of teaching Junior everything since Greg had recently taken a new position at work and now had to report to Key West every day. He had formerly worked just a couple of miles down the street, but now he'd be commuting two hours in addition to to his regular shift.

After Greg and I decided the best way to handle setting boundaries with Junior, we told him he had to get a full-time job. Since he had a driver license but no car, he applied at the Walgreens store a mile up the road. Junior had come to us pretty beaten down because he and his mother had been fighting a lot toward the end. Instead of helping him learn how to be an adult, she bitched at him all of the time. That did nothing to help him grow up, so we approached it differently. Greg and I explained that we would treat him like an adult as long as he pulled his weight. He was very excited when he was offered the job at Walgreens, but one of the conditions was that he had to get paid by direct deposit. He had no idea what that meant. I told him it wasn't a big deal, that direct deposit was just a more efficient way to get paid. I was surprised to learn that he didn't have a bank account, and had never had one. When I was sixteen, I couldn't wait to get a job and open my own bank account, but apparently times had changed. I told him he should accept the job and I would take him to the bank. The nice thing about Marathon was that people took the time to help each other. That is one thing I really miss about living there back then. The banker at Marine Bank took the time to teach Junior everything he needed to know about his new checking account, direct deposit and his ATM card. It felt good to see Junior blossom. He was such a nice young man. I wanted to give him every opportunity to succeed, especially since I didn't have anyone to help me like that.

ANOTHER NEW BEGINNING

Nita and I had gotten closer since I now lived only two blocks from her. As I got to know her better, I learned of her personal struggles. She told me of the fruitful lives she and her late husband had. At one point, they owned a bar that she managed. When they sold it off, they purchased their home in Marathon, their boat, their show car and retired. They were all set for the rest of their lives until he was diagnosed with cancer. His treatments and care drained their savings, because their insurance only paid a percentage of the hefty cost. She then sold their home in West Palm Beach, bought herself a new little pickup truck, and moved to Marathon. She lived quite well for the first few years, but she never learned how to invest her money to make it work for her. Like most people, she put it in the bank and lived off of it, and that only lasts for so long.

Like Nita, I had no retirement savings, and at thirty-six years old, I knew I needed to figure something out. The fear of struggling financially pushed me to start looking for a job that offered medical benefits and paid time off, which were the only two things Hall's didn't offer. At that time, Florida Fish & Wildlife had a dispatch center in Marathon. It was hidden within a government complex back off of the main road, so a lot of people didn't know it was there. The agency was hiring law enforcement dispatchers, so I applied. It paid a little less than I made at Hall's, but it offered paid time off, retirement and insurance. I knew the benefits outweighed the loss, so I had to try to get it. I also told everyone that I was selling my trailer in Grassy Key. I felt confident that my relationship with Greg was going to last, and there was no need to continue to pay lot rent for a place that I no longer needed.

It had been a few months before I heard anything about my application, but one day I got a phone call. A lady asked me if I was still interested in the job, and I told her yes. She invited me for an interview and scenario test, whatever that was, and we set an appointment.

When I arrived, they questioned the heck out of me and asked me a lot of random questions about myself. I was given a typing test, but since I could type as fast as they could talk, they quickly realized it was not necessary. I was then seated at a desk in a private office and given a handheld police radio and me a couple of different scenarios. As the scenarios played out, I'd be answering a phone call while an officer would stick their head in my office to ask for something, and then another officer would be calling me on the radio. The goal was to see if I could prioritize the order of events being thrown at me effectively. I accepted the challenge with confidence. I knew I could handle it.

After we were finished they laughed as they told me I handled it better than some of their current employees could have. I was flattered, but knew in the back of my mind that compared to some of the things I'd been through in my previous jobs, this was a cake walk. I found it fun to be challenged. They clearly liked my performance and said I'd be hearing from them soon.

When I got the call offering me the position, I told them my boss required me to give thirty days notice. They said they couldn't wait that long, but they could give me three weeks, so I accepted. I dreaded telling the man I'd spent two years sitting next to in a small office that I was leaving him. I hated even more that I couldn't give him the amount of notice I'd agreed to when I was hired. Although he was tough on me, we had a healthy respect for each other. He knew that at my age I would make stupid mistakes, but he talked me through them like no one ever had before. He was an amazing influence in my life and he'd taught me so much more than my own parents. It broke my heart to leave him.

I told him of my plight and he understood, but he had a strict policy that departing employees must give thirty days notice. I told him I'd tried to get him the thirty days notice, but they just couldn't hold the position for that long. In true form for him, he said I'd never be eligible for re-hire because I broke a company policy. I told him I understood, and I told him I would do all that I could to help make the transition as smooth as possible.

Leaving was hard but I was excited to start a new adventure. I had a new home, new boyfriend and step sons, and now a new career. It was a lot of new for me, but I looked forward to it.

STORMY START

y first day of work was filled with paperwork and learning the computer system. My training officer was great. Donna was very experienced and had a sweet disposition. She was a talented dispatcher who cared about her officers. Because she had such a passion for the job, she was a great teacher. She taught me exactly what to do and I picked it up quickly. I really loved the job. The officers were nice, and I really liked my new boss. She was strict but fair, and in my opinion there's nothing better.

It was 2004 and it had been a busy year for hurricanes in Florida. Just a week after I started working, Hurricane Frances struck Martin County, located in the middle of the east coast. Hurricane Charley had devastated Punta Gorda, on Florida's southwest coast on August 13, just two weeks before I started. FWC had deployed officers to both Punta Gorda and Martin County to assist because a lot of the officers in those areas had damage to their homes. We were also dispatching the officers of the Palm Beach/Martin County region because their dispatch center had been damaged and many of the dispatchers had damage to their homes.

I was told that Hurricane Charley was so devastating that our officers were deployed there to search damaged homes for injured or dead people. They also called in to keep us informed of what they were doing. They said there were a lot of loose pets that were left behind so they were trying to round them up and feed them. They were also removing debris and downed trees from roads and driveways, delivering water and checking on anyone that stayed behind. There were a lot of elderly people that stayed and became trapped in their homes without power or water. They were doing the best they could to help everyone. Now we were deploying more to assist in Martin County as well. We were told a road on South Hutchinson Island had washed out and an entire community was cut off by the loss of that road. They were going to have to set up a ferry service to rescue those who were trapped.

On September 25, Hurricane Jeanne made landfall in Martin County in the same area Hurricane Frances has devastated just twenty days earlier. From what we were told, it was bad. Frances had caused a lot of damage, and Jeanne hit pretty much the same area. On September 28, Hurricane Ivan made landfall in Fort Myers, which is just south of Punta Gorda, which had been devastated by Hurricane Charley in August. Our officers would report in and tell us stories of the things they were seeing. I couldn't even imagine seeing anything like they described. I'd lived in Florida for almost ten years and had been fortunate. I'd never been through a major storm.

When a natural disaster is forecasted, law enforcement employees, including dispatchers, are put on what are called Alpha/Bravo shifts. That means the workforce is divided in half, and each half works a fixed twelve hour shift. This allows full shifts on both day and night shifts, which is important in a natural disaster situation. There are no days off during these situations until the affected areas are stabilized. It is not uncommon to work a week or two straight, because it usually takes law enforcement and emergency services that long to get things back under control. However if there is an extended power outage, as there was with these storms, it could be a month before anyone gets days off. This was one of those situations. I'd been working twelve hour days for three weeks straight before I was able to get a day off. I wasn't complaining because I knew how lucky I was. I had electricity, running water, and a nice warm bed at home. Our officers were out in the heat without running water or electricity, and they didn't get the luxury of time off. Many of them had to drive long distances just to get to sleep in a bed for a few hours, before they had to get up and do it all over again.

The good thing about the intense work schedule is that I was able to get all of my required policy reading out of the way and got pretty proficient on the radio. They'd released me from training during hurricane duty, which felt like a huge accomplishment.

Greg was almost as happy as I was to see me back on a normal work schedule. He had gotten used to me cooking him breakfast before he left for work, and had been having to rely on McDonald's lately. I missed our routine as well. We would now be able to resume our Friday and Saturday nights at the Monkey watching Freddie's band play.

HAVING A BALL!

The next couple of months flew by. Before I knew it, fall was upon us and we were planning for the holidays. Greg told me he'd been invited to attend the Coast Guard Ball in Key West. He asked if I'd like to be his date and told me he really wanted to go, and so did I, so I said yes. I didn't have a lot of time to prepare, but knew I would have to go to Miami to try to find a dress, so I made a weekend out of it and stayed with Jo and Bill. It was nice to get off the rock, as we called our island, on occasion. Jo and I found a great dress that was both fitting for the occasion and affordable.

Greg had his own preparations he'd been working on. He was helping the Monroe County Sheriff's Explorers troop learn how to perform as an honor guard, so they could perform at the Coast Guard Ball. The Explorers are a group of high school students that are interested in a career in law enforcement. They are uniformed, trained in police tactics, taught how march, and help the community by volunteering to assist with local events. They'd been practicing for the Ball for weeks. They were a great group of kids, and participating in the pomp and circumstance that goes with such a prestigious event would be a great experience for them. We had learned the Vice Admiral of the Coast Guard would be coming from Washington DC to attend the ball, so that added an extra layer of excitement for everyone. I explained to the Explorers who he was, which helped them understand just how important it was for them to be invited. It was as if we were going to meet a celebrity!

After the Explorers put on a flawless performance, the Vice Admiral was gracious enough to introduce himself and take the time to shake hands with each of them. He congratulated them on a perfect performance. It was nothing short of a fairy tale event.

NEW TRADITIONS

*A*fter we enjoyed a great family Thanksgiving, I introduced my new family to my favorite Christmas tradition. Christmas has always been my favorite holiday, so I always wanted to get it started as soon as possible. Thanksgiving seemed like a great time to do it, so instead of sitting on my ass after eating way too much turkey, I'd put up the tree and start to decorate the house. I have always been partial to artificial trees. We had a real tree a couple of times when I was a child, but after dealing with tree sap and falling needles everywhere, I decided that artificial trees were the way to go.

We cleared a place for the tree and started testing all thirty strands of Christmas lights. You can never have too many lights on a Christmas tree. The boys eventually got excited about it and joined me. By the time the weekend was over, we'd gone to Kmart no less than three times and the whole front yard was decorated. I could tell none of them had ever taken Christmas as seriously as I do.

Internet shopping was getting popular in 2004, but Amazon sold only books. We had to get most of the gifts from eBay. I had a blast buying all kinds of presents for the boys. It was exciting to have kids to buy for, and these boys had suffered a lot of disappointment in their lives, so I wanted to make this a magical Christmas for them. That is something no child should ever be denied.

Christmas Eve for Greg and I was spent assembling toys and gifts for the boys until the wee hours of the morning...and I do mean wee hours. I don't think we got to bed until around 4:00 a.m. There was this bicycle that just would not go together, and we were both so tired, it kicked our ass. Just as we were about to give up, the Christmas Angels showed up and helped us get it assembled. I'm not sure what they downloaded into our brains, but whatever it was helped us figure out what we'd been doing wrong. We finally went to bed, only to be awakened just three hours later.

Although we were dragging, we had a great day with the boys, who were amazed that Santa hadn't forgotten them. We enjoyed a big traditional Christmas breakfast of eggs and white sauce, my family's tradition, and then Greg and I snuck in a quick nap before I had to start cooking the turkey.

ENERGY SHIFT

hortly after the holidays passed, the energy in our home shifted. I didn't know what it was, but it was pretty uncomfortable. The seven year old son was acting out and causing me to have to discipline him. I would make him sit in a kitchen chair, quietly and still, for ten minutes. It was a harmless way to teach him that he had a responsibility to behave or there would be negative consequences. The older boy was spending all of his time in his room playing video games when he wasn't at work. Greg seemed to be agitated a lot. Something had definitely changed.

Greg and I had been dating for just over six months at that point. I'd only been officially living there for three months, but after analyzing it, I didn't feel like me moving in was the issue. My work schedule had been really messed up since the hurricanes, so I worked Alpha/Bravo shifts until Thanksgiving. Because things were getting under control and we'd become fully staffed at work, we began to get more days off. My final work schedule ended up being four days per week, ten hours per day, so I had Saturday, Sunday and Monday off. My shift ended at 4:00 p.m., so I was home in time to have a nice dinner on the table by the time Greg arrived.

Back to the change of energy in the house...it was about then when I realized Greg's mother had recently been around a lot more than she had been in the past, at least since I lived there. I would get home from work and she'd be sitting at our kitchen table. I didn't care because she was part of the family, so I'd ask her if she needed anything. She always said she didn't, then would tell me she was just waiting for Greg to get home. Happy to hear there was nothing required of me, I went about my business.

A few weeks earlier, we'd been notified by Greg's sister that his father had been sick. Greg's father lived in Virginia, near his daughter and son-in-law, where he remained after he'd retired from the Coast Guard years earlier. He'd been a heavy smoker and had just been diagnosed with pneumonia, so we were concerned.

Greg's parents had gotten a divorce about ten years earlier. His father had already been retired, so his mother got a small alimony settlement and moved to the Keys into a cheap rental across the street from Greg's rental house. She never had a driver license since she grew up in New York City and she had always lived in walking distance of necessities. Fortunately at that time, that was also possible in Marathon. Greg attempted to teach her to drive, but that brought more frustration and anger than he could handle, so he bought her a small scooter. A week later she wrecked it. After hearing the story of how it happened, I wasn't so sure it was an accident. That was enough to convince me to keep my distance.

It was about the time we'd learned about Greg's father that my parents came to stay with us for awhile. They had been at my sister's house in Lake Worth for about a month, and needed a break from her and her lovely husband. Although we had a big house, we also had a big family. To keep things simple, Greg and I slept on the sleeper sofa and gave my parents our room. Once they realized they were putting us out of our bed, they decided to stay only two weeks. They needed those two weeks to recover from being at my sister's.

Once my parents arrived, Greg's mother made it a point to continue to hang out at our kitchen table. My mom asked me about her situation, then she gave me her take on it. She noticed Greg's mother kept fingering a gold necklace with a ring on it that she was wearing. My mom could tell she was doing it to bring attention to it and hopefully get to tell the story that went along with it. My mom finally put her out of her misery on the second day she was there, and asked her about the necklace. Greg's mother told my mom it was her ex-husband's ring. It was some award ring he'd gotten from the Coast Guard that she kept after the divorce. She further explained that she'd worn it for such a long time that she never took it off after the divorce. That's when I realized it was Greg's father that initiated the divorce.

PLANNING FOR THE FUTURE

G reg and I continued to go out on Friday and Saturday to the Monkey and resorted to fooling around in the back of my Blazer, because it was our only option for privacy with company in the house. During my time off, I enjoyed showing my parents around Marathon, and they spent the rest of their time hanging around the house and fixing things, like midwestern parents do. This was their second trip to the Keys. They visited me the previous year when I lived in Grassy Key in the apartment with Tom. They stayed for a whole month on that trip because my neighbor had moved in with his girlfriend and let them stay in his apartment next door to us. They seemed to be ashamed of my life at that time, and my mom spent a week convincing me that I needed to drive something better than the van I owned before I caved. I let her talk me into trading in my paid off van for a two door Chevy Blazer and a hefty car payment, because she didn't like the appearance of my van. My mom was hung up on the exact thing I wasn't, appearances. My parents were very happy that I'd secured a government job and a government boyfriend, so all was well with the world in their eyes. The question remained…was all well in the world in mine.

Greg had served in the Coast Guard for eighteen and a half years. He planned to retire once he completed twenty years. We had received an offer in the mail from a timeshare company offering us a free long weekend in the Cape Canaveral area. Since Greg had mentioned that he wanted to look into getting a job at NASA or Cape Canaveral after he retired, I suggested we take the trip to explore the area. Greg and I never left the Keys together, so I convinced him we should take advantage of the free accommodations. I also told him he should consider buying a house before prices went up, which they always do in Florida. He could rent it out until he retired. That would allow him to be a local applicant as opposed to someone that would have to relocate. Being a local certainly wouldn't hurt his chances of getting hired. He loved the idea, so we started looking online for houses and found a local real estate agent to help us. We planned our timeshare visit and arranged to house hunt with her for a full day. It was crazy how easily it all fell into place.

We decided that Merritt Island was the best place for him to look. If I ended up going with him, which was not a guarantee yet, I could ask for a transfer to the Orlando dispatch center with my job. The commute from Cocoa to Orlando wasn't short, but it was doable. Greg had talked about us getting engaged, and since we were always watching our money, I offered to use my previous wedding ring to save us money. He thought about it and came back with the response, "I don't want to sound like a cheapskate, but I think the opportunity to save that money is valuable and we can put it toward the house." I accepted that answer, and the plan was in place that he'd figure out when he wanted to propose and surprise me. My feelings were mixed…I was excited to be wanted by Greg, but I wasn't sure I wanted to be wanted by Greg.

Since check in wasn't until 3:00 p.m., we arrived early so we could meet our real estate agent. She showed us around the area and told us what to expect living in various neighborhoods. We looked at four great houses, and fell in love with the last one. We told our agent we'd give her an answer in a couple of days. This was a big decision for Greg. He'd enlisted in the Coast Guard right after high school and the Coast Guard took care of his housing, whether he lived on base or in a rental. I tried to put his mind at ease by telling him I'd owned a home jut like the one we loved, and with a Veteran's Administration (VA) loan, he could purchase it with very little out-of-pocket expense. The interest rates were good and the rental market on Merritt Island was really strong, so it would be a win-win situation for him. I could tell he liked the idea of having somewhere to go after his retirement, and the house we loved was a four bedroom with plenty of room for the boys. I also reminded him that our current home was paid for by the Coast Guard and it wasn't cheap, so staying there wouldn't be an option.

We suffered through the timeshare presentation that dragged on for four hours. We finally convinced them we couldn't afford their timeshare because we had just decided to buy a house, so they let us go. As we walked out, Greg said he was ready to call the agent and put in an offer on the house we both loved.

The next morning, we stopped by the real estate office on our way out of town and Greg signed the necessary paperwork. We were somewhere around West Palm Beach when we got a call from the real estate agent telling us the sellers had accepted Greg's offer on the house. We were so excited we could hardly contain ourselves! Fortunately, our real estate agent was very experienced and helped us maneuver through the inspections without any issues, and referred Greg to a lender that got him through the loan process flawlessly. With Greg being active duty, the VA loan process was very easy. Before we knew it, he was the proud owner of a beautiful four bedroom home on Merritt Island.

We travelled back to Merritt Island for the closing on his house a month later. We decided to stay in a motel for just one night, attend the closing, and then head back home. It was that night when Greg's sister called from Virginia. Greg's father had been under the care of Hospice, and had just passed away.

As soon as we got home, we had to turn right back around to drive up to Virginia. It was an interesting trip, and I got to see a side of Greg I'd not seen previously. He spent most of our drive trying to explain why he had a contentious relationship with most of his family members. I knew there was no way I was going to be able to remember who to avoid and who was nice, so I was friendly to everyone. They all seemed like nice people to me.

We were in Newport News, Virginia, which I really enjoyed, with the exception of the cold weather. We had the opportunity to visit a Coast Guard base in Virginia that was much larger than the ones I'd been to in the Keys and Miami Beach. We got to go to their commissary so Greg could buy some new uniform pieces, and I got to see some Navy ships, which were absolutely huge. We also visited a Civil War battlefield. I never realized just how much history and military presence was in Virginia. That comes from the naivety of growing up in rural Ohio. I really enjoyed it because there was just so much to see.

Once we got home, Greg asked me to join him while he went through the things his father left for him. I was again surprised at what I learned. Greg always had a somewhat arrogant demeanor, which is why he had more acquaintances than friends, but seeing him cry as he shared his father's stories from his Coast Guard days was quite eye opening. Greg said his father came to him in a dream just before he died and told Greg he was crossing the Bar. Greg explained to me that crossing the Bar referred to the Columbia Bar, which is a training both he and his father had been through. Crossing the Columbia Bar is a very dangerous and challenging feat. Coast Guardsmen are sent to training there in some circumstances and the term "Crossing the Bar" in Greg's dream meant his father had crossed over to the Other Side. I could tell the dream gave Greg a sense of peace after he learned his father had passed.

IT'S NOT FAIR

As spring approached, I'd begun to tire of many things in our lives. I was tired of Greg not taking an interest in my life, only expecting me to take an interest in his. When I'd invite him to any type of function that had to do with my job or my membership in the Legion, he wouldn't go. He had absolutely no interest in my life or activities. That alone left me feeling deflated. When your partner takes no interest in your life, it's disappointing, and I had become very disappointed. The shiny new of our relationship and having an instant family had worn off. No one in the house appreciated my efforts to cook and clean for them. I knew no one would care whether I cooked or threw a bag of burgers and fries on the table every night. Everyone was just into their own lives. We didn't mesh. I remember when we'd first got together, Greg had told me early on that as long as he was happy in the bedroom, nothing else mattered, which turned out to be very true. I learned to make it work for me. I deserved that. Feelings of unrest gave me the sense that something was brewing. I just wondered if I was prepared to find out what it was. Whatever it was brought back unhappy memories of my childhood and feeling like everything was so unfair.

A few months passed, which rendered me even more unhappy. I'd begun to work a lot of overtime just so I could be away from the house. It also gave me the opportunity to pay off the bills I'd incurred over Christmas. My absence forced the boys to take care of themselves, which took a lot of the burden off of me. As these changes were happening, smoking no longer held the same appeal it once had. One day I lit a cigarette and it tasted like crap. I knew it would be a great way to save money, so I decided to quit. I was surprised when Greg told me he wanted to try to quit as well. We immediately stopped smoking in the house and moved all of our ashtrays outside, which helped deter the cravings. I also told Greg I wanted to cut back on my drinking because my body was telling me it was time. I wanted to limit my drinking to Friday and Saturday nights only. We didn't need to drink during the week, so he agreed. We started off strong, but Greg eventually spent more time outside smoking than he did inside the house. I just observed.

As my feelings of unease continued to grow, I tried to ignore them because I wasn't in the financial condition to be on my own. Housing prices had risen drastically in the two years I'd lived in Marathon, and I really didn't want to deal with living with another roommate, so I continued to work as much as I could. I did know that I wouldn't be moving to Merritt Island with Greg. I also knew I didn't want to marry him, so I was secretly glad that he hadn't asked. It had been months since we had talked about getting engaged, and it never came up again. The longer this went on, the more unsettled I felt. I knew something wasn't right, but I just couldn't figure out what it was. I was kind of afraid to try.

I have always enjoyed getting psychic readings and learned a lot from them over the years. I had a longtime friend that taught me that I could go inside myself and hear my intuition if I quieted myself and raised my vibration. I'd been too busy to practice in the past, but thought this would be a great time to implement my training. It was hard to quiet my busy mind, but as I practiced I discovered a "knowing" that just came to me. I can't put it in words, but it was a feeling that I knew something life changing was about to happen. I begrudgingly continued to sit tight until more was revealed to me.

Greg seemed to pick up on my unease and gradually started to detach from me. Because he had to drive to Key West, he had to leave for work around 5:30 in the morning and didn't return home until after 6:00 p.m. There were a few days he didn't come home at all and he gave me the excuse he had overnight duty, and eventually the arrival times home became later and later. He blamed it on taking on temporary duties as a supervisor. I had no way to know if that were true or not, so I continued working all of the overtime I could get.

About another month passed when it suddenly hit me. I knew at that moment that our relationship was over. It was a Friday night. I had just opened a bottle of beer and taken my first swig. It didn't taste right. I didn't want it. I felt like I was drinking it, or attempting to drink it, out of habit. As we were getting ready to head to the Monkey to see our friends and Freddy's band, we'd have a beer or two, then get a cab and head to the bar. But not tonight. Just like I knew I wasn't going to Merritt Island with Greg, I knew I wasn't going to the Monkey, and I knew that we were finished. Now if I could only get my mouth to say what I needed to say, it would all be better, but it wasn't going to be easy. I kept moving around the house in an effort to avoid Greg as my mind raced to process what was happening.

As I worked through what I was feeling, my intuition was rattling my entire body. I was aware now of what I had always known deep down inside. Our manufactured relationship was temporary. It was created to suit a purpose, but wasn't ever meant to be a long term thing. It was yet another stepping stone in my life. It allowed me a place to try out being a mom and allowed Greg the opportunity to have some stability in his life. The boys benefited as well, I believe. They got to see what another female perspective could offer them and gave them the opportunity to learn from an outsider. I learned a lot from them as well. Using what I'd been through growing up, I made sure they felt loved and knew that if they were punished it was to teach them to be better people, not just to feed a need to be vindictive. But now, all of that was over. Our lessons and experiences were coming to an abrupt end right here, right now.

As all of that raced through my mind, I found myself back in the living room. Greg was outside finishing a cigarette and turned to come back inside. The nagging feeling to tell him it was over got stronger and stronger. My heart was pounding so loud it blocked out my hearing. I couldn't even hear the stereo playing because my inner voice was sending me such a strong message. It was forcing me to get the words out. I couldn't hold it back any longer. I took a deep breath and spat out the words, "I can't do this."

Greg, as he had become programmed to do, rolled right into an instant reply and said, "If you don't want to go out tonight, I'll go alone." I believe that he knew something was brewing as well, he just wasn't sure what it was. I think he was attributing it to one of my horrific bouts of PMS coming on.

When my cycle was coming, I got hungry, moody, and mean. When it actually started, I was in such pain that I would take 800 mg Motrin by the handful, which never helped but it was what was on hand. Greg said it was the drug of choice for the Coast Guard so he had a lifetime supply for his knee pain. But this wasn't a case of PMS. It was a combination of my guides, my intuition and my guardian angels telling me it was time to end this stage of my life and move on. It was just one week before our one-year anniversary. As I relived our time together, it became clear that Greg had been using me. He never offered me any support, whether it was when I got a black eye from a lady at the Legion because I told her something she didn't want to hear, or when I was installed as the President of the Legion Auxiliary, or if I was invited to a function from work. He was never interested. He was never there for me, but he fully expected me to be there for him. Greg missed having a wife, and I happened to be the best option available when he was looking. I should have realized it when he told me he loved me just a couple of weeks after we'd started seeing each other by saying, "I know you need to hear this, so I love you." I DID know it, I just refused to see it. Boy, had I been an idiot...again. I was really frustrated with myself because I had allowed myself to get into another bad relationship.

Greg was still under the impression that I meant I just didn't want to go to the bar, so I clarified it for him. I told him I couldn't be in a relationship with him any longer, and while those words were coming out of my mouth, I also decided right then and there that I wasn't going to let leaving financially ruin me again. I told him I would be staying in the house until I could arrange to find somewhere else to go, because I wasn't going to put myself in financial peril. He just stood there and calmly looked at me as he shook his head up and down. Everything seemed to be happening in slow motion. I felt two different emotions at the same time. On one hand, I felt like a fool for letting this go on for so long. But on the other hand, I felt triumphant. I'd listened to my gut and been able to say what I needed to say.

Greg walked out the front door after he just said, "Okay." I'm not even sure if he waited for the taxi or walked the mile to the bar so he could clear his head. I didn't care. I was just happy it was over. A huge weight had been lifted off of my shoulders, and I was so happy I wanted to jump up and down. As I commended myself for not wanting a cigarette, I sat down to process what had just happened. As I reflected back on the past year, I realized it hadn't been so bad. I'd had fun with Greg for the most part, and had fun being a stepmom to the boys. At least I wasn't making the mistake of going to Merritt Island with him.

Since I worked for the State of Florida, I had a lot of options. I could transfer to another FWC dispatch center, or apply to work at another agency. I just had to figure out where to go.

NO LOOKING BACK

Once again, I was blessed to have everything fall into place without a hitch. My friend Twila, who had bought my house in North Palm Beach from me, called me out of the blue. When I told her of my plight, she said, "Just come here. You can stay in the guest room as long as you like. I could use your help with my business on your off time, and it won't cost you anything."

The next thing I had to do was find out if I could transfer to the West Palm Beach dispatch center. I went to my boss and told her what was going on. She was wonderful. She made a call and learned West Palm had a vacancy, and she helped me submit my transfer request.

All I had left to do was pack, because I had a lot of stuff. I hired a moving company and arranged for my stuff to go into a storage unit near Twila's, and booked a date for the move.

When moving day arrived, I went to the bank to close my account. There wasn't any use staying with my bank because they were only located the Keys. I stopped at the gas station and filled up the Blazer then went back to the house to wait for the movers. They showed up shortly after I got back from my errands and had me packed and on the road in an hour. Just like that, my life in Marathon was over. As I followed the moving truck out of town, I made sure to look in my rear view mirror one last time. This place that had saved me from my second divorce and felt like such a great home was now just a reflection in my rear view mirror. Wherever will I end up next?

Printed in the United States
by Baker & Taylor Publisher Services